ROMAN

27 B...

LIFE OF PAUL
from conversion in 34 AD to 64 AD

34-35 AD	Paul is converted -*Acts 9:1-19*
37-38 AD	Visits Jerusalem -*Acts 9:26-29*
48 AD	Second visit to Jerusalem *A-cts 11:27-30*
48-50 AD	First missionary journey (Cyprus, Galatia) He writes Galatians -*Acts 13-14*
50 AD	The Council at Jerusalem -*Acts 15*
51-53 AD	Second missionary journey (Galatia, Macedonia, Greece) He writes I and II Thessalonians -*Acts 16:1-18:22*
54-57 AD	Third missionary journey (Greece, Macedonia). He writes I and II Cornithians, Romans -*Acts 18-23-21:14*
58-60 AD	Arrest in Jerusalem; Tied and imprisoned in Caesarea -*Acts 21:15-26:32*
60-63 AD	Paul in Rome writes Philemon, Colossians, Ephesians, Philipians
64 AD	Final imprisonment and death. He writes I Timothy, Titus, II Timothy

FAMILY CONNECTIONS
relations explained

EMPEROR CLAUDIUS
CLAUDIUS was married four times.

He married URGANILLA.

> They had no children.

He married AELIA, a marriage in name only.

He married MESSALINA when she was 14 and he was 57

> They had two children: BRITANNICUS and OCTAVIA.

He married AGRIPPINA who brought into their marriage NERO, her son from a former marriage.

EMPEROR NERO
NERO married OCTAVIA.

> They had no children.

He married POPPEA, but had her put to death when she was with child.

CARADOC/CARACTACUS
CARADOC (CARACTACUS) married ERGAIN

> They had four children: CYNON, LINUS, ERGAIN and GLADYS (CLAUDIA).

AARON
PRISCILLA married AARON.

> They had two children, SAUL (PAUL) and REBEKAH.

PRISCILLA was widowed and then married QUINTUS CORNELIUS PUDENS.

> They had one son, RUFUS PUDENS PUDENTIA.

RUFUS PUDENS PUDENTIA
RUFUS PUDENS married GLADYS (CLAUDIA)

> They had four children: TIMOTHEUS, NOVATUS, PRAXEDES and PUDENTIANA

THEIRS IS THE KINGDOM

Roberta M. Damon

GREYSTONE PRESS
Edmond, Oklahoma
2004

Theirs is the Kingdom
Copyright © 2004 by Roberta M. Damon

Library of Congress Cataloging-in-Publication Data
Inspiration, Historical Fiction, Christian History

Library of Congress Catalog Number
2003111274

ISBN#: 0-9669682-8-x
Softcover: alk. paper

Cover by Lane Nelson

Book Design by Mia Blake

GREYSTONE PRESS
2220 N. E. 131st Street
Edmond, Oklahoma 73013

To THOSE MARTYRED IN THE CAUSE OF CHRIST. . .

THEIRS IS THE KINGDOM.

"Blessed are those which are

persecuted for righteousness' sake,

for theirs is the kingdom of heaven."

Jesus of Nazareth

Matthew 5:10

ACKNOWLEDGMENTS

Heartfelt thanks to:

Carolyn Plampin, dear old friend and missionary colleague, who discovered Claudia and gave me the idea;

Dr. Gladys Lewis, my heart friend and partner in crime, who birthed this baby;

Dr. David Thomas, my friend, who kept me supplied with background material and advised lovingly and wisely;

Dr. Peter James Flamming, pastor of First Baptist Church, Richmond, Virginia who trusted me enough to put me on his staff (oh, happy years) and asked what it is I do that makes God smile;

Ed Clemmons, who reminded me of *I, Claudius*;

Carolyn Hott Spencer, Latin teacher and photographer extraordinaire, who showed me Rome and the University of Richmond library;

Ralph Starling, my dear friend and colleague, who measured the Mamertine prison for me;

Martha Cloe, Patti Asby and Elizabeth Spencer, my delightful fellow travelers in Rome;

Sister Pearl Lopez, of The Church of Saint Pudentiana in Rome who promised to show me the first century house under the church if I bring an emergency lamp to scare away the snakes;

Mario Antonucci, at Saint Pudentiana's, who let us photograph his photographs;

Tiffin Mabee, and others on staff, at the William Smith Morgan Library at Union Theological Seminary Richmond;

Sandra Higgins, at the library of the International Mission Board in Richmond, who told me where to find rare books;

The staff at Virginia Commonwealth University Library;

The staff at Boatwright Library at the University of Richmond (I do love all librarians!);

The staff at The Cathedral of the Sacred Heart, Richmond, who loaned me books.

Acknowledgments

Unending gratitude for all those who listened:

Dr. Wilbur Lewis, whom I love and admire, reviewed the obstetrical chapters and made suggestions;

Jay Christie, sweetest spirit I know, in his hospital room;

Phil Mitchell, gifted church musician who helped me with worship in the early church and put his head on his desk while I read aloud the part about Paul's execution;

Douglas Johnson, who listens with her heart;

Beverly Morgan, soul friend;

Joyce Chrismon, who thought this book seemed like a good idea at the time;

Marie Davis, a soul sister, who brings joy to my heart;

Dr. Ron Dubois, who told me years ago that I ought to write a book;

Don and Mary McBride, my beloved brother and sister-in-law, who let me read to them;

Suzanne Shonnard, who told me about a splendid thing;

Deborah Edgar, who cried as I read to her from the manuscript (always a good sign);

Margaret Taylor, who went with me to the mountain;

Jerrie Lohr, my friend and favorite English teacher;

My friends in the Builder's Class, who kept asking, "When will it be published?"

Earlene Jesse, and her wonderful women of the Women's Missionary Union of Virginia who have given me a platform;

And most of all, my deepest gratitude to Bill Damon, my husband and technical guru, who is happy when I write.

As a professional in literature and its study, I have long
been enchanted by the sound of the human voice in print
media. Literature is simple: the public forum for examina-
tion of life in all of its expressions. As such, the canon of
literature is never closed. Attitudes toward what should
be included in our publicly recognized archives of linguis-
tic art change. Methods for study evolve to enhance understanding of even minimal contributors. Closer correspondence between so-called high art and popular culture
becomes apparent. Back of all discourse about writing
rests a truth. New voices continually surface as candi-
dates for inclusion in our literary history and reservoir.

Because of my keen sense of the shared humanity in
written voices and my interest in what they contribute to
knowledge about ourselves, this venture comes. The work
of writers who never published still rings with a voice and
a story to tell. And so do the voices of those about whom
they write. We learn from and govern ourselves with our
stories, a practice as old as the Bible and Homer. With
commitment to opening a stage for their performance, the
curtain goes up on *Recovered Voices* with its third actor,
Theirs is the Kingdom, by Roberta McBride Damon who
writes her version of the ancient story of family by meticulous research into a particular ancient family. Almost
two decades ago, she became interested, first, in the story
of Claudia, mentioned in the New Testament in association with the first Christian church of Gentiles in Rome. In
the beginning, she had a feminist perspective, trying to
determine the prominence of the woman so named, obviously with an importance that went beyond the surface
text. For the past ten years, I have been party to her research and findings as she has uncovered amazing facts
and startling information which only rise from deep, per-
sistent investigation and study. This historical novel based
on the solid data which has emerged has wrapped around

all women and all men who have the sensitivity of spirit and calling to be named followers of The Way. Moreover, the information which becomes available from this fictional account of historical evidence serves to enforce the faith of those followers as they understand the price paid by countless numbers to insure that the message of the Christ who promised The Kingdom through sacrifice and denial not be diminished, but heralded forward with victory.

Roberta Damon has given voice to many in the first century of Christianity by learning who they are, where and how they lived and died, and the character she has captured in their voices which she assumes and reproduces for her readers. She meshes the history of place with the personality of people to produce an ambiance of credible witness to New Testament, Roman, and British events which continue to influence contemporary society and faith practice.

In this third act of the series, you will meet people in conversation and family relationship with such notables as the Apostle Paul, Emperor Claudius, the poet Martial, and mad Nero. You will learn about one family's efforts to honor the slain martyrs in Rome's Coliseum. Witness the execution of Paul, the faithful example of one patrician Roman family, and the touching romance between a real British princess and a Roman Senator. Read the close correspondence between the writings of such lofty figures as the Venerable Bede, Tacitus, Tertullian, and Josephus. With a firm confidence that you will find a compelling interest on each page, I offer the third in the series, *Recovered Voices*, with *Theirs is the Kingdom*.

–Gladys S. Lewis, Publisher

PREFACE

When Roman Emperor Claudius ordered his legions to invade Britain in 43 AD, young Rufus Pudens went to war as aide to General Aulus Plautius. Their most formidable foe was the King of Siluria (Wales), Caradoc, called Caractacus by the Romans. A scant four years before the Roman invasion, as a result of persecution, preachers from Jerusalem, Eubulus and Joseph of Arimathea among them, went to Britain preaching a new gospel. Members of the British royal family embraced Christianity as a result of that preaching.

For seven years, Caradoc held off the Roman armies. Never conquered, but most foully betrayed by a kins-woman, he and all his family were carried captive into Rome. There, he stood before the Roman Senate to plead for his life. No woman had ever stood before that tribunal, but Caradoc's daughter, Gladys, just sixteen, bravely stood beside her father as he addressed the Senate. After granting Caradoc clemency, Claudius adopted young Gladys and gave her the name Claudia, after himself, thus sealing an alliance between Britain and Rome.

The family was housed for the seven years of Caradoc's sentence at the grand villa of Senator Rufus Pudens Pudentia. His home became known as the *Paladium Britanicum* and later *The Apostolorum,* the house church of the gentiles in Rome. There Paul, half brother to Rufus Pudens, lived at times with his family. During Paul's imprisonment, the family ministered to him. When he was executed, they followed with him to the block and claimed his body which they interred in the family tombs.

Rufus Pudens and Claudia married and had four children. Their two daughters, Praxedes and Pudentiana, grew up to do God's work–recovering and burying remains of many martyred Christians. They themselves were ultimately martyred along with other members of their family. Claudia, alone, died a natural death. Christians around the world owe a debt of gratitude to those early believers.

Theirs is the Kingdom is a fictionalized account of the story of the British royal family, their captivity, and their becoming a part of the first gentile Christian church in Rome. The book is set against a dual background: court life in Rome during one of the most turbulent periods of history, and the life and writings of Paul, the great apostle to the gentiles.

TABLE OF CONTENTS

"Nero fastened the guilt and inflicted the most exquisite tortures on a class hated for their abominations, called Christians by the populace. *Chrisus,* from whom the name had its origin, suffered the extreme penalty during the reign of Tiberius at the hands of one of our procurators, Pontius Pilate, and a most mischievous superstition, thus checked for the moment, again broke out not only in Judaea, the first source of the evil, but even in Rome, where all things hideous and shameful from every part of the world find their centre and become popular. Accordingly, an arrest was first made of those who pleaded guilty; then, upon their information, an immense multitude was convicted, not so much of the crime of firing the city, as it was of hatred against mankind. Mockery of every sort was added to their deaths. Covered with the skins of beasts, they were torn by dogs and perished, or were nailed to crosses, or were doomed to the flames and burnt, to serve as a nightly illumination, when daylight had expired. Nero offered his gardens for the spectacle, and was exhibiting a show in the circus, while he mingled with the people in the dress of a charioteer or stood aloft on a car. Hence, even for criminals who deserved extreme and exemplary punishment, there arose a feeling of compassion; for it was not, as it seemed, for the public good, but to glut one man's cruelty, that they were being destroyed."

Tacitus, *Annals,* McHenry (43-51)

"Do thy diligence to come before winter. Eubulus greeteth thee, and Pudens, and Linus and Claudia, and all the brethren."

II Timothy 4:21

1

"Salute Rufus, chosen in the Lord, and his mother and mine."
Romans 16:13

"The cradle of the ancient British Church was a royal one; herein being distinguished from all other churches, for it proceeded from the daughter of the British king, Caractacus, Claudia Rufina, a royal virgin, the same who was afterward the wife of Aulus Rufus Pudens, the Roman senator, and the mother of a family of saints and martyrs."
Moncaeus Atrebas, *In Syntagma* (38) as quoted in *St. Paul in Britain* by Richard Morgan (3)

"Ecclesia Britannica ab incanabulis Regia et Apostolica."
("The British Church was from its cradle Apostolical and Royal.")
As quoted in Andrew Gray, *The Origin and Early History of Christianity in Britain* (38)

THE LEGEND

"The *triquetra* is an ancient symbol dating back at least five thousand years. Many cultures and religions consider the number three holy or divine."

Barbara Walker

Before anyone thought of recording time, when life was short and the world was dangerous, people had just begun to live in families. Women planted and men hunted, but some men worked with metals.

An artisan, Aethelwredd by name, was, upon a day, returning to his keep. He saw movement in the grass. He stopped, listened, and then, laughing, ran toward his child whose hair glinted gold and red in the setting sun. The child startled. She took one step toward the running man, arms upflung in welcome. At that moment, they both saw the coiled serpent. As quick as a lightening flash, Aethelwredd picked up the child and flung her aside. At the same instant, the fangs of the serpent found their mark in Aethelwredd's heel. The man was felled. His leg numbed as the venom worked its paralyzing evil. He cried out for help, his voice joining the screams of the terrified child.

Hildreth came with rock in hand. She crushed the head of the serpent, ground his head under her heel and cut him in two parts. One part she threw to the setting sun. One part she cast into the tall grass. She slashed with flint the flesh of Aethelwredd and squeezed the wound til blood flowed free. Putting her mouth to his heel, she sucked blood and venom. She spit out vile poison. She tied a cord around Aethelwredd's leg and swung the child to her shoulders. She carried the child on her back while she dragged Aethelwredd to the keep. Day and night she kept her vigil. Aethelwredd lived.

In gratitude, he fashioned for her a talisman–a circle of gold. Within it, he placed three oblong shapes, saying, "One for me. One for you. One for the child. The circle is the keep wherein we dwell secure."

This legend was lost until 2003 when "The Ballad of the Savior Wife" was discovered and translated by Old English scholar, Marianne Booker.

The Ballad of the Savior Wife

O sing the might of Aethelwredd
Who saved the child from serpent fangs.
The fangs found flesh of Aethelwredd.
Deep plunged the fangs, the death blow dealt.

O sing the might of Aethelwredd
Who dying cried a curse on curse.
O sing the greater might of she
Who heard his cries and running came
To crush the head of serpent coiled
And cut the flesh of Aethelwredd.

O sing of greater might of she
Who sucked the blood and venom mixed.
She saved the life of Aethelwredd
And gathered up her child and he
Who saved the child from evil fate.

O sing praise of Aethelwredd,
The child, the wife of strength and might.
O sing his praise who fashioned fair
The amulet of golden light.

Sing praises to the savior wife
Who wears the talisman of gold,
A circle fastening up the ones
Who dwell secure within the fold.*

*A better translation for "fold" would be "keep." Keep, n. The strongest and most secure place in the castle; often used as a place of residence, especially during a siege.

NARRATORS

Bran: Father of Caradoc; former King of Siluria; arch Druid; sometimes called Bran the Blessed

Carádoc (Caractacus): King of Siluria; father to Cynon, Linus, Ergain and Gladys (Claudia)

Ergain: Queen, wife of Caradoc; mother to Gladys (Claudia), Cynon, Linus, and daughter Ergain

Ergain: Sister of Claudia, Linus, and Cynon

Eubulus: Simon Peter's father-in-law; one of the seventy Jesus sent out, early preacher in Britain

Evelyn St. Claire: Tourist

Gladys (Claudia): Youngest child of Caradoc and Ergain; wife of Rufus Pudens; mother of Timotheus, Novatus, Praxedes and Pudentiana

Gwynedd: Servant to Gladys (Claudia)

Hermas: Pastor of gentile church in Rome; mentioned by Paul in his letter to the Romans

Joseph of Arimathea: Uncle to Mary, mother of Jesus; Roman *decurio* in Siluria; one who preached in Britain after Stephen's martyrdom (all except the apostles were scattered abroad preaching the gospel)

Marianne Booker: Tourist, university professor

Novatus: Second son of Claudia and Rufus Pudens

Onisemus: Slave

Priscilla: Mother of Saul and Rebekah by her first husband, Aaron; mother to Rufus Pudens by her second husband, Quintus Cornelius Pudens

Pudens: Rufus Pudens Pudentia, Roman Senator, husband to Claudia; son of Quintus Cornelius Pudens and his wife, Priscilla

Pudentiana: Younger daughter of Claudia and Rufus Pudens

The Builder: Unnamed architect

Timotheus: First son of Claudia and Rufus Pudens

ROBERTA M. DAMON

"The Christian religion began in Britain within fifty years of Christ's ascension."

> Robert Parsons, *Three Conversions of England* (I, 26) as quoted in Andrew Gray, *The Origin and History of Christianity in Britain* (6)

"*Interea glaciali frigore rigenti insulae, et velut longiore terrarum secessu soli visibili non proximae verus ille Sol, non de firmamento solum temporali, sed de summa etiam coelorum arce cuncta tempora excedente, orbi universo praefulgidum sui coruscum ostentans, temppore ut scimus, summo Tiberii Caesaris, quo absque ullo impedimento ejus propagaba ature religio, comminata, senatu nolente, a princepe morte dilatoribus militum ejusdem, radios suos primum indulget, id est sua praecepta Christus.*" ("These islands, stiff with cold and frost, and in distant region of the world, remote from the visible sun, received the beams of light from Christ, the True Sun. He afforded his light, the knowledge of his holy precepts, in the last year of the reign of Tiberius Caesar.")

> Gildas Badonicus as quoted by Andrew Gray in *The Origin and Early History of Christianity in Britain* (6)

"Christianity was brought to Britain by Joseph of Arimathea, c. A.D. 36-39."

> Andrew Gray, *The Origin and Early History of Chrisianity in Britain (3)*

"Christianity was privately confessed elsewhere, but the first nation that proclaimed it as their religion and called it Christian after the name of Christ, was Britain."

> Sabellus *Enno* (lib vii c.5) as quoted in Morgan, *St. Paul in Britain* (64)

"Joseph ab Arimathea nobiio decurio in insula Avallonia cum xi." ("Joseph of Arimathaea, the noble decurion, received his everlasting rest with his eleven associates in the Isle of Avalon."

> *Thick vellum Cottonian MS.,* quoted also by Usher, *Melchini Fragmentum,* as quoted in Morgan, *Saint Paul in Britain* (64)

"The regions in Britain which the Roman arms had failed to penetrate professed Christianity for their religion."

> Tertullian, *Def. Fidei* (179) as quoted in Morgan, *St. Paul in Britain* (112)

"When *all* the disciples, except the Apostles, were "scattered abroad," after the persecution which arose about Stephen, and went "everywhere preaching the Word," it is but natural that some of them should go to Britain, the land of the Druids, where the Roman Governors could not persecute, and where the Druids would extend to them religious toleration."

> Andrew Gray, *The Origin and Early History of Christianity in Britain* (33)

THE PREACHER   39AD   792 AUC

JOSEPH SPEAKS:

 We walked through the fields of wheat and barley. The crops were plentiful and well tended. The land was lush, the soil fertile. We lifted our eyes to the green hills and lifted our voices in psalms. Josephus, has a strong voice and he sings with enthusiasm. We passed farmers tending their crops. We passed flocks of sheep and herds of cattle. We passed merchants with their carts and wagons carrying their produce into the towns.

I served as a *decurio*–a provincial Roman Senator in charge of the management of Rome's mining interests in Britain. I was responsible for a fleet of ships which plied the waters of the Roman world. The ships loaded at the mines in the southernmost tip of Anglia and, from there, they carried the ore to ports around the world. I have attained both wealth and respect. I am a Jew from Ramah, the birthplace of the prophet Samuel. Ramah–also called Arimathaim. I have always tried to be an honorable man. I have been privileged to be a member of the great Sanhedrin. I have maintained a residence in my home town, of course, but also in Jerusalem, and for years in Insula Avalonia in Britain. The latter community provides a respite of peace in an increasingly violent world. Not that I plan to rest.

I am a follower of The Way. It was, after all, my great nephew, the son of Mary, my brother's daughter, who taught a new gospel, healed the sick, raised the dead, and for all his goodness was put to death in Jerusalem by Roman crucifixion. I spoke before the Sanhedrin in defense of my great nephew–all to no avail. It was I who asked the Procurator Pontius Pilate for the body. And it was in my own tomb that they laid him. Our family and all his followers were devastated by the brutality of the death. Brutality is Rome's way, but I believe in miracles. I am a witness. It was for this my son and I walked the Silurian roads. We were going to see the king.

The road to the royal residence was lined with trees. Four small children played among them under the supervision of a nurse. As we approached, the children ran to us laughing.

Their nurse hurried behind as if to shield them from harm.

"Good day to you," I smiled. "What a lovely sight these children are. My name is Joseph and this is my son, Josephus."

Josephus knelt down in the grass and searched his pockets. He pulled out glass beads and a ball on a string. The children gathered about him under the watchful eye of their caretaker.

The oldest boy spoke. "I am Cynon. I am nine and I can read. That is my brother Linus. He runs faster than anyone. The girls are Ergain–she's five, and the little one is Gladys."

"And how old are you, Gladys?"

The child was sucking one grubby thumb. She hid behind the skirts of her nurse and shyly poked three little fingers upright.

"Three years old. My, what a big girl you are."

Ergain looked at me with big eyes and forthrightly asked me, "Are you old?"

"Well," I cleared my throat. "Yes, I am."

"You look old. You look as old as our grandfather."

"I'll venture it is your grandfather that I have come to visit. Is King Bran your grandfather?"

"Yes, he is the king, but he is our dear Papa."

The children ran toward the house, calling for their grandfather. A servant came to usher us into the salon.

"Please, make yourselves comfortable here." A second servant appeared with towels and a ewer of water with which we could wash our hands and faces. Yet another entered with a tray of bread, butter and cheese. There were cups of milk and a large bowl of berries.

King Bran entered the chamber.

"Welcome, my friends. Joseph, it is good to see you again. I hear that you have settled in Siluria. What a welcomed addition to our fair land. And this must be your son."

Josephus bowed his head in respect.

"I am Josephus, sir. We have just met your grandchildren. They are beautiful."

"Oh, yes. They are very dear to me. They are the children of my son, Caradoc. Well, young Josephus. I remember you when you were the same age as Cynon. Time has a way of changing all of us. You have grown into a fine young man. I hope you are as honorable as your father. In all our dealings, I have found him to be worthy of trust."

"Thank you, King Bran," I smiled my thanks. "You and your people have always been most gracious to me."

The preliminaries over, the servants removed the trays and retired to the kitchen. Bran asked the reason for the call.

"Are you here on business, then?

"No. It is something of a more important nature."

"More important than business? Come, Joseph, surely among the Romans there is nothing more important than making money." Bran smiled inquiringly.

"If I may, I would like to speak to you about spiritual matters."

At that moment, Bran's daughter appeared at the doorway.

"Oh, I am sorry. I didn't mean to intrude." She turned to step back into the hallway.

"No, Gladys, my dear, do come in. You may remember Joseph from Ramah. He was the Roman *decurio* managing the mining interests in our district. He was just speaking of spiritual matters. You must come in and hear him."

"If I am not in your way."

"Dear lady, I would be so pleased if you would stay."

13

I smiled at her. "I believe there is a very little girl playing outside under the trees who bears your name."

"Yes, she is my niece and my namesake." I settled myself upon the bench.

"She is delightful. Now, with your permission I shall speak of the important matters I came to address. I know that you are Druid. I am greatly impressed by your search for the truth. Your people are well educated. Your life revolves around a great system of ritual, worship, parliament, courts, and centers of learning. I know that you believe in one God, Creator and Preserver, and of man's high origin and final immortality. I know that you teach reverence to the Deity, abstinence from evil, and valiant behavior according to the three grand articles. The very word "Druid" derives from the word "Truth.""

"You are well informed, Joseph, about our beliefs." Bran nodded. I acknowledged my host who sat with hands folded, listening intently. I continued.

"Your great motto I have learned and pondered, 'Truth against the world.' Your great educational system is ancient in origin. I am aware that you are worshipers, not of the heavenly bodies, but of the great Creator of the Great Lights. I know that you worship the one great Supreme Being. I do not come to destroy your magnificent system. It has served you well. Rather, I come to proclaim One who declared Himself truth."

"And who is this one?"

"His name is Yeshua. He was a prophet who healed the sick and raised the dead. He proclaimed that He is the way, the truth, and the life–the very Son of God. My own people rose up against Him and He was crucified. He died on a Roman cross, but on the third day he arose from the tomb that I, myself, provided. He walked among us for some days after his resurrection, and then ascended into heaven to God the Father. We were left awed and desolate. At the great feast, his chosen disciples and followers met to pray in an upper room. One of his disciples preached that day to the multitudes. I tell you the very air was alive with his words. Suddenly, there came a mighty, rushing wind, and flames of fire sat upon the heads of all those who believed. It was the great Spirit of God who came that day. The very foundations of the earth seem to shake. All the followers began to speak of Yesu, and every person there from all over the world, could understand the words that were spoken. Three thousand fell on their faces before the preacher confessing their belief in the crucified One–the One who died to take away our sins. I tell you, I was there, and my poor words cannot begin to express what happened to us all. God poured out his spirit on all flesh, just as the old Jewish prophets had predicted long ago. I'm telling you, it happened. Many of the Jews are beginning to believe that he is their Messiah. I am here to proclaim him to you. He gave his life willingly that all who believe might live fully. This Yesu promises to all who will follow him life abundant and life eternal."

Bran listened with tears in his eyes.

"Do you not know that one of our names for God is Yesu? Surely, you are speaking of him. My heart tells me that he is Truth. I believe the words you have spoken."

I turned to the lady Gladys. "And do you also believe in this One who is Truth?"

"I believe." Together King Bran and his daughter bowed before me to receive my blessing. I laid my hands upon their heads and lifted my heart to God in a prayer of thanksgiving. Who knew how these two might influence their world? Who knew what they might suffer?

15

ROBERTA M. DAMON

PAUL TO HIS MOTHER, PRISCILLA 40 *AD* 793 *AUC*

 I, Paul, an Apostle of Jesus Christ, write unto you, my mother and dearly beloved, from Arabia. I have seen the Lord. I must stay here until my way is made plain. While I was traveling to Damascus breathing curses on his followers, I was blinded by a great light. I heard the voice of the crucified One. He told me to go into the city and wait. A certain man, Ananias by name, saw a vision. He was told that he was to care for me because I am God's chosen vessel to bear his name before the gentiles, to the Jews, and to kings. He also said that I would suffer. When Ananias came to me, he called me "Brother Saul," and I received my sight. I preached in the synagogues in Damascus. The Jews rose up against me, whereupon I escaped to Jerusalem. The believers would not receive me until they were convinced that I had been transformed. I do not know how long I shall tarry here. I am no longer Saul, but Paul. I bear witness that whereas once I persecuted followers of Christ, I now proclaim him Lord. He died and rose again that all who believe might have eternal life. Greet Rebekah and little Aaron. Greet Rufus, my brother. May every tongue confess him whose name is above every name, and who gives life to everyone who believes.

"In omni Gallia eorum hominum, qui aliquo sunt numero atque honore, genera sunt duo. Sed de his duobus generibus alterum est druidum, alterum equitum. Illi rebus divinis intersunt sacrificia publica ae privata procurant, religiones interpretantur: ad hos magnus adulescentium numerus disciplinae causa concurrit, magnoque hi sunt apud eos honore. Disciplina in Britannia reperta atque inde in Galliam translata esse existimatur, et nunc, qui diligentius eam rem cognoscere volunt, plerumque illo discendi causa proficiscuntur. Druides a bello abesse consuerunt neque tributa una cum reliquis pendunt; militiae vacationem omniumque rerum babent immunitatem. Tantis excitai praemiis et sua sponte multi in disciplinam conveniunt et a parentibus propinquisque mittuntur. Magnum ibi numerum versuum ediscere dicuntur. Itaque annos nonnulli vicenas in disciplina permanent. Neque fas esse existimant ea litteris mandore, cum in reliquis fere rebus, publicis privatisque rationibus Graecis litteris utantur. Id mihi duabus de causis instituisse videntur, quod neque in vulgum disciplinam efferi velint neque eos, qui discunt, litteris confisos minus memoriae studere: quod fere plerisque accidit, ut praesidio litterarum diligentium in perdiscendo ac memoriam remittant. In primis hoc volunt persuadere, non interire animas, sed ab aliis post portem transire ad alios, atque hoc maxime ad virtutem excitori putant metu mortis neglecto. Multa praeterea de siderbus atque eorum motu, de mundi ac terrarum magnitudine, de rerum natura, de deorum immortalium vi ac potestate disputant et iuventuti tradunt."
("Throughout Gaul there are two classes of persons of definite account and dignity–one consists of the Druids, the other of knights. The former are concerned with divine worship, and due performance of sacrifices, public and private, and the interpretation of ritual questions: a

great number of young men gather about them for the sake of instruction and hold them in great honor. In fact, it is they who decide in almost all disputes public and private. It is believed their rule of life was discovered in Britain and transferred thence to Gaul, and today those who would study the subject more accurately journey, as a rule, to Britain to learn it. The Druids usually hold aloof from war, and do not pay war-taxes with the rest; they are excused from military service and exempt from all liabilities. Tempted by these great rewards, many young men assemble of their own motion to receive their training; many are sent by parents and relatives. Report says that in the schools of the Druids they learn by heart a great number of verses and therefore, some persons remain twenty years under training. And they do not think it proper to commit these utterances to writing, although in almost all other matters, and in their public and private accounts, they make use of Greek letters. I believe they have adopted the practice for two reasons–they do not wish the rule to become common property, nor those who lean the rule to rely on writing and so neglect the cultivation of the memory. And, in fact, it does usually happen that the assistance of writing tends to relax the diligence of the student and the action of the memory. The cardinal doctrine which they seek to teach is that souls do not die, but after death pass from one life to another; and this belief as a fear of death is thereby cast aside, they hold to be the greatest incentive to valor. Besides this, they have many discussions as touching the stars and their movement, the size of the universe and of the earth, the order of nature, the strength and the powers of the immortal gods, and hand down their lore to the young men.")

Caesar, *Commentary* (335-339)

"Penitus religionem Druidarum abolevit Claudius."
("Claudius declared Druidism a capital offence.")
Seutonius in *Vita Claudius* (53-54)

"The Druids teach that by none other way than the ransoming of man's life by the life of man is reconciliation with the Divine Justice of the Immortal Gods possible."
Julius Caesar, *Commentaries* lib. v (335-336)

THE DRUIDS 40 *AD* 793 *AUC*

QUEEN ERGAIN SPEAKS:

 A group of children, my child among them, sat in a semicircle. The priest, dressed in his white robe, stood before them. He asked questions of the children. They answered him by rote. The little ones recited their lessons in a high-pitched, sing-song unison. There is nothing more important in our land than the education of our children. From the earliest age, students memorize the triads. Holding up three fingers, the priest intoned: "What are the three duties of every man?"

The children responded: "The three duties of every man are to worship God, to be just to all men, and to die for your country."

"What three things should all men love?"

"There are three things all men should love: mother nature; rational works of art; and faces of little children."

"Very good. What three things came into being at once?"

"The three things that came into being at once are: light, men, and moral choice."

The triads are reminders of the great triune God of the Druids. We encourage the children to memorize. Our tribal bards can recite the genealogies of every member of the community back into the far reaches of time–a stunning accomplishment. Memorization sharpens the mind and encourages logical thought. I am proud of my children. Gladys is my youngest. She loves her lessons. Formal schooling begins at the age of five, but Gladys began learning as soon as she could talk. I was her first teacher. When Gladys was a baby, I often held up three fingers and counted: one, two, three. Before she was a year old, she could hold up her own fingers for me to count.

Gladys is fascinated by the small circle of three golden petals I wear. It is a part of her earliest memory, as it was a part of mine. I loved it when it glittered in the sunlight, or when it caught the firelight's gleam in winter's cold as I rested my head on my mother's breast. When my child is fifteen, I shall give it to her.

"Where did you get it, Mama?"

"From my mother."

"Where did your mother get it?"

"From her mother."

"What makes it shine?"

"It's made of gold."

"It goes around and around and around."

"Yes, little one. It's like the sun, like the moon, like grandmother to mother to daughter." The amulet has passed through the family from mother to last daughter for as long as anyone can remember.

The priest continued the day's lesson: "What do we know of the universe?"

"The universe is infinite; out of himself the creator created it; the creator now pervades it and rules it."

"What is the essence of the creator?"

"The essence of the creator is pure light. He is called the one without darkness. His real name is mystery and so is his nature."

"Who is the Supreme Being?"

"He is creator to the past, savior and preserver in the present, and recreator in the future."

"Let us stand and repeat our motto three times." The children stood straight and tall. They placed their hands over their hearts and repeated together: "Truth against the world. Truth against the world. Truth against the world."

"Very good. You recited well today, children." They lined up to receive their teacher's blessing. He placed his hands on each child's head and murmured a prayer.

Gladys ran to me. We walked the path toward home.

"Tell me the story about the flood, Mama."

"Oh, that's one of my favorite stories. I heard it from my grandfather when I was a little girl. Once, there were many animals and people on the earth, but the people were not good. The Creator was not pleased and so the rains came on the earth. It rained so much that it covered the trees and the mountains. Everything was destroyed. But there was one good family who built a boat. They saved all the members of their family and many plants and animals. When the rains stopped and the waters subsided, the whole world was washed clean. And the good family and all the animals came out to live in the new world."

"Tell me about when the world was all ice." Gladys held tightly to my hand.

"The sun went to war against the heavens. The sun was so unhappy that he hid himself and all the earth grew cold. It was so cold that everything was covered with ice– the trees, the grass, the rivers, and the lakes. One day, the sun appeared again and the earth was soon filled with green trees, and birds, and flowers once again."

"It's like winter and spring, mama. When the ice melts, the flowers bloom."

"That's right. What a smart girl you are." I smiled into my child's eyes. "We must be gentle with the earth. All of our food comes from the ground. We must help take care of all the creatures."

"And all trees and flowers."

I love to teach my child life lessons. She is so eager to learn. I want her to know about our family. I want her to know that people in our community, not kin to her by blood, are nevertheless, related to her. I want her to know that among our race, there is a kinship of heart, intellect, and spirit. She must learn that all gentle folk are related in love.

Learning is of such importance. I can still recite lessons from my own childhood: "What are the three ways man differs from God? Man is finite–God is infinite. Man has a beginning–God, none. Man changes–God is unchanging. Without freedom of will, there is no humanity. Man is master of his own spiritual destiny. Man can choose good or evil."

I want my children to grow up knowing they are valued. They are growing up with stability of family, affirmation of personhood, and the discipline of study. I want my children to love learning. I want them to place a high value on education. Above all, I want them to have a nobility of spirit, a desire to search for truth, and a reverence for life.

My children love the annual religious celebrations. The vernal festival falls on the first day of May. I climb the hills with my four little ones and watch the celebration of the rebirth of life after the ice and snow. We delight in the flowers the girls wear in their hair. We watch the graceful, intricate dances and sing and clap our hands to the music. Spring comes to us accompanied by the playing of the flute–bright notes that shimmer in the air like drops of water. In autumn, our family participates in the harvest festivals when the crops are in. We offer a portion in the high place to the Supreme Being. Autumn is beautiful in Siluria. It is the season of crisp air and rising mists. Trees turn to gold, red, and rust, and the apples are heavy and sweet with juice. We love the midwinter festival, too, always white with frost and snow, when the archdruid himself gathers mistletoe from high up in the branches of the trees.

We worship at the high places–the temples open above and on every side. The huge temple stones are so old their surfaces are soft with moss and lichen. Those stones were brought from far away in ancient times–so ancient that no one remembers just how they arrived at their present site. Our national religious processions are led by our priests resplendent in their canonicals of white and gold. Most of all, we pay homage to the benign and gentle Deity who watches over us all, who blesses the earth with abundance, and who is truth and goodness.

When Joseph and the other Apostles came to Siluria

from across the sea to preach the new religion, it sounded very much like what we had always believed, so that there was not so much a turning away from the old and an embracing of the new, but rather, an instant recognition and affirmation of the Truth as it was now more fully revealed to us. It was not a violent ripping away of the old beliefs. It was rather a gentle merging and transforming of a basic foundation of love into Love.

"The British Isles which are beyond the sea, and which lie in the ocean, have received the virtue of the Word. Churches are there founded and altars erected. Though thou shouldst go to the ocean, to the British Isles, there thou shouldst hear all men everywhere discoursing matters out of the Scriptures, with another voice, indeed, but not another faith, with a different tongue but the same judgment."

> Chrystostom of Constantanople as quoted in Morgan, *St. Paul in Britain* (108)

"The apostles passed beyond the ocean to the isles called the Brittanic Isles."

> Eusebius *De Demonstratione Evangelii* (lib. iii) as quoted in Andrew Gray, *Origin and Early History of Chritianity in Britain* (25)

THE CHOICE   44 *AD*   797*AUC*

EUBULUS SPEAKS:

 I am old. I have lived more than sixty years. My hair and beard are white with age and my skin is wrinkled. I sat in the shade of an oak sipping cool water from a nearby spring. Lucas, my companion, sat beside me on the ground.

"How far to the market square?" Lucas called out to a passing Silurian farmer.

"Not far," came the answer. "Go down that road. You should be there when the sun is high." The man gave a wave and continued on his way.

"Do you think you can walk it, Eubulus?"

I smiled. "Do you think I've never walked before? I've been walking since I was a baby of two and that's been many a year."

"It has that." Lucas laughed as he helped me to my feet. We brushed grass and dirt off our garments and fell into step together. "Tell me what it was like to follow Jesus," said Lucas.

"I've told you that story over and over. Do you really want to hear it again?"

"I never get tired of it. Tell about the time He sent you out."

"Yes. Well, there were seventy of us. We were just common folks–fishermen, farmers, tradesmen–no one special, you know. He sent us out two by two. He said it was good to have a partner so that if one got into trouble, the other could pull him out. He said we were not to take any money with us. He said God would provide for our needs. He said we were not even to take any extra clothes. We were not to take a walking stick. You talk about faith. We had to have it. He said that people would receive us gladly, and if there were some folks who did not want to listen to what we had to say, we were just to shake off the dust of our sandals and leave that place and go on to the next where we would have a good reception. I tell you, it was amazing. We never went hungry. We never wanted for something to eat. We always found a place to sleep. Sometimes we slept with the farm animals, but we made out just fine. People were eager to hear the good news. Once we met a woman who had just taken freshly baked bread out of the oven. We preached to her about the Bread of life. She opened her heart to believe, and then she gave us bread for our journey. We would knock on a door and explain to the folks that Jesus said he was the Door. They would stop whatever they were doing and they would listen to us and pray with us to receive our words. I tell you, it was as if the great Spirit of God went before us and prepared the way. I've been preaching ever since. Now, I'm not the preacher that my son-in-law is. That Simon Peter can preach the ears off a camel–and get him to believe, too. No, I'm not the preacher he is. Once I get started telling my story, it is hard to stop. I tell you, I remember when the Lord called him–you know, Simon, from his fishing business. He had several boats and he had men working for him. Well, along came Jesus one day and said that Simon was to follow and he did. And he took his wife with him. Yes sir, my daughter, Perpetua, went with her husband. Off they went with Jesus, first all over Galilee. For three years, they traveled with him everywhere. There were twelve men especially chosen and there were women who went along to help out. Finally, they all went up to Jerusalem. Right up to the day he was put on that Roman cross, they went. Well, if truth be told, it was my daughter and the other women from Gallilee that followed all the way to the cross." I shook my head. "It was a terrible time. During the trials, Simon denied the Lord, just like Jesus told him he would. Simon never believed he was capable of doing such a thing until it happened. It just about broke his heart, and he has spent the rest of his life trying to make up for it. Simon is a good man. He's always been a bit quick-tempered, but he's a good man–and a good preacher. When he tells what Jesus did for him, and that he saw the Lord after he came back from the dead, I tell you, it is a powerful message."

"It is the power of the Spirit of God." Lucas pointed ahead. "Look, Eubulus. I think that must be the place up ahead. Let us pray that they will receive us today as others have received you in the past."

We stopped on the road and I prayed.

"Oh, Lord, You have entrusted us with carrying your word to these gentiles. Open hearts today, Lord, that our words might find a good lodging. In Christ's name we pray."

Lucas added, "Amen."

We approached the market square. We stood in the middle and announced: "We come as friends. We are followers of The Way. Come and hear our message." The people gathered– men, women, children. I looked at the children in the crowd.

"We come from far across the ocean. I came to your country on a ship with big sails and lots of mice."

The children laughed delightedly.

"And did you bring a mouse with you?" asked one small boy.

"No, but I fed some of my bread to a mouse who became quite friendly with me."

"You should have brought him with you. We would give him some of our bread." The crowd clapped and laughed.

"The next time, I'll bring a mouse. Today I will tell you a true story. There is a man named Jesus who is the Son of the true God. He was kind and good. He loved everyone– poor people, little children, even sinners. He would go into a town and everyone would come out to hear him. I often heard him teach. I saw many wonders and miracles.

He healed my wife when she was so sick with fever she couldn't lift her head up. When Jesus came into our house, he laid his hand on her brow, and the fever left her immediately. She got up and prepared dinner for us all. It was a good dinner, too. I can't tell you how many sick people Jesus healed. He even raised people from the dead. He was truly a miracle worker. People came from far and near and brought their sick children. One woman, bent over double for almost twenty years, was healed by Him one day. She could barely walk before she met Jesus. After she was healed, she danced for joy. Another woman was healed just by touching the hem of His robe. I tell you, it was wonderful to see. People flocked to hear Him teach. He had a new way of looking at life. Instead of just keeping the rules, He said that it is what is in our hearts that really matters. My family has been connected to Jesus from the time he began to preach and teach and heal. My son-in-law was one of twelve men Jesus chose. Both he and my daughter were his followers. Men came to him and asked the question, "What must I do to inherit eternal life?"

"And what was the answer?" someone shouted.

"Once, He said that we must be born again–born of the Spirit. He told one young man that he had to sell everything he had, but that was because the man was too much concerned with what he owned–or what owned him. To inherit eternal life, you just have to believe that Jesus really was God's own Son, and that when He died, it was because He loved you. And when we do that, our hearts are never the same again, and we learn to love like Jesus did. Even a child can believe in Jesus. I remember once that there were mothers who brought their children to him for his blessing. His followers wanted to turn them away, but Jesus told them to let the children come to him. And when the little ones ran to Him, He put His hands on their heads, He looked into their eyes, and He blessed them with his love."

Children came pushing their way through the crowd, elbowing adults and stepping on their feet. The oldest child stepped up to me and spoke in a clear voice.

"My name is Linus. I believe in Him." The child had deep blue eyes and a shock of hair that was as golden as a field of wheat. "I'm going to be His follower." I nodded and put my hands on his head in blessing. A girl almost as tall as he stood beside him. She spoke confidently.

"I believe the stories you told about Jesus."

"And what is your name, child?"

"Ergain." I smiled at her, put my hand on her head, and murmured a prayer. At last, the smallest girl whispered, "I wish I could give him a hug. I love him."

"And your name, dear?"

"Gladys." It was so softly spoken I had to bend to hear her. I put my hand on her head. She tilted her chin upward and looked at me with shining eyes. In that moment, I thought of his teaching: Unless we become as little children, we will not enter the kingdom of heaven.

Roberta M. Damon

PAUL'S LETTER TO HIS MOTHER FROM PHILIPPI
51 *AD*   804 *AUC*

From Paul, an Apostle of the Lord Jesus Christ, to my beloved mother who is my sister in the faith, from the church that is in Lydia's house: I greet you in the name of the Lord. Young Timothy is with me. I give thanks for the Lord Christ who works in him. In Troas, I saw a vision. A man of Macedonia, called to us to come over and help. We set sail and by the power of the Spirit of God, we came to Philippi. On the Sabbath day, we found women praying by the river. Lydia, a wealthy woman, brought us into her own house where we proclaimed Christ unto her. She and her household received our words with joy. We have suffered imprisonment, beatings, and deprivation. We do so gladly for the glory of the Lord Christ who has cleansed us from all unrighteousness. We find rest in Lydia's house. May the God of all righteousness give you peace and comfort and strengthen you in your time of suffering. Greet all the brethren in your house.

ROBERTA M. DAMON

THE ANOINTING 51 *AD* 804 *AUC*

GLADYS SPEAKS:

 I open my eyes in the half light. I see Gwynedd moving around the room, laying out the ritual garments. Now, suddenly, I am wide awake. This day, I shall be officially ushered into the clan.

"Is my father in from the field?" I rub the sleep from my eyes and kick the covers aside.

"Yes, my lady. The king arrived late last night." Gwynedd held a robe warmed by the open fire for me.

"Poor man. He was so weary. He barely touched his food. Here, my lady, put on this robe. You mustn't catch a chill." Gwynedd was present at my birth. She has cared for me all my life.

"Thank you, Gwynedd. Please tell my mother I'm awake. Then you may call the women."

"Yes, my lady." She pushed the draperies aside. It is customary for the wise women of the clan to gather for the anointing just as the first rays of the sun appear on the horizon. Their incantations hold special power at daybreak. The official ceremony will take place at noon in the high place of worship. All the members of the community will be there, but this ceremony is for the women. It will be held in my bedchamber. When a girl turns fifteen, the wise women gather to bestow their blessing upon her. No one remembers just when this custom began. It is very old–as old as the earth. My mother was blessed on her fifteenth birthday and my grandmother and her mother before her–all the way back to when no one can remember anymore. They do it to call forth all good spirits.

I hear my mother's footsteps. My mother is a true queen. I love to look at her. People think I look like her.

She makes me proud. She has taught me to walk tall as she does, with head held high. She says it is the mark of royalty.

"Good morning, mother."

"Good morning, daughter. Did you sleep well?"

"Yes, and I dreamed of roses in a green meadow full of galloping white horses."

"Roses are sweet and horses are swift. Both are beautiful. A dream of sweetness, strength and beauty is a good omen for your initiation day. Are you ready for the ceremony? Here, let me brush your hair."

Mother set aside the flask of scented oil and the sash of red lambs wool she carried in her hands. She picked up the brush and began gently to brush the tangles from my hair. She rubbed my neck and shoulders. I love my mother's hands. I look at her hands, sometimes, when she does not know I am watching. Her hands are busy, gentle, soft as they caress, strong in reprimand. Her fingers are long, the nails oiled and buffed. Her hands are clean. They smell of spices. Most of all I love my mother's hands as they cup my face so that when I look at her, I see her looking back at me, looking deep into my eyes with such love as I never hope to find on this earth again.

At the sound of a rustling skirt I look up to see my Aunt Gladys standing at my bedside with a crown of blossoms in her hands. I love my Aunt Gladys. I am her namesake. My older sister is named for our mother. But I am named for Gladys. She is more like a big sister than an aunt. She is funny and fun, always ready for adventure.

"Good morning, Bright Eyes." She grinned at me. "I understand that there is a beautiful young princess who is fifteen today and is ready to be initiated. Have you seen anyone that fits such a description?"

"Good morning, Aunt Glad. I think you must be thinking about me. I'm fifteen." I smiled up at her. When do we begin?"

Gladys smiled. "I saw the crones gathering as I came in. We begin when they say we begin."

Three old women entered my room bringing spices, holy water and wine. The women spread sheepskin on the floor and bid me sit upon it. They placed the wreath of flowers on my brow and formed a circle around me and began to chant in unison:

Bless, O Chief of generous chiefs,
Myself and everything anear me,
Bless me in all my actions,
Make Thou me safe for ever,
Make Thou me safe for ever.

The oldest of the crones held up a cup of wine. Her voice was thin, but she did not falter in her incantation. She faced me and bid me bow my head. With every line spoken she dipped her thumb into the cup and anointed forehead, temples, cheeks, chin, shoulders, throat, breasts, belly and feet.

From every brownie and banshee,
From every evil wish and sorrow,
From every nymph and water wraith,
From every fairy-mouse and grass-mouse.
From every troll among the hills,
From every siren hard pressing me,
From every ghoul within the glens,

The other women joined her, their voices rising like mist from the river:

Oh! Save me till the end of my day.
Oh! Save me till the end of my day.

The women circled me about, placing their hands upon my head. They anointed me with oil. They bade me sip from the cup of wine. They sprinkled my shoulders with spices and my hands with drops of wine.

I bathe thy palms
In showers of wine,

In the lustral fire,
In the seven elements,
In the juice of the rasps,
In the milk of honey.
And I place the nine pure choice graces
In thy fair fond face.

Each crone pronounced a grace while placing her hands upon my head in blessing. As one finished speaking, she stepped aside and another took her place, circling, ever circling:
The grace of form,
The grace of voice,
The grace of fortune,
The grace of goodness,
The grace of wisdom,
The grace of charity,
The grace of choice maidenliness,
The grace of whole-souled loveliness,
The grace of goodly speech.

They stepped aside beckoning to my mother. Queenly in every respect, she knelt before me. She placed the red woolen sash around my shoulders. She smiled through tears as she chanted:
Thou art the joy of all joyous things,
Thou art the light of the beam of the sun,
I responded:
Thou art the door of the chief of hospitality,
Thou art the surpassing star of guidance,
Thou art the step of the deer of the hill,
Thou art the step of the steed of the plain.
And then, my mother spoke again:
Thou art the grace of the swan of swimming,
Thou art the loveliness of all lovely desires.

Then, all the women chanted in unison:
The best hour of the day be thine.
The best day of the week be thine.
The best week of the year be thine.
Shield this child from sin.
Shield this child from ill.
May all fruitfulness be hers.
May all blessing be hers.

Gently, my mother took from around her neck the talisman her mother had given to her on the occasion of her anointing. My mother had worn it since the day she was fifteen. She kissed it and placed it around my neck. I felt as if I had been crowned.

"Oh, mother, it is so beautiful."

"Wear it in love until you pass it on to your own daughter." My mother's smile warmed my heart.

"When I was little, I thought it looked like a flower. See the petals?"

"Your grandmother told me that it represents the three stages of a woman's life: maiden, mother, and crone. I think of it as representing body, mind and spirit in perfect balance. If you put your finger on any part of it, you will trace it forever. It never ends. One part flows into another, like life. It is eternal, just as love is eternal."

"I'll take good care of it. I do thank you with all my heart." She kissed me gently on the forehead.

The sunlight streamed into the whitewashed chamber. The women embraced me and then bowed before me and my mother. Then they retired and left us alone. My mother spoke with a tremor in her voice. "I do wish you every good thing, my dear child."

"And I you, mother."

"I have every good thing. My children bless me. My husband protects me."

"Gwynedd says that my father is in from the field."

"Yes. He wouldn't miss this day." A shadow passed over her face and she shivered slightly.

"Do you worry, mother?"

"Yes, of course, I worry."

"I worry about him, too. I know my father fights for the honor of Siluria. I just wish they would leave us alone. Why do they have to own the whole world? I can barely remember a time when my father was not at risk in battle."

"I know. You were only–dear me, how old were you when the war began–six? Seven?"

"Seven, I think. Oh, I do remember when I was really little and father would carry me on his shoulders and let me pick quince and haws and blackberries."

"I remember that. You came home with juice staining your face and hands and clothes, your hair tangled and your bare feet dirty. You were a disgrace. But what joyful laughter in those days. There has been too little laughter these last years."

"But today there'll be laughter again. He's home safe."

"Yes, he's safe for now. Well, let's have a look at your robe. I see Gwynedd sewed up the hem."

Mother held up the garment I would wear later in the day. It is of the finest white linen and is intricately embroidered with gold thread. "It's beautiful and so are you. My heart's desire is that you shall be as beautiful in your attitude and in your actions as you are today in form and face. True beauty is of the heart, you know. True nobility comes from within."

"You have always taught me so. I am grateful to you. I want you and my father to be proud of me."

"Oh, my dear. You are a source of such joy and pride to us both." For a moment, my mother held me fast in her arms, my face against her breast. I bid farewell to my childhood in those moments. Now I am a woman. My fingers sought the small gold disc at my throat. It felt warm to my touch. Warm, like my mother's smile.

At high noon we lined up–fifteen-year-old boys and girls, eager to enter into the adult privilege and responsibility of the clan. The priests led the way to the high place down the long avenue lined with huge monoliths. Stones, so ancient no one remembers how or when they were placed on the hill, encircle the open place of worship. The priests chant incantations to the heavens, to the great lights, and to the fecund earth. One by one, we step up to face the bard who stands behind the altar and chants each initiate's genealogy back through nine generations of free Britons. All challengers are invited to come forward with any objection. As I listen to the bard retell my own family history, I smile. My father's family pedigree can be traced back into antiquity hundreds of years. Our family began to keep a record of our generations long before the founding of Rome. I don't know why the Roman armies are in our country causing trouble. I would like to tell them to go back to where they came from and let my father come home to stay. The bard completes his chant. It is time for the priests to ask the questions. One by one, we respond with the correct answers and we are anointed with oil. They pronounce blessings. We are embraced by the priests and welcomed into the clan.

I am of the royal line. My mother stands tall and proud beside my father. My father is a good king. At the name of Caradoc, all knees bow in homage. I burst with pride when I look at him. He is a big man–massively built, every bit the warrior-king. I can see, out of the corner of my eye, my older brothers and my sister. They would make me laugh if they could. They are proud of me, but that doesn't mean they have stopped teasing me. Now that I am officially a member of the clan, they must treat me more respectfully. Today is my day. Tomorrow, my father will take the field again and we shall all be sad and worried for him. But today is mine. Today is a day for celebration.

Roberta M. Damon

"Itum inde in Siluras, super propriam ferociam Carataci viribus confisos, quem multa ambigua, multa prospera extulerant, ut ceteros Britannorum imperatores praeemineret." ("The march proceeded against the Silurians, whose native boldness was heightened by their confidence in the prowess of Caractacus; whose many successes, partial or complete, had raised him to a pinnacle above the other British leaders.")

Tacitus, *Annales* (lib xii) c 33; Jackson (361)

"Caesar's original intention was to carry the war into the interior, but finding his forces inadequate to cope with the British in the field, he abruptly determined to close the campaign."

Don Cassius (lib xxxix 115), 1606 folio as quoted in Morgan, *St. Paul in Britain* (30)

"In 1723, whilst excavating for the foundation of some houses, the monument generally known as the *Chichester Stone,* was discovered. The inscription, which was partly mutilated, and is cut in very bold characters, as restored by Horseley and Gale, is as follows:

Neptuno et Minervae Templum
Pro Salute Domus Divinae
Ex Aucoritate Tib: Claudii
Cogiduni Regis Legati Augusti in Britannia
Collegium Babrorum et qui in eo
A sacris sunt de suo dedicaverunt
Conate Arcam Pudente Pudentini Filio.

The temple was erected about A.D. 50 before the conversion of Pudens and before his marriage with Claudia."

Andrew Gray, *The Origin and Early History of Christianity in Britain* (17)

43

"Enimvero Caratacus huc illuc volitans illum diem, illam aciem testabatur aut reciperandae libertatis aut servitutis aeternae initium fore; Haec ataque taliadicenti adstrepere vulgus, gentili quisque religione obstringi, non telis, non vulneribus cessuros." ("As for Caractacus, he flew hither and thither, protesting that that day and that battle, would be the beginning of the recovery of their freedom, or of everlasting bondage. The host shouted applause. Every warrior bound himself by his national oath not to shrink from weapons or wounds."

Tacitus, *Annals* (lib. xii), McHenry (29-38)

THE WAR   42-52 *AD*   795-805 *AUC*

CARADOC SPEAKS:

 An arch of triumph stands in Rome and another in Gaul, built by the Roman army corps of engineers. The arches are dedicated to Claudius. The arch in Rome is in honor of his great victory over Britain. The one in Gaul is there because it was from Gaul that the largest expeditionary force Rome ever sent out set sail from there. On both arches, these words are cut into marble: *"ARCUS CLAUDII: He received the surrender of eleven British kings who had been defeated without loss in battle, and was the first to bring barbarian people from across the Ocean under the sway of the Roman people."* The inscription infers it was an easy victory. Such was not the case. The phrase "without loss in battle" is sheer fiction. The Roman losses were staggering. Claudius was in Britain only sixteen days. And even after he rushed back to Rome to proclaim to the Roman senate that Britain was under their domination, the war continued for another seven years. The senate had no way of knowing the war was far from over. They conferred on both Claudius and his son the name of *"Britannicus."* They voted that there should be a national holiday to commemorate the emperor's great triumph. When he arrived in Rome, he ascended the steps of the capitol on his knees, supported on each side. He held a grand triumphal festival which included horse racing, bear killing, athletic events, and gladiatorial contests in which British prisoners, along with other foreigners, fought to the death. It was a great day in Rome.

Claudius was well aware that his "victory" was partial at best. As for Rome's defeating the "barbarians," well, I could argue him down on that point. Britons are far from barbaric. It is not we who hack each other to death for entertainment. Our queens do not poison their relatives as the Romans do. No, Claudius knew that it would take more than his presence to put us under Rome's heel.

I suppose if one tries to understand this war, it is necessary to look back to other attempts on our island. Julius Caesar tried to conquer Britain almost a hundred years before Claudius became emperor. Caesar had his eye on the riches of Britain–its wheat and barley, its iron, tin, bronze and gold, its wool and linen goods. During that invasion, in fifty-five days of battle, the Roman battalions managed to advance only seven miles. The second Julian invasion involved more than a thousand Roman ships carrying their army. That campaign lasted four months. The Romans managed to advance only seventy miles inland, and they took no hostage or prisoner of status. The second attempt was more of a failure than the first. The defeat of Julius Caesar by our little island is unparalleled in history. After that, for ninety-seven years, no other Roman attempted to set foot on our land. Rome still remembers the Julian campaign with distaste. For Britain, it is the stuff of which legends are made.

Our island is small compared to the Roman Empire, but our warriors have always been as brave as the legionnaires. Britain is famous for its breed of horses and its daring charioteers. The British fleet, too, was, even then, formidable and her mariners sailed their waters with steady eye and hand. The armies were well–trained and well–manned. Rome was the world and the world was Rome, with the exception of our island to their west.

During the reign of Augustus and Tiberius, Rome spent her manpower in building roads from the capitol westward to Calais, and eastward to the Persian Gulf. The Roman Empire extended across the earth and a hundred and twenty million paid homage and taxes to it. Rome maintained a military complex such as the world had never seen. Her armies were highly disciplined and in a constant state of preparedness.

At one time, during Augustus' reign, war seemed imminent. Augustus sent ambassadors to our island demanding the reinstatement of the properties of three traitors to Britain. The demand was refused on the grounds that Rome had no right to dictate Britain's internal matters. Augustus moved half of his forces within striking distance of our island, but he obviously had no real intention of invading. A British fleet swept the Channel. Augustus was warned by his own advisors that he was courting disaster and so retreated. My grandfather, King Lear, requested a conference with Augustus–his old tutor and honored friend. The result was a triumph of diplomacy. The emperor retracted his demands and reduced the heavy duties imposed on British goods to a light tariff. Diplomatic relations were reinstated and British nobility again resumed their lives in the Roman capitol.

Then there was Caligula. He was the first since Julius Caesar to attempt an invasion. He did it to celebrate his birthday. He was mad, of course. He ordered the armies of Gaul and the Rhine to rendezvous at Boulogne. When the Roman flotilla was moored and prepared to embark, Caligula saw the British fleet gathered to oppose his army and suddenly, he had a change of heart. He began to make light of the whole operation. He held a grand review of his troops on the sands of the shores of Boulogne. Suddenly, he turned to his soldiers and said, "Let us, my comrades, leave these Britons unmolested. To war beyond the bounds of nature is not courage, but impiety. Let us rather load ourselves with the bloodless spoils of the Atlantic ocean which the same beneficent goddess of nature pours on these sands so lavishly at our feet. Follow the example of your emperor. Behold, I wreathe for laurel this garland of green sea weed around my immortal brow, and I fill my helm with these smooth and brilliant shells. Decorated with these we will return to Rome, and, instead of a British King, Neptune and Nereus, the gods of ocean themselves shall follow captives to the Capitol behind our triumphal car." He then promised a year's extra wages to his troops. The British fleet stood scandalized as Roman soldiers in full battle dress began, laughing and shouting like children, and gathering sea shells and sea weed. Caligula's own officers were angered by his antics, but feared to oppose him. He led a grand procession through the streets of Rome on his birthday. Caligula was assassinated the next year– not that the British had anything to do with that, although there were many people who were glad to see him dead. Claudius, rather reluctantly I'm told, succeeded Caligula as emperor.

Two years after Caligula's farcical attempt, Claudius decided to invade in earnest. My armies were prepared to meet the enemy. I stood before my troops to encourage them: "This day, my fellow warriors, this very day, decides the fate of Britain. The era of liberty, or eternal bondage, begins from this hour. Remember your brave and warlike ancestors, who met Julius Caesar in open combat, and chased him from the coast of Britain. They were the men who freed their country from a foreign yoke, who delivered the land from taxes imposed at the will of a master; who banished from your sight the *fasces* and the Roman axes; and above all, who rescued your wives and daughters from violation."

We were battle ready. We would stand and fight. We would die, if necessary, to protect our families, our homes, our freedom. Rome was not at that time engaged in any other war so the entire might of the Roman Empire was thrown against us. Claudius was no Caligula. When Claudius decided to invade Britain, he was as serious as death.

PUDENS SPEAKS:

 I was eighteen when I went to war. My father, the senator, arranged an assignment for me to be aide to General Plautius. I was wild with excitement. I knew that one day I would assume the position of my father in the senate, but my interest had always been engineering. This was my opportunity to observe the army engineers at work in time of war–an invaluable part of my education. From my childhood, I have built things. When I was a boy, I built a bridge over the creek that fed the baths beside our property. I was always interested in watching the road crews lay the stones in the road beds. As soon as I was old enough to ride by myself, I spent my days marveling at the roads, the buildings, the monuments that cover the face of our city. How did they do it? How were they able hundreds of years ago to move so many huge stones and put them in place to form the roads? How did they build the public baths? How did they build the temples? Augustus said he found Rome built of bricks and left it covered in marble. It really is magnificent. I've been to the quarries. They are enormous. I traveled to Luna northwest of Rome to observe the workers cutting the *carrara* marble. It is fine grained with a smooth surface. It is used by both sculptors and builders. I have seen the quarries of the Alban Hills. I walked the miles to Tibur to watch the workers cut the travertine limestone. I loved nothing so much as watching the men clearing the harbor or examining the aquaducts and conduits that bring water into Rome from springs far away. It is rumored that Claudius has great plans. He has plans for a new aquaduct, I know. Everyone is saying that he has resurrected the plans of Julius Caesar for a sea wall at Ostia.

At eighteen, I was off to war. I believed we would strike, overcome the British, and be back in Rome for a grand parade before my next birthday. I stood behind the general, ready for any command. This campaign was triggered by Claudius' refusal to receive ambassadors from Britain. Our troops were already gathering at Bologne. The total invasion force numbered between forty and fifty thousand men. It was before dawn of a hot July day. Our ships were in the harbor ready to board our troops.

"Look, young Pudens." General Plautius pointed out to the Channel. "You are about to see the approach of the British navy. If they are wise, they will turn around and run back home. Watch with me."

I had some difficulty seeing anything through the morning fog, but then I saw the shape of a ship, and another and then another. The general turned to me. "Go down to the dock. Tell the captain to pass the word that the British ships are on their way." I nodded and ran as fast as I could.

"General Plautius commands that you pass the word that the British ships are in the harbor." I was breathless from excitement and from running. Calmly, the captain responded.

"Yes. Message received." My task complete, I ran back up to the observation post. My father could not have chosen a better mentor for me than my general. Aulus Plautius, was a man known to all as being of fine character and dedication to duty. He was an excellent leader and well respected by his men. Now, I stood beside him, proud to be under his command. We stood watch together.

"It won't be long before we know whether they will engage or retreat. My guess is that when they see they are outnumbered they will retreat." We waited and watched. Before the sun was fully risen, slowly, silently their ships slid back in the direction from which they had come. No attempt was made by our ships to stop them. A shout was heard from our armies. With the British navy in retreat, we were ready to embark.

Plautius gave the command for the troops to board. Suddenly, and for no reason I could see, someone shouted, "No!" Others took up the cry. Officers began shouting orders. The orders were disobeyed or ignored. Appeals to duty had no effect. Someone shouted, and the shout was repeated by others: "We will follow you anywhere in the world, but not out of it." A rumor spread that if our ships sailed too far, they would topple into the abyss. Plautius was apoplectic. This was mutiny. The general sent a senior officer to Rome to report to Claudius. We waited for orders from the emperor. The troops were immovable. I'll never forget, days later, when Narcissus hurried in from Rome. He was Claudius' trusted advisor. Narcissus is a eunuch, plump as a girl. He curls his hair and paints his face. I'll never know if Claudius planned for Narcissus to have the effect he did, but the result was immediate and decisive. As soon as Narcissus pranced up to the podium to harangue the troops declaring that he, himself, would lead them into battle, to a man they rose up and demanded that General Plautius assume command. Suddenly, they were ready to fight. Plautius quickly took advantage of their change of attitude. The army embarked in four divisions, I Augusta, the XIV Gemina, the XX Valeria, and the IX Hispania. They landed two days afterward at Rutupium. The war was on.

We made camp. Our engineers set to work overseeing the digging of huge earthworks. With my general's permission, I consulted with the army corps of engineers. They designed and built a temple to Nepture and Minerva. They cut in stone the following words:

NEPTUNE AND MINERVA
A TEMPLE
THE COLLEGE OF ENGINEERS AND MINISTERS OF RELIGION ATTACHED TO IT, BY PERMISSION OF TIBERIUS CLAUDIUS COGIDUNUS, THE KING, LEGATE OF AUGUSTUS IN BRITAIN, HAVE DEDICATED AT THEIR OWN EXPENSE, IN

HONOR OF THE IMPERIAL FAMILY THIS TEMPLE TO NEP-
TUNE AND MINERVA. THE SITE WAS GIVEN BY PUDENS,
SON OF PUDENTINUS.

Romans do not go into battle without paying homage
to the gods.

I listened and learned. General Plautius and his advisors allowed me to sit in on strategy planning. As Caesar
had directed his march along the Sarn, so Plautius moved
his own troops. Our first encounter was with Guiderius
and Caradoc at Southfleet across the river on the flats
between the hills of Kent and the Thames. The Britons
retreated. In that battle, Guiderius fell. His brother,
Arviragus, succeeded him. The British elected Caradoc
Pendragon–their military dictator. He became Rome's
nemesis. Three times Plautius attempted to force his way
across the Thames. Three times he was foiled. Caradoc
was a formidable foe. For two days of desperate fighting,
he was able to hold off three Roman generals–Plautius,
Vespasian and Geta. Caradoc did not quit. He regrouped.
Plautius was forced to send messages to Rome for instructions and reinforcements. The emperor, himself, came to
Britain. He brought with him his Praetorian guards, the
eighth legion, and a detachment of elephants. Yes, elephants. They were to confound the British horses, which,
I must say, they did. Their odor so confused the horses
that the British chariots were soon in total disarray. So,
there was a decisive victory for us at Colchester. The
emperor soon left Britain for Rome. He announced to the
Senate that Britain was now under Roman rule. That was
not entirely true. The war was just beginning.

Theirs Is The Kingdom

"*Anno autem ab Urb condita septingentesimo nonaagesimo octavo Claudius imperador, ab Augusto quartus, cupiens se utilem reipublicae ostentare principem, bellum ubique, et victorium, undecumque quaecivit. Itaque expeditionem in Brittanium movit. . .Hoc autem bellus quarto imperii sui anno complevit, qui est annus ab incarnatione Domini quadragesimus sextus quo etiam anno fames gravissima per Syriam facta est, quae in Actibus Apostolorum per prophetam Agabum praedicta esse memoratur.*" ("Now in the 798th year from the building of Rome, Claudius, the fourth emperor after Augustus, being much desirous to show himself a prince profitable unto the commonwealth, sought war on all sides and victory whencesoever it might come. And so he made a voyage unto Britain. . .This war was brought to an end in the fourth year of his empire; which was the forty sixth year of the incarnation of our Lord: in the which year also there fell in the Acts of the Apostles, is shewed to be fore-spoken by the mouth of Agabus the prophet.")

Bede, *Historical Works* from Thomas Stapelton, 1565 (26-27)

"And there stood up one of them named Agabus, and signified by the spirit that there should be great dearth throughout all the world: which came to pass in the days of Claudius Caesar."

Acts 11:28

THE PEACE WEAVERS   45*AD*   798 *AUC*

PUDENS SPEAKS:

Plautius appeared in the doorway of his tent and called for his leaders. Officers and advisors gathered. I stood just behind the general and listened to their discussion.

"We are badly bloodied. Our troops are decimated. Winter is coming on. You may recall from last winter's ice that winter in Britain is like nothing we ever experienced in Rome.

We need time to regroup. The British are far stronger than we anticipated and they are not going to give up." Plautius paused. "We can ask for a truce and try to settle our differences with diplomacy. Or we can rest our men and horses, wait out the winter, and in the spring, fight on. One thing is certain. We cannot fight now without massive reinforcements. The decision is mine, but I welcome your opinions. What say you?"

"I say we fight on and fight now. If we are bloodied, so are they." Drusis Tullius was young and ambitious. "Diplomacy never conquers."

"I disagree. Our men are in no condition to mount another attack. And if supplies do not arrive soon, we will be in danger of running low on food. The soldiers are battle weary. We cannot risk another battle. We need fresh troops." The opinion was voiced by Aulus Tyrenius, a veteran of many campaigns.

"If we call for reinforcements when can we expect them to be battle ready and in place?"

"The tenth legion can be here before Spring."

I listened as each man expressed his opinion. War is not what I expected it to be. When I was assigned to General Plautius, I thought only of the adventure. I have discovered that war is made up of long periods of tedium broken by horrifying battles. We have been in Britain for three years now. We have engaged the enemy in nine major battles and innumerable skirmishes. I have seen men and horses hacked to pieces. I have seen forests burned and villages sacked. There is no army on earth like ours, but these Britons are determined to stand their ground. I don't know what Plautius will do. Going into winter quarters means keeping men and horses fit and maintaining military discipline. Even I agree that fighting now is out of the question. My attention wandered until I was abruptly brought back to the discussion at hand.

"Pudens, call for a scribe."

"Yes, general." I ran through the camp to the tent of my friend, Marcus.

"Marcus, the general is calling for you."

"Ah, so the general needs me. The fate of Rome is now in my hands."

"Don't stop to play games. General Plautius is in no mood for foolishness." Marcus gathered up his writing materials.

"Patience, young Pudens. Rome will not fall in the next hour." I pulled at his sleeve.

"Hurry. Follow me." I ran back to the general's tent with Marcus trailing behind.

"We are calling for a truce." General Plautius looked at me. Rufus, you will deliver the message to Caradoc's camp.

"I am honored." My heart beat fast as I thought of going into the enemy camp. General Plautius dictated while Marcus wrote:

"To Caradoc, King of Siluria, General of the Armies of Britian: This is to inform you that I am willing to call a halt to our hostilities so that we may negotiate our differences. I request that you send your response by the hand of my aide, Rufus Pudens Pudentia."

"Sign that 'Aulus Plautius, Commanding General of the Armies of Rome.'" Marcus wrote carefully. He blotted the scroll, rolled it and tied it with a leather thong.

The general handed me the rolled message.

"The gods go with you, Pudens. Do not fail in this mission."

"I will not fail you, general." I tucked the message inside my tunic. I felt excitement and dread. I had no weapons. I carried a flag as a signal that my purpose was peaceful. I mounted my horse and rode toward the enemy camp.

Everything was eerily quiet. I rode alone through open country, through deep meadows flanked by woods. Up hills and through gullies, I heard only the clatter of my horse's hooves and the beating of my own heart. Nothing moved. I felt the eyes of the enemy on my back. From the moment I crested the highest hill, I knew the woods around me were full of British fighters. I lifted my banner and called out, "Truce!" I carefully and slowly spurred my horse onward. Suddenly, I was knocked from my mount. Two blue-painted warriors grabbed me under the arms and propelled me forward. My mind whirled. Surely, I would die.

"I am unarmed." They half carried half dragged me to the edge of the woods. Suddenly, I saw the tents of the British forces. The soldiers held both my arms in their strong grip. I offered no resistance. They took me directly to their general's tent.

I shall never forget my first sight of King Caradoc. When he stood, he towered over me. His shoulders were broad and his arms and legs muscular and as big around as logs. His hair, whitened with lime, stood in spikes. His mustaches were magnificent and were also caked with the white powder. His bearing was erect and regal. Dressed in a fine woolen tunic and a heavy cloak, he exuded power. I felt fear, but did not show it. He spoke in a voice that was deep and commanding.

"Who are you?"

"Rufus Pudens Pudentia, aide to General Aulus Plautius."

"And what is your business here?"

"I bring a message from my general to you, sir."

"What is this message?"

"It is underneath my tunic. I am unarmed. May I give it to you?"

"You may." Only then, did the two British fighters let go of my arms. I felt bruised. I slowly reached into my tunic and handed the message to Caradoc. I had been told that he was educated in Rome and not only reads Latin, but uses our language eloquently. He read, called for a quill and wrote one word across the face of Plautius' message: TRUCE. He handed it back to me.

"Take this to your general. We shall negotiate the truce three days from now at sun up in my tent."

Someone brought me my horse. I mounted with relief. I would live. I rode back to report to Plautius. Had Caradoc refused to negotiate, his men would have cut off my head and sent my horse back with my headless body–his message to my general. I spurred my horse onward. As I rode toward our camp, I saw my general on the crest of the hill, waiting and watching.

"So a truce it is, Pudens," he shouted. I spurred my mount and rode up the hill. I reigned in and dismounted. Plautius clapped me on the shoulder.

"Welcome back. Well done." I saluted and handed him the message from Caradoc. Suddenly, my knees felt weak. I began to shake. Plautius roared with laughteer.

"Bring this soldier wine." He turned to me. "Sit down, young friend. You've gone pale as a girl." Someone handed me a cup of wine. Gratefully, I drank. I was surrounded by my compatriots. They cheered. They laughed. They embraced me and each other. I was lucky to be alive.

Three days later, General Plautius and his advisors met with Caradoc and his staff. There, in Caradoc's camp, they negotiated the terms of the truce as follows:

In order to insure peace, it shall be agreed that neither Rome nor Britain will use arms against the other.

Caradoc shall go to Rome to negotiate peace with the

Emperor Claudius and his advisors. He will argue for the sovereignty of Britain and plead for a lowering of tariffs on British goods.

Within a half a year, all Roman troops shall leave Britain.

British citizens living in Rome shall not be molested.

Educational exchange will be encouraged.

Trade between Rome and Britain shall resume.

Diplomatic relations between Rome and Britain shall be restored.

To seal the bargain, Aulus Plautius will be married to Caradoc's sister, Gladys, and Claudius will give his niece, Venus Julia, in marriage to Arviragus.

If the truce holds, Britain may yet enjoy a cordial relationship with Rome while, at the same time, refusing to relinquish her sovereignty. We shall see.

GLADYS SPEAKS:

I have always loved my Aunt Gladys. I am named for her. Our name means "princess." And, of course, we both are truly princesses. Her father is King Bran who is my grandfather. My father is King Caradoc, Aunt Gladys' brother. Sometimes I watch her as she studies. She is a Greek scholar and a writer. Perhaps that's where I get my interest in poetry. I can remember when I was little that my Aunt Gladys taught me my letters. I know some words in Greek and can write it. I do know Latin well. My father taught all us children Latin almost as soon as we could talk. My mother tried to teach me to weave tapestries, but I'm not good at it and it doesn't interest me.

"Gladys, come." My Aunt Gladys called to me from our front door. "Let's find a quiet place to sit. I feel I haven't had a moment's rest these last few days." I nodded agreement and fell into step with her.

We walked the path through our woods until we came to our special place, a bower of moss-covered ground beside a quiet little stream surrounded by great trees which shut out the sun in summer. We discovered it long ago. Sometimes we sail boats of leaves in the stream. Sometimes we build a dam with stones and mud and twigs. We sit on the bank and dangle our feet in the cold, clear water. Sometimes, I put my face close to the surface. I can see the sandy bottom rolling with pebbles smoothed and polished. I love to watch the tiny fish darting to and fro. This is our secret place, perfect for hiding or talking or giggling. I think of it as a girls' place. My aunt settled herself on the grassy bank and took sweets from the basket she carried. She smiled as she gave me a small cake, but somehow, behind her smile, I thought I saw sadness. We've always known, without words, what the other is thinking and feeling.

I took the sweet with thanks. "You are different." It was a statement, not a question.

"Yes."

"Tell me, then."

My aunt sighed. "I hardly know where to begin. This is going to be difficult for both of us."

"Has something happened?"

"Yes." She took a deep breath. "Gladys, dear little one, I am going away."

"Away? Where?"

"I am going to live in Rome."

"What do you mean? You can't live in Rome. Rome is our enemy." Suddenly, I felt a tightness in my chest.

"Gladys, do you understand what a truce is."

"I know the armies have stopped fighting. Is a truce the end of the war?"

"Not exactly. A truce is more a temporary peace. Both armies agree to stop fighting and they negotiate. Do you know the word 'negotiate'?" She looked at me inquiringly.

"I'm not sure."

"Negotiate is when they try to work something out. One side agrees to something and then the other side agrees to something and maybe the war will end. As a part of the truce, the daughter of the Roman Emperor will be married to our General Arviragus. And the other side of that agreement is that I shall be married to the Roman General, Aulus Plautius." She looked at me, her eyes pleading for my understanding. "And then, after we are married, he will take me to Rome to be part of his family."

"Why? You don't have to do this. I'll talk to my father. He won't make you do this."

"It's already settled. I shall marry General Aulus Plautius and we shall live in Rome."

I felt I was smothering. "Please, don't go. What shall I do without you? I hate this. It's not fair. You don't even know General Plautius. Why is my father making you do this?"

"Gladys, don't be angry with your father. I do this for Siluria. Do you know about the peace weavers?"

"I don't know what you are talking about."

"Let me tell you. Men fight wars, child. They fight for gain. They fight for freedom. They fight to protect their families. They fight to protect their domains. Sometimes they fight to conquer and to acquire new territory. Women wait. Women have never loved war. Women have always been a part of the spoils of war, but they weep to send their husbands and sons to battle. Women of high estate have often been traded for peace. We call ourselves the peace weavers. Think of it, Gladys. There is a quiet power in peace weaving. If, by my marrying General Plautius, the war will end, think of the good things that will come of it. Your father will come home to stay. Our men will not die at the hands of the Romans. There will be no more killing. Peace is better. If I can be a part of making peace, I will."

"I can't live without you."

61

"Yes, you can. And you can come to visit me in Rome. And I can come home to Siluria to visit. It won't be so bad. You'll see."

"It will be bad. It won't be like it always has been. I will miss you."

"I will miss you, too."

"I can't believe you are going to be married."

"I know. I can hardly believe it myself. But, I believe it is right. I am at peace within my self." She offered me another sweet cake, but I wasn't hungry anymore.

"Is he handsome?"

"I suppose so. He is not so tall, but broad and muscular."

"Is he rich?"

"I imagine Rome has paid him well."

"Are you going to have babies?"

"Perhaps."

"What shall I call him?"

"He will be your uncle."

"Uncle Plautius? Uncle Aulus?"

"You will have opportunity to ask him. Oh, I must tell you. I have been asked to take a Roman name."

"You won't be my Aunt Gladys anymore?"

"I'll always be your Aunt Gladys. The name I have chosen is a beautiful one, I think."

"What is it?"

"I shall be known in Rome as Pomponia–Pomponia Graecina."

"Pomponia Graecina." The name tasted like honey in my mouth. "Pomponia Graecina." It has the sound of dignity and grace. "When will you be married?"

"Soon."

I stood and brushed the dirt from my clothes. I tried not to cry. I hugged my Aunt Gladys Pomponia Graecina. She hugged me back.

"Be happy, Gladys. Remember the peace weavers. It is a splendid thing."

PUDENS SPEAKS:

I finished brushing the general's cloak. He paced nervously.

"Well, Pudens. Today I shall be married. We must be at the royal residence by midday." The general was as excited as if he had chosen the bride himself.

"Yes, general." He was dressed in full military regalia. I placed his cloak around his shoulders. "What do you know about your bride?"

"She is of royal blood, the sister of King Caradoc. I have seen her only once. She is comely in the British way. She is intelligent. I understand that she is a Greek scholar. I shall have to see to it that she is instructed in the ways of Roman domesticity. She will bear me many sons."

"And the emperor's daughter will marry Arviragus?"

"Correct. Next month in Rome, Claudius is giving Venus Julia to Britain's second in command. Too bad Caradoc is already married. He might have been the one to be wed to Julia. With my marriage and with Julia's, the alliance between Rome and Britain will be doubly sealed."

"Shall you keep your command?" If Plautius was recalled to Rome, I, too, would be ending my military service.

"As long as the truce holds, I will remain at this post. If hostilities should break out again, I will be recalled. Claudius will not allow the brother-in-law of the British king to remain as commander-in-chief of Rome's armies. Well, we shall hope the alliance holds, though I must admit I would like to go home. The British are more stubborn than we imagined. I trust that stubbornness does not extend to my bride." He laughed. "That is one Briton I shall conquer."

Plautius mounted his horse. A column of Roman officers followed him. They rode, backs straight, chins in, heels down, in perfect cadence, toward the British royal residence. Every horse was curried, every breastplate and epaulet was shined to a high gloss. This was a wedding procession. The Roman general was to receive his royal British bride.

The wedding took place in their high place of worship. The druidic priests, dressed in white and gold, chanted blessings on the couple. The bride was, indeed, comely if a bit delicate. All these British women have golden hair and blue eyes. They are not nearly as voluptuous as our Roman women. Give me a woman with black hair, dark eyes and flesh on her body. These British women are bones covered with pale skin. This bride may be a princess, but she doesn't look capable of bearing sons for the general– maybe a daughter or two. Oh well! Any sacrifice for the glory of Rome!

CARADOC SPEAKS:

 The truce held for six months. During the break in the war, I went to Rome. I did not bow before Claudius. Hostilities broke out again over some small misunderstanding. There is no trust between Britain and Rome. Plautius was recalled to Rome. Claudius took a dim view of my brother-in-law's keeping his command. He and my sister left for Rome where she, no doubt, learned to be a proper Roman matron. I am proud of my sister. She showed her allegiance to Siluria. She did her duty. The truce seems a hundred years ago, though it has been only seven.

I have fought thirty battles with the Romans–nine before the truce and the others after. I have often been outnumbered, but never outmaneuvered. I know the terrain. I know every corner of this island. I also know the Romans are more prone to use brute force than finesse. My forces faced a hundred thousand men, and we did not fail.

We relied on surprise attacks. I encountered Rome's best–
Plautius, Geta, Vespasian, Ostorius Scapula. Once I had
Vespasian at sword's point in his own tent, when his son,
Titus, led the first cohort of the fourteenth legion to his
rescue. Even the Roman chronicles record my victories.
Never was I conquered. I was, however, most foully be-
trayed.

ROBERTA M. DAMON

PAUL TO RUFUS PUDENS FROM GALATIA: 51 *AD*   804 *AUC*

 I, Paul, write these things to you, Rufus, my brother, that you may know the truth that you may have liberty in the Lord Jesus Christ. I hear that you completed your service to Rome and have returned to your household. My prayers have been for you, for I know that you can be a useful vessel, fit for service in His name. I would that you not only be my brother in the flesh, but that you also be my son, begotten by me into eternal life. I proclaim to you Jesus Christ, who was, in the fulness of time, born of a virgin, nourished in the Law, lived a perfect life, worked many signs and wonders, was arrested, tried, and convicted, and suffered death on the cross, laid in the tomb, and rose again the third day. Believing this, Rufus, you may have eternal life. Grace be to you. I long for you that you may know the joy of the Lord. Greet our mother who has prayed unceasingly for you. Salute those of your household.

"Clara ea victoria fuit, captaque uxor et filia Carataci fratresque in deditionem accepti." ("It was a glorious victory; the wife and daughters of Caractacus were captured, and their brothers, too, were admitted to surrender."
Tacitus, *Annals*, lib xii, McHenry (29-38)

THE CAPTURE · 51 *AD* · 804 *AUC*

BRAN SPEAKS:

 Everyone huddled together in the great hall. I stood to address the gathering. I saw Gladys touch the gold circle at her throat. She moved close to her mother. I was not going to convince anyone that we were not in danger, but I wanted to avoid an outbreak of panic.

"This is the time for bravery." I kept my voice low. "We know that the Roman armies are coming here. They are on their way even as we speak." The air was thick with tension. No one moved.

"What will happen to us?" My granddaughter is brave. Her question was asked in a clear voice that did not tremble.

"Stay calm and listen to me. We men will meet them at the gate. We will be unarmed and we will let them know that we are willing to talk peace. While the king is in the field, Cynon, Linus, and I are the male leaders of this family." All eyes fell on the three of us. What they saw was one frail old man and two beardless boys–not a reassuring sight.

"What will happen if they are unwilling to listen to you?"

"You are not to concern yourself with that. All male servants will stand with us. We will protect our women and children. Queen Ergain, Gladys, and little Ergain will be responsible for keeping everyone calm inside the house." I lifted my face and hands toward heaven.

"Great Lord of life, keep this house from evil." Gwynedd began to weep softly. Gladys reached out to her.

"Don't cry, Gwynedd. Stay close to me. Listen to my grandfather and do as he says."

I looked around the room. "Let us remember, we put our trust in God. Truth against the world." Everyone repeated it in unison. Their voices did not waver: "Truth against the world." Thus fortified, I motioned to the men. We moved out to meet the Roman legionnaires

We stood silently under the trees. We did not have long to wait. In the distance, we could see a contingent of what looked to be a hundred men in battle dress, well mounted, and galloping at full speed straight toward us. The hooves of the horses sounded like thunder across the meadow. A hundred yards from the gate, the centurion held up his hand and called his men to a halt. Everything stopped. There was no noise except an occasional whinny from the horses and the sound of their stamping feet. The centurion dismounted. He walked toward us. I squared my shoulders, lifted my head, and went out to meet him.

"Who is in the house?" The centurion barked the question.

"Women and children only. No one here is armed."

"Is the queen here?"

"Yes."

"Are her children with her?"

"They are." The centurion picked up a sharp stick from the ground. He made marks in the dirt and handed the stick to me.

"Draw a diagram of the house. Show me where the entrances are located."

"Yes, Commander. As I took the stick, I looked down at the marks the Roman had made. I saw in the dirt, two curved lines forming a simple fish. I looked into the impassive face of the Roman commander. I thought I detected a slight nod of the head, though it might have been my imagination. I looked into the man's eyes trying to read a message in the expressionless face. I took the stick and drew the requested diagram.

"There are entrances here, here, here, and here." I drew two curved marks at the top of the drawing. The message was clear to us both. The centurion feigned interest in the diagram, and then he turned to his cohort.

"Surround the house. Harm no one. The goods and

people are to be saved. Take family members and their personal servants hostage. The others may go free. Do not burn. Do not take spoil. Leave the women unharmed. I have instructions to deliver the hostages safely into the hands of Ostorius Scapula. The man who harms one hair on the heads of any one of these prisoners will be executed by my own hand. Do not draw your swords. You have your orders."

The soldiers surrounded the house. Four of them went in to round up the members of the royal family. They were almost obsequious in their treatment of them. The soldiers put each hostage on the back of a horse behind a legionnaire: Queen Ergain, her daughters, her sons. I stepped forward.

"I'm going with you."

"Get out of the way, old man."

"I demand to be taken with you. I am responsible for the safety of this family."

"You?" It was a hoot of derision.

"Take him." It was a command shouted by the captain. I nodded my thanks. In what looked like sleight of hand, a soldier lifted me and threw me onto the back of a horse.

We took courage. We were not to be harmed. We had no news of the battle, nor of Caradoc. We rode toward the *castra.*

"Ipse, ut ferme intuta sunt adversa, cum fidem, Cartimanduae reginae Brigantum petivisset, vinctus ac victoribus traditus est,nono post anno, quam bellum in Britannia coeptum." ("Caractucus himself–for adversity seldom finds a refuge–after seeking the protection of the Briganian queen Cartimandua (Arregwedd), was arrested and handed to the victors, in the ninth year from the opening of the war in Britain.")

        Tacitus, *Annales.* (lib xii, c 36) as quoted in Jackson
           (364-365)

"In Britannia Romanos post Caractaci captivitatem ab una tantum Siluram civitate sawpius victos et profligatos." ("In Britain, after the captivity of Caractacus, the Romans were repeatedly conquered and put to the rout by the single state of the Silures alone.")

        Tacitus *Annals* (lib. v. c. 28) as quoted in McHenry
           (29-30)

"Cartismandua Brigantibus imperitabat, pollens nobilitate; et auxerat protentiam, postquam capto per dolum rege Carataco instruxisse triumphum Claudii Casesaris videbatur." ("Cartismandua [Arregwedd] strengthened her throne when, by the treacherous capture of King Caractacus, she was regarded as having given its chief distinction to the triumph of Claudius Caesar.")

        Tacitus *Annals* (lib. iii) as quoted in McHenry (38-46)

THE BETRAYAL   51 *AD*   804*AUC*

CARADOC SPEAKS:

 We were half dead from exhaustion, our faces covered with dirt, sweat and drying blood. We rode our lathered horses to the nearest shelter. We were, by my calculations, due north of Siluria, close to Caer Evroc. Finally, after days of heavy battle, the Roman army, under the command of Ostorius Scapula, had, for the moment, at least, prevailed. Regan and I reigned in our mounts. Regan, my loyal aide, has been with me through many a battle. When I face danger, I am happy to have my old companion at my side. We stopped under a protecting grove of elms. Our horses were trembling with fatigue.

"Look." I pointed to the north. "A rider." We waited, alert to danger. "He sees us. Keep your sword ready." The rider approached us and reined in his mount.

"You are Caradoc, King of Siluria?"

"Who asks?"

"Kerick, a servant of Queen Aregwedd of the Brigantes. I bring news. Are you Caradoc?"

"I am. What news do you bring and from whence do you ride?"

"I am in the service of your kinswoman. I bring this letter written in her own hand."

Regan approached the messenger, took the missive and handed it to me   I opened it and read:

"To Caradoc, esteemed cousin, by the hand of my servant, Kerick, I, Aregwedd, write unto you to inform you of the calamity which had befallen you, your wife, and your children. Ostorius is victorious in the field. Your armies are routed. Your wife, your daughters, your sons, and your father have fallen into the hands of your enemy. Your fam-

73

ily has been carried to the *castra* at Uriconium where they are being held prisoner. I solicit you, not for the first time, to come and find shelter and restoration at my compound. Do not seek at this time to attempt to rescue your family members. It would be reckless and would put them in mortal danger. Let me assure you that according to the intelligence I have received, they are being well treated. Caradoc, dear cousin, come to my palace to rest. I can help you to free your family. I have a plan. Trust me. All will be well. Farewell."

I rolled up the letter and put it in my saddle pouch.

"What shall you do?" Regan's eyes questioned me. I thought fast. Aregwedd was not to be trusted. She is loyal to Rome. She is last in a long line of traitors to Britain. Her political leanings reach back to Caswollan's victory over the Tribunates when Mandubratius fled to Rome to save his own neck–traitorous coward that he was. Aregwedd is of that branch of the family. They are vipers, always ready to curry favor with Rome. The woman is my cousin, and queen of the Brigantes. I don't trust her, but she has news of my family. Regan waited for my answer.

"We ride to Aregwedd's compound–and we keep our wits about us." I instructed the messenger to lead the way. We mounted our exhausted steeds and spurred them to-ward Caer Evroc. In an hour of hard riding, we arrived at my cousin's gates. Aregwedd herself came to meet us.

"Dear cousin," she saw the blood on my forehead, "You are wounded."

"It's nothing. What news of my family?"

"Come. You must be calm. Refresh yourself. Wash. Eat. We have ointments for your wounds. I have sent a servant to acquire the latest news of your family. You will feel more at ease when you are clean and you have a full belly." She commanded a servant to see to the horses. He bowed and led the animals toward a stall where they would be fed, watered, and rubbed down.

We were offered the comforts of the house–water, ointments, food. After a meal at which we drank a goodly
portion of red wine, we lay down to sleep. I do not know
how long I slept. Sometime in the blackness of the night, I
opened my eyes. I sensed the presence of someone in the
room with me. The hair on the back of my neck rose. I
came fully awake to a room full of Roman soldiers. I
struggled to sit up. Before I could get to my feet, they slit
Regan's throat. I tried to shout, but no sound came. I felt
a sword's point at my own throat as ten men fettered me
with iron chains. They dragged me to the floor. I kicked
and struggled against the chains. Aregwedd stood to one
side observing it all. I saw her face. Never have I seen a
look of such hateful malice.

"Kill him," she hissed.

"Oh, no. This one will be delivered to our general. The
soldiers surrounded me. I looked into my cousin's eyes.

"Traitor!" I strained with all my strength against the
fetters.

"How the mighty have fallen." She taunted me. "You
have caused Rome much grief with your horses and your
armies. Claudius now owes me a debt I do not intend to
let him forget. All Rome will applaud me. Everyone will
say that it was a frail little woman who brought the great
warrior to his knees. And I will never walk in your shadow
again as long as I live." She turned to leave, but not before she saw me spit on the floor at her feet.

"If harm comes to my wife or my children, their blood
is on your hands. I shall not rest until I avenge this treachery." I heard her caustic laugh.

The soldiers led me away, bound hand and foot, still
struggling.

"Quiet him," shouted the captain. In obedience, someone picked up a large rock and knocked me senseless. I was
mercifully unconscious most of the ride to the *castra* at
Uriconium where I was delivered to the tender mercies of

Ostorius Scapula. As I struggled toward consciousness, I was aware that every bone and muscle in my body ached. The slightest movement caused me pain. I heard someone shout.

"Bring in the prisoner." The captain barked the orders. Four men carried me into the presence of their general.

"Sir, shall we make plans for his execution?"

"Oh, no. Claudius has been waiting a long time for this moment. He may have plans to torture this one before his execution. I'm certain the suffering will be prolonged. Oh no. We don't kill him. We let the emperor decide how he dies. We send to Rome for instructions. Keep him chained. Assign four men at every watch to guard him. Call for a scribe."

Presently, the scribe bustled in with papyrus and ink and arranged himself at a low table. He waited, pen poised. Scapula dictated: "To our great emperor, Claudius, from Uriconium: Hail! I, Ostorio Scapula, inform you, oh most revered Caesar, that I have in my custody, Caradoc-Caractacus and his family. I await your instruction. Honor unto Caesar."

They did let me see my family. My wife and children were brought to me. We were silent until the guards turned their backs. Then my father, my wife and the children gathered around me.

"Have they harmed you or our daughters?" Urgently, I clasped my wife's hands.

"No. They have not harmed us. They have treated us well. But, you, oh my husband, I fear you have been ill-treated." She examined the scrapes and cuts and bruises on my face and head. My daughters and sons embraced me.

"Father, you are wounded." Gladys and Ergain tearfully fluttered around me. I reassured them. "Do not let them see tears. They will take it as weakness. I do not fear for myself. Be strong."

"We shall follow your example, Father."

Linus spoke. "What will they do with us?"

"They will do nothing until they hear from Claudius.

They have wanted to capture me for years. I have cost Rome dearly. Only Claudius will decide what shall be done with me. While we wait, let us be brave. Let us show these Romans British royalty. No groveling. No weeping. Heads held high and hearts of courage."

Gladys whispered to me. "I have concealed my mother's talisman in the folds of my cloak. I shall carry it with me wherever they take us. It gives me strength." And then she whispered in my ear: "Truth against the world."

I smiled at my daughter and responded: "Truth against the world."

For a month we were kept under guard at the *castra*. Finally, word came from the Emperor Claudius: "Bring them to Rome."

THE ARRANGEMENT: 52 *AD* 805 *AUC*

PUDENS SPEAKS:

 I was in a hurry. My thoughts were on the words I would use to frame my request to the emperor. On some level I was aware of my toga ruffling in the breeze against by legs and my sandaled feet making slapping noises on the polished marble corridor. I walked toward the anteroom of the emperor's chambers. I paused and nodded. A praetorian saluted, searched me for weapons, and led me into the presence of Claudius. The emperor was sitting at his writing table, pen in hand, laboring over a document. Claudius serves Rome well. I hear that he arises hours before dawn to begin the day's work. I knelt before him.

He waved me to my feet, and stammered, "S-s-s-enator P-p-p-udens, welcome to my l-l-library. Wh-wh-what brings you here, my son?"

"It is good of you to receive me on such short notice. I come to ask a favor, Caesar."

"And how much will this f-f-f-favor cost me?" Claudius smiled, his mouth drawn downward, his eyebrows raised sardonically, his head bobbing slightly.

"You will be glad to hear that it will cost you nothing. In fact, in a way, I would be the one bestowing the favor. My idea will save you money."

"S-s-so," said the emperor. "Just what is this favor we can do for each other?"

"It has to do with the Briton." I looked earnestly into my sovereign's face. "It is about Caradoc and his family."

"Caradoc? You mean Caractacus? I hope you can do something to s-s-save me m-m-money. He has cost us dearly in the past seven years. D-do you have any idea what s-s-seven years of warfare has cost us in men and materiel? B-b-by the gods, everything costs money. And everybody c-c-complains. Do you know what the Fucine Lake project has c-c-cost us? Eleven years and thirty thousand men d-digging through solid rock and the thing doesn't w-work. D-d-do you know h-how humiliating it is to st-stage a great sp-spectacle, to c-c-celebrate the opening of the sl-sluices and n-nothing happens?"

"But the principle is sound. We are even now redigging the tunnel and the lake will be drained. It will work, Caesar. It will provide needed farmland." I was present at what was supposed to be the grand opening of the draining of the lake. Claudius ordered a naval battle with real ships and nineteen thousand combatants divided into opposing navies–the 'Sicilians' and the 'Rhodians." They were to reenact a battle. We built stands around the entire lake to accommodate the spectators. Claudius, Nero, and Agrippina appeared in full military regalia. We were all horrified when we opened the sluices and discovered that the channel had not been dug below the level of the lake. It was not our finest hour. I hope never to be the recipient of the kind of anger Claudius displayed that day. I spoke to soothe him. "The lake project is just as important as the aquaducts or the canals. You have brought glory to Rome, Caesar, not only with your projects, but look how you have expanded the empire. Look at the good laws you have passed. Under your leadership conquered people become citizens of Rome."

"G-glory will n-n-not pay for these p-projects. Do you know how much we've spent in ten years on the canals alone? We're nowhere near finished with it. But I'm still convinced it is the best thing for Rome to have a p-p-port closer than Ostia. To t-t-trans-ship our merchandise is foolish and outmoded. I know it costs m-money to build a new system, but I also know it's worth it. Listen Pudens. When I came to this exalted p-position Rome was on the verge of f-famine. You are too young to remember, but by Jove, I re-re-remember. We had eight day's s-supply of grain for over four million p-people. I had t-t-to do s-something immediately. Grain shipment wasn't due to b-b-begin until March s-so I offered to insure any vessel that w-w-would supply Rome. A t-t-temporary s-s-solution, b-but it worked. It will n-n-never happen again with the n-new harbor. In spite of m-my advisors, I ordered it d-d-done. They said it was too c-c-costly. W-Well it is c-c-costly, b-but it had to be d-done. I don't regret it."

I watched as he became more agitated. "Caesar, your plans for a port are nothing short of visionary. Both Julius Caesar and Augustus drew plans, but you are the one who put the thing in working order. The sea walls are magnificent. I have been honored to help design the granaries. And they will make life in Rome–not simply more convenient, but possible. Tomorrow, we expect a shipment of ten thousand *modii* of wheat. The forty-five arcades are almost complete. We will number the arcades. Tickets will be issued with matching numbers so there will be fair distribution to the populace." I spoke out of conviction, but I also hoped to placate him into listening to my idea.

"J-just so, P-p-pudens. I'm glad you bring your s-skills to the project. It's g-g-good to hear a v-v-voice of s-support. So, how are you going to save me m-money?"

"You may recall, Caesar, I served as aide to General Plautius in the Silurian campaign. When I arrived in Britain, my first deed was to arrange for a temple to be built in honor of Nep- tune and Minerva, erected by the legion's engineers. It bears my name in honor of my father."

"Yes, your father. Quintus was a distinguished senator and a pious man. The gods smiled on him. He and I agreed on m-m-most issues. Yes. A fine man and one who could be trusted. You come from good stock, young Pudens. May the gods bless you as they blessed your father."

"Thank you, Caesar. Well, I was in Britain during the six

month truce."

Claudius looked up from under bushy brows. "Ah, the double wedding–my niece to a British king and Plautius to Caradoc's sister. Marriages seal our negotiations, Pudens. We trade women for peace. The sister of Caractacus–her British name was Gladys, was it not?

"It was."

"She assumed the Roman name of Pomponia?"

"Correct. Pomponia Graecina."

"That truce!" The veins stood out at the emperor's temples. Foamy saliva formed in the corners of his mouth. "By Jove, that was the year C-c-caractacus visited Rome–by way of the n-n-new canals, as it happened. C-c-caractacus! What an insolent fellow! To the senate he said he ordered every tree in Siluria felled so we Romans would know it was British strength and not their forests which had defeated us. And when he saw our public buildings he said, "Rome's buildings are magnificent. Why should Rome envy me my soldier's tent in Britain? I didn't begrudge him his tent. I wanted his domains." Claudius sighed. "It is a costly war, but Rome will win. With generals such as Plautius, Geta, and Vespasian, how can we fail?"

"Of course, Rome shall conquer." I spoke reassuring words. "It was a privilege to serve under Plautius. Yes, I remember the truce well. Of course, when the fighting resumed my general was recalled to Rome."

Claudius tapped his fingers on the table top. "He had to be recalled. Can you imagine leaving him there in command, now the brother-in-law of our enemy? Caractacus would have had his spy system built-in." He turned to me. I sensed his impatience. "What has all this to do with you and a f-f-favor?

"When I was in Briton as aide to Plautius, during the truce, as a part of the wedding festivities, I was invited to the Silurian palace. The king and queen were most hospitable and their children were kind, as well. The sons, like their father, studied here in Rome. The daughters are gentle and proud of their family. I would ask, Caesar, that you grant me the privilege and the responsibility of taking them to my villa when they are brought to Rome. *Domus Pudens* is far enough away from the center of the city that there will be less likelihood of an unfortunate event. The *Carcer* is no fit prison for the British royal family–particularly the women. I realize they are political prisoners. There will certainly be a be a trial. Until you decide what punishment will be given to Caractacus, let them live with me. I will pay all their expenses, lodging, food, and whatever else they will need. I will be personally responsible for their conduct."

Claudius pursed his lips. He closed his eyes and rubbed his forehead with his fingertips. He must know that the Briton's arrival in Rome will be the occasion of some degree of upheaval. Claudius thought awhile and then turned to me.

"The p-populace will be eager to catch a glimpse of the b-barbarian–the Beast of Briton. Better, perhaps, that he be housed away from public view. You may take him and his f-family members to your villa, but Caractacus must stay under armed guard at all t-times. I will order the Praetorians to pull that d-d-duty. I will hold you personally responsible for their s-safety and their conduct."

"Thank you, Caesar. Then it is agreed?"

"Agreed, young Pudens." Claudius stood with difficulty and took me by the arm, leaning heavily on me for support. He hobbled to a nearby bookshelf. "I s-s-say, have you seen the books I have written on the history of the Etruscans? Most f-f-fascinating. Also, I have completed a history of Carthage. I wasn't always emperor, you know. I spent thirty-five years as a historian. Perhaps, that shall be as much my legacy as this exalted position I now hold." He smiled sardonically. "C-c-come, let me show you. You s-s-seem well informed about historical matters."

83

I spent the rest of the afternoon listening as he told me, in minute detail, more than I wanted to know of the history of the early settlers of Rome. Withal, I could not help but admire the emperor his indefatigable efforts at recording this history, and his insightful commentary on his research. His engineering projects are simply magnificent. Claudius has multiple physical handicaps, but his mind is sharp as a two-edged sword.

THEIRS IS THE KINGDOM

RoBERTA M. DAMON

"Roma catenatum tremuit spectare Britannum." ("Rome trembled when she saw the Briton, though fast in chains.") Tacitus, *Annals* (lib. xii) in McHenry (29-38)

"Vocatus quippe ut ad insigne spectaculum populus: stetere in armis praetoriae cohortes campo, quo castra praeiacet. Tunc incedentibus regiis clientulis phalerae. Non Caratacus aut vultu demisso aut verbis misericordiam requirens." ("The people were summoned to a grand spectacle; the praetorian cohorts were drawn up under arms. Then came a procession of the royal vassals. Caractacus did not stoop in supplication. He, neither by humble look nor speech, sought compassion."
Tacitus, *Annals,* (lib. xii) in McHenry (29-38)

THE ARRIVAL · · · · · · · 52 *AD* · · · · · · · 805 *AUC*

CARADOC SPEAKS:

 We were marched like criminals on display. The populace lined up along the avenues for the spectacle–three million of them they told me later, sweating in the hot sun, jostling for position to better see the Beast of Britain. Rome is a whore, drunk on excess. Rome is glutted with too much of everything–too much wealth, too much power, too much of everything, entertainment, wine, cruelty, intrigue, blood–too much, too much. I loathe Rome. I felt the excitement in the air. The crowds shouted and jeered.

"Bring him on. Bring on the great warrior."

"Let's have a look at him."

"He's not so great now."

"I guess Rome showed him he can't forever win."

"Rome conquers all."

"Hail Caesar!"

"Their shouts echoed from the Palatine to the Capitoline across the Forum, bouncing from the public buildings–temples, basilicas, colonnades and triumphal arches until there was one enormous and continuous roar of sound, as if the forces of hell were let loose on this one particular golden Italian day. I heard someone shout:

"Here they come."

Charioteers in full regalia stood tall behind their steeds which they controlled with a flick of the whip. The iron wheels made a deafening thunderous sound on the stone roadway. Trumpets and banners and soldiers without number marching in perfect cadence made a colorful and impressive spectacle indeed. I heard it from every direction:

"Hail Caesar! Hail Caesar!"

It was shouted in unison until it became a litany burned into the brain and sinew.

"Hail to the emperor Claudius." We were marched through the wide avenues. At last, I caught sight of the emperor. He sat, waiting and calm, at the main entrance to the Basilica Julia–the largest basilica of the Forum. The building itself was meant to intimidate. I've seen this building. I've been in Rome before, though certainly not under these circumstances. Julius Caesar laid the cornerstone to this one a hundred years ago. The great judicial building of Rome houses the civil court. I know about it. And I can guess that Claudius chose it because he felt it made an impressive backdrop for a god. I'm sure he thinks he'll join the pantheon after they deify him. He does not look godlike. His head bobs incessantly. His knees shake under that pristine toga. He is afflicted with a mouth that drools a thick, foamy saliva. Everyone knows that his own mother called him "my son, the imbecile." Claudius has his physical afflictions, but he is no imbecile. I respect his mind. He is sharp, meticulous, and cruel. I, of all people, know that he holds life and death power over most of the world. There he sits, surrounded by members of the Senate and the Praetorian guards. One of the senators shouted again: "Here they come!"

Claudius, with the assistance of two Praetorians, rose to his feet. The ranks parted, opening a corridor to make way for our entourage. A detail of five soldiers escorted me. One soldier led the group. The other four formed a square, and in the center of the square, I marched. I was followed by the other members of my family. Weighed down by shackles, my ankles and wrists were encircled by iron cuffs and the chains were so arranged as to hobble me as I walked. Even so, the populace seemed terrified at my appearing. Britons stand head and shoulders over even the tallest Roman. British men are well-muscled. As I passed along the parade route, there was a collective and audible gasp.

"By the gods. Look at him. He's enormous."

"No wonder we haven't been able to take him before now."

"He is a most admirable foe."

"Look how fiercely he struggles against the chains."

"His eyes are full of rage. I'd hate to meet him on a dark night."

"They say the Britons are well-trained and well-armed."

"He has led battalions into war against Rome. I'll wager his fate is sealed."

"It would be no disgrace to fall in battle to so brave a one."

"I hear he was betrayed by a kinswoman."

"He'll be condemned by the Senate. Surely, they will not let him live."

"Look how strong he is. Never have I seen such a body."

I stand tall. I was trained from childhood in the strengthening of body and in swift and accurate martial arts. How must I appear to this Roman rabble? My hair is long, my skin fairer that Roman men's, but deeply tanned from months and years of living close to earth and sun. I am an excellent runner. As a boy, I learned to swim and to climb. I am trained to bear pain and fatigue with dignity. I live for my own honor and for the honor of my country. I am trained not to show fear. All the forces of Rome cannot shake me.

How ludicrous that Rome considers me a barbarian. I was educated not only in the British centers of learning, but in Rome as well. I know their language as I know my own. All the nobility of Britain and Gaul study in Rome– some in the emperor's palace. Our own educational system requires twenty years to master the circle of knowledge. I studied philosophy, astronomy, geometry, jurisprudence, medicine, poetry and oratory among other subjects. I can say, with certainty, that I am no barbarian. Rome, drunk on bloodlust, seems more accurately to fit that description. As I struggled through the Roman streets,

I was sustained by our motto: "Truth against the world. Truth against the world."

My father followed me in this travesty of a procession. How could it be that the blessed, Bran, Arch Druid of Siluria, former king and honored chief of the Silurian university should be subjected to such an ordeal. How I love and respect my father. He put aside his crown so that I might rise to the throne. I have always honored him–more so now. Even in his old age, he walks with pride. His steps are made firm by his conviction of the righteousness of our cause. Behind him came my queen. She is brave and beautiful. Any worry she felt for me or for our children, she concealed behind a mask of serenity and peace. Behind her came the children walking two by two. The boys, Linus and Cynon, vowed to protect their mother and their sisters. At last, the girls, Ergain, and Gladys, followed behind the rest of the group. They are young and beautiful. They emulate their mother. This day they walked firmly without display of fear. Unmindful of the harsh and jeering multitude, we walked with heads held high through the indignities of the day. The Roman men, laughing coarsely, made crude remarks. Perhaps they think we cannot understand their language.

"I'd like to meet her in the dark."

"By Jupiter. I could do something with that."

"I like the young one best. She looks ripe enough to be plucked."

"Hey, beauty. Look my way."

I wanted to get my hands around their fat, sweaty necks. As for my women, the jeers fell on deaf ears–the crudity beneath their noting. Ah! These Romans. They call us barbarians. Who is barbarous after all?

Claudius raised his hand. Instantly, a hush fell across the Forum.

"What say you? Who comes here?"

A guard stepped smartly up and handed a rolled letter

to the Praetorian who passed it to the emperor. He read:

"To the Emperor of Rome, Tiberius Claudius Drusus Nero Germanicus, Hail!

I, Ostorius Scapula, deliver into your hands, the Briton, Caractacus, known as Caradoc, King of Siluria. My battalions were victorious over the British armies. The family of Caradoc was captured at the royal residence. We received intelligence that Caradoc, himself, took refuge at Caer Evroc with Aregwedd, Queen of the Brigantes, known to Rome as Cartismandua, a kinswoman of the prisoner and a friend of Rome. By her orders, the Briton was seized in his sleep, fettered and delivered into my hands. According to your orders, I hereby deliver him and his family captives into your presence. Hail Caesar!

Claudius handed the missive to his guard and addressed me.

"What s-say you? Are you an enemy of Rome?"

"I am."

"You shall be s-sentenced three days hence in the S-senate of Rome. Whom do you wish to speak in your d-defense?"

"I shall speak for myself."

"Are you certain you do not w-wish to have an advocate?

"I shall speak for myself."

"V-very well. I have nothing more to s-say at this t-time. We are dismissed until such time this p-prisoner appears before the Senate.

Claudius and his guards turned to leave. Rufus Pudens caught the eye of the emperor and raised his eyebrows in questioning permission. The emperor nodded, yes, and hobbled out of the hot sun toward the comfort of his palace.

The young senator approached the guards. "By order of the emperor, the prisoners are to be conducted to *Domus Pudens.*" We were taken to the villa.

91

"Adjacent to the palace were baths on a corresponding scale, known subsequently as *Thermae Timothinae* and *Thermae Novatianae.* The palace baths and grounds were bequeathed by Timotheus to the Church at Rome. And these were the only buildings of any magnitude possessed by the Roman Church until the reign of Constantine. Hermas terms the *Titulus "amplissima Pudentes domus."* It was the hospitium for Christians from all parts of the world."

Williams Morgan, *Saint Paul in Britain* (56)

THE VILLA 52 *AD* 805 *AUC*

QUEEN ERGAIN SPEAKS:

 Our family was conducted to the senator's villa. As soon as we were settled in the sedan, young Pudens ordered Caradoc released from his chains. The Praetorian demurred. The senator looked at him in astonishment. "By the gods, man. He is unarmed. All of the Roman army stands between him and Britain. Do you think he will escape? I alone am responsible to the emperor for him. Take off the chains."

Reluctantly, the guard did as he was bidden. I gasped when I saw the skin rubbed raw from my husband's wrists and ankles. Pudens spoke comfortingly to me and to all the family.

"We'll soon be at my home. You are my most welcome guests. You will find everything you need there. We have ointments for your cuts and bruises. We have water for bathing and clean clothes for all of you. My servants are preparing a meal for you. I well remember your hospitality to me when I was in Siluria during the truce. Please, set your minds and hearts at ease. I will extend to you every comfort. My mother, the lady Priscilla, is eagerly awaiting your arrival."

I looked at him with gratitude.

"You are most kind. My daughters are fainting with fatigue. If you can give us a place to rest, we will be most grateful."

"I am your servant, madam."

Caradoc was fuming. "What a humiliation to be paraded through the streets of Rome like a common criminal." His hands clenched and unclenched in an effort to get the blood circulating again.

Gladys looked at her father's bleeding wrists and was

appalled. "Please, Senator Pudens, do you have a clean kerchief we can use to bind up my father's wounds?"

"No need for that," her father insisted. "I'm not a baby. I'll be all right."

"But, of course." He pulled a clean square of linen from the fold of his toga. I watched my daughter as she applied the linen to her father's cuts and bruises. I watched her gentle attention to her task. My daughter is beautiful and kind.

We traveled east for some time. When we topped a hill, the senator announced, "We have arrived. This is the entrance to my villa." The gate was opened by servants who bowed to our group. We were escorted through lawns and gardens to the door of the large main house. The senator's mother was waiting to welcome us.

"Do come in. You must be exhausted." She smiled and opened her arms to us.

"This is my mother, the Lady Priscilla."

I looked into his mother's welcoming eyes and returned her smile.

"You are kind to take us in. We are frightfully unkempt and we are so weary. We don't want to impose on you."

"Not at all. It is our pleasure to have you here."

The senator's family home is impressive. He pointed to the baths adjoining the living area. "Please make yourselves at home. You will be shown to your apartments and there will be servants who will conduct you to the baths. I'm sure you will find everything you need."

We women were left to the care of the lady, Priscilla, and her servants. My husband was conducted, still under guard, to a bedchamber. We were escorted to our bedroom, a quiet place, full of flowers. A large platter of fresh fruit sat on a low table, some of which we did not recognize. Towels of linen, a basin of water, oils and spices, and, best of all, a clean, large bed waited invitingly. A servant girl appeared and conducted us to the bath house where we bathed in warm spring water. Afterward, we were oiled and massaged by expert hands. What luxury! What a pleasure to get rid of soiled clothes and the grime of travel. What comfort for sore, tired muscles to be soothed by the servant girls. After our capture, we lived in a Roman *castra* for a month before sailing to Rome under arrest–and in conditions not fit for women. Here, in this house, we are treated as guests, not prisoners. These servant girls are trained to be gentle. They warmed the fragrant oils before they were applied to our tired bodies and wiped down with soft cloths. Our hair was brushed and braided and we emerged feeling clean, sleepy, and grateful. We put on the clothing that was laid out for us and, then, we slept. For two hours, we napped before we were summoned to the atrium, the large central open space in the house. We women were taken to a dining room for the evening meal. The men were conducted to their own dining area, the *triclinium*.

We have no idea what the future holds for us. I may be a widow in a few days. No one knows what the Roman emperor will decide. I am fearful, but I must not show my fear. I am grateful for this place and for the kindness shown to us. *Domus Pudens* is to us, at least for the present, both safety and comfort.

PUDENS SPEAKS:

 We reclined at table. Conversation over dinner ranged from memories of the truce in Britain to the upcoming trial of Caradoc. Huge platters of fish, fruits, and vegetables were carried into our dining room on the shoulders of young men. Wine flowed freely.

"I'll never forget bringing you the truce proposal. I must confess that I was terrified." I smiled at my guest.

"I remember you. You had reason to be afraid. I was

impressed by your demeanor. You did not show fear." Caradoc raised his cup. "Let us drink to feigned courage. It often accomplishes as much as the real thing." We raised our cups and drank.

"You must accustom yourself to being called by your Roman name. Here in Rome, you are known as Caractacus. It has a noble ring to it."

"Caractacus it is, then, I suppose. But my Silurian name has served me well."

"What will you say before the Senate?"

"I shall tell the truth, and I shall be eloquent."

"Rarely does one goes before that tribunal alone without an advocate to plead his cause."

"I imagine that it is not often that a king and an innocent and honorable man goes before that tribunal." The Briton rose from the table. Two Praetorians stood just behind him, watchful, hands on their swords. "If you do not mind, Senator Pudens, I believe I shall take my leave. I have work to do before I sleep. I have a speech to write."

"Of course. You will find writing materials in your chamber. I do hope you rest well." I stood as Caractacus was led from the banquet hall.

"Unde fama eius evecta insulas et proximas provincias pervagata per Italiam quoque celebrabatur, avebantque visere, quis ille tot per annos opes nostras sprevisset. Ne Romae quidem ignobile Carataci nomen erat." ("Through resistance, his reputation had gone beyond the islands, had overspread the nearest provinces, and was familiar in Italy itself where there was curiosity to see what manner of man it was that had for so many years scorned our power. Even in Rome, the name of Caractacus was not without honor.")

Tacitus, *Annales,* (lib xii, c 35) in Jackson (365)

"Vocati posthac patres multa et magnifica super captivitate Carataci disseruere." ("The Fathers, who were convened later, delivered long and florid orations on the capture of Caractacus.")

Tacitus, *Annales,* (lib xii c 38) in Jackson (367)

"Si quanta nobilitas et fortuna mihi fuit, tanta rerum prosperarum moderatio fuisset, amicus patuis in hanc urbem quam captus venissem, neque dedignatus esses claris maiorbus ortum, pluribus gentibus imperitantem foedere in pacem accipere. Praesens sors mea ut mihi informis, sic tibi magnifica est. Habui equos viros, arma opes: quid mirum, si haec invitus amisi? Nam si vos omnibus imperitare vultis, sequitur ut omnes servitutem accipiant? Si statim deditus traherer, neque mea fortuna meque tua gloria inclaruisset; et supplicium mei oblivio sequeretur: at si incolumem servaveris, acternum exemplar clementiae ero." ("Had my government in Britain been directed solely with a view to the preservation of my hereditary domains or the aggrandizement of my own family, I might long since have en-

tered this city an ally, not a prisoner; nor would you have disdained for a friend a king descended from illustrious ancestors and the director of many nations. My present condition, stript of its former majesty, is as adverse to myself as it is a cause of triumph to you. What then? I was lord of men, horses, arms, wealth; what wonder if at your dictation I refused to resign them? Does it follow, that because the Romans aspire to universal dominion, every nation is to accept the vassalage they would impose? I am now in your power–betrayed, not conquered. Had I, like others, yielded without resistance, where would have been the name of Caradoc? Where your glory? Oblivion would have buried both in the same tomb. Bid me live, I shall survive forever in history one example at least of Roman clemency.")

> Caractacus' Defense before the Roman Senate and Emperor Claudius, Tacitus, *Annales*, as quoted in Jackson (365-366)

THE PLEA 52 *AD* 805 *AUC*

PUDENS SPEAKS:

 The day of the trial arrived. Everyone in the family went to the Curia–the Senate's meeting hall, to be near Caradoc. The Curia stands on hallowed ground. The original building was planned and erected by Rome's third king, Tulius Hostilius, and stood–remodeled and revised, to be sure–for five hundred years. Fire destroyed it twice. Julius Caesar planned and began the third major rebuilding, but when he was assassinated, it was left to Augustus to complete it. It stands within a grand complex of buildings and is sacred to our history. It is known now as "Curia Julia," after the great Caesar. Many of the senators pause in the small temple in the courtyard west of the Curia to offer sacrifice and pray before entering the hall where deliberations take place. They arrive by way of the colonnaded walkways. Only senators, their guests and invited speakers may go into the building. Caradoc's family wanted to witness these proceedings, but when they arrived their entry was barred. The meeting was closed. They were invited to stand on the porch beyond the open doors. The chamber is built with huge bronze doors commissioned by Julius Caesar and installed by Augustus. These are traditionally left open so that the *spectatori* and *auditori* may gather on the porches. This day, we senators were all present–seated along both sides of the tiered chamber on long marble benches. Claudius sat elevated above us. The trial was ready to begin. Conversations stopped. A reverential hush fell over the chamber.

"Bring in the prisoner."

"There is one small difficulty, sir."

"And what might that b-b-be?" Claudius looked impatient.

99

"It is a matter of the prisoner's daughter, Caesar."

The hair on the back of my neck rose.

Claudius sighed. "And what is her p-p-problem?"

"She insists on standing beside her father while he pleads his case. No woman has ever stood before the Roman senate." All eyes turned toward Agrippina sitting, silently for once, in the shadows. No woman indeed, yet here was the emperor's wife pushing her way in, not willing to miss this trial of the century. She was, no doubt, here with the permission of her husband–or at least his acquiescence. Agrippina does what she wants to do. "What shall we do about the prisoner's daughter?"

Claudius laughed. "How old is this woman?"

"Sixteen."

"Bring her in."

I must confess I was seized by a moment of anxiety. Gladys could be executed as a part of her father's humiliation. I know Claudius. He may appear avuncular, but he is remorseless. More than thirty senators and hundreds of military officers have been executed for mere suspicion of disloyalty. Caradoc's life is at stake and now, Gladys, too is in danger. This kind of impertinence would not be overlooked.

The guards conducted Gladys into the senate chamber. She looked straight at the emperor. She neither bowed nor nodded. Her chin and her mouth were set firmly. Her hand rose momentarily to the small gold object at her throat as if it could impart courage. I held my breath.

"By Jupiter. Who is this pretty one? What is your name, child?" Claudius smiled at the sight of her.

She lifted her head proudly. "Princess Gladys, daughter of Caradoc, King of Siluria." Her voice did not waver.

"And how old are you, Gladys, daughter of the King? They tell me you are sixteen. Is that right?"

"Yes."

"Well, why do you want to attend this proceeding?"

"I stand beside my father in support of his cause. He is innocent of any wrong against Rome. You are the ones who invaded us." There was an audible gasp from the assembled senators.

Claudius laughed out loud. A sigh passed through the room like a wave. The senators laughed retroactively.

"What do you want, Gladys?"

"I want to stand beside my father as he addresses this body."

A voice from the back of the chamber was raised in displeasure. "Objection." The voice belonged to Persius Gaius, old nemesis to the emperor. "It is not fit that she should be present." Several senators murmured their agreement.

"I will stay." Gladys looked like a small fierce animal ready to pounce. Arch enemies sometimes have a way of making our decisions for us. At Gaius' objection, Claudius knew immediately what he would decide.

"Granted. You may stay. I like your spirit. Call Caractacus." I realized I was sitting on the edge of my bench, every muscle and nerve strained toward the proceedings, as if my own life were at stake.

The guards brought Caradoc into the chamber. He stood tall, the hero of forty battles. Nothing in his character or demeanor could cause him shame. Everyone present recognized his nobility. He planted his feet firmly, squared his massive shoulders, lifted his chin, looked at his daughter with pride, nodded to the emperor, and began to speak.

"Had my government in Britain been directed solely with a view to the preservation of my hereditary domains or the aggrandizement of my own family, I might long since have entered this city an ally, not a prisoner; nor would you have disdained for a friend a king descended from illustrious ancestors and the director of many nations. My present condition, stript of its former majesty, is as adverse to myself as it is a cause of triumph to you. What then? I was lord of men, horses, arms, wealth: what wonder if at your dictation I refused to resign them? Does it follow, that because the Romans aspire to universal dominion, every nation is to accept the vassalage they would impose? I am now in your power–betrayed, not conquered. Had I, like others, yielded without resistance, where would have been the name of Caradoc? Where your glory? Oblivion would have buried both in the same tomb. Bid me live, I shall survive forever in history one example at least of Roman clemency."

He stopped, bowed his head, and waited. The senate to a man, accustomed to hearing great oratory, sat stunned at the persuasive skill of the Briton and at his poetic command of their language. We looked toward Claudius. The emperor paused. The whole world seemed to stop. Everyone knew that clemency was seldom granted. In case after case, men were routinely condemned to death for much less crime than Caradoc's. Certainly, none lived who had caused Rome so much grief in defeat. Suddenly, Claudius smiled and, in a radical departure from the norm, jabbed his thumb upward. Cheers erupted from the senators. Gladys threw herself into her father's arms.

Claudius lifted his hand. The silence was immediate. Now the emperor would pronounce the sentence. Everyone leaned forward to hear.

"I grant you your life. You will be a prisoner in Rome for seven years. You will be in *libera custodia*–free captivity. You will not be confined, but may go about Rome at will. You will not leave the city. You will be able to receive funds and goods from your homeland." Claudius paused. "The most important stipulation of all is this; you will never take up arms against Rome again. Do you understand the verdict?"

"I understand."

"Do you accept the conditions of this sentence?

"I accept."

"One more thing," said Claudius. "I hereby adopt this young woman, Gladys. She shall henceforth enjoy the privileges of being the daughter to the emperor. Also, she shall be known from this day, not as Gladys, but as Claudia–after me. Come, Claudia, and embrace your new father."

I felt pride and relief. Claudius was clever. To seal an alliance, if one can't marry, one adopts. Gladys stepped in front of the emperor. She bowed low before him, her long hair falling like a silken veil, hiding her face. Gracefully, she rose to her feet and gave the commanded embrace. I heard her words, softly, but clearly spoken.

"Thank you, for sparing my father's life. Thank you for being kind to me. I shall try to be a good and obedient daughter to you, my second father."

"In so doing, my dear child, you have sworn allegiance to Rome. You are now and f-f-forever under Rome's p-p-protection." Everyone present understood that Claudius had scored a triple triumph: victory over the Briton with a promise he would not oppose Rome again; vengeance on an old enemy; and a new alliance sealed with the adoption of his enemy's daughter. Who said Claudius is an imbecile? Amid cheers, the royal family left the Senate chamber to return to my villa.

I sat in my chambers that night, a vision playing over and over in my mind. It was the vision of the Briton standing straight and tall before the Roman Senate pleading for his life. I thought of the daughter standing beside her father. What courage! What poise! What presence! Before I slept, my mind played the scene over and over again. Caradoc, Caractactus. Gladys, Claudia. Who are these people?

ROBERTA M. DAMON

THE MUSINGS   53 *AD*   806 *AUC*

CLAUDIA SPEAKS:

 I find it hard to believe that we have been in Rome a year. I sometimes long for Siluria, but my father says we should live our lives as pleasantly as possible while we are here. We will be here for another six years. Six years! An eternity. The lady Priscilla has befriended my mother, and she has taken a great interest in me and my sister. She said she will teach us how to please a Roman husband. Priscilla often sits in the atrium with her needlework. She lets Ergain and me sit and watch. Her hands are swift and delicate as they weave the complicated tapestry pattern. She let me try it once.

"I don't see how you do it. I keep tangling my threads until it is impossible to know which thread goes where. I'll never be able to do this." By the time she helped me untangle the knots, I was trembling with vexation. She is patient and kind. "You are the mistress of the needle, my lady. I fear I will never master it."

"Patience, my dear. You'll learn yet. We all have our talents and skills. I could never write poetry as you do."

"I do love to write poetry."

"See? We are different in our abilities. I can teach you needlework. A good Roman wife must be skilled at weaving and cooking. Tomorrow, we will work in the kitchen. I will teach you how to make *passum*. Oh, Claudia, we'll make a fine Roman wife of you, yet. You will bear many sons for your husband, and he will respect and honor you." She smiled and nodded.

I wonder what life holds for me. While growing up in Siluria, I never dreamed I would be in Rome. Our coming here has changed many things for us and for others. Even the name of the villa has changed. Since our arrival, it is less frequently called *Domus Pudens* and is now known as the *Paladium Britanicum*. Drenched in sunshine, the villa sits high on what is known as Viminilus Hill. The view from the front lawn is spectacular. I love to sit and look at the rolling countryside. Often, I take my writing materials and sit on a bench to think and write. Life is pleasant for us in Rome, always with something to do. I am learning to like Roman food, plentiful and with a new treat to taste, always. The cooks never stop working. Four hundred servants assure the management of this place.

Guests are forever dropping in. Family members come and go. My Aunt Gladys, Pomponia Graecina, comes often to spend an afternoon, and sometimes, her husband with her. Dear Uncle Plautius. He surprised me with a gift, my father's battle shield. General Scapula took it from my father at the time of his capture. The general passed it on to his predecessor, my Uncle Plautius, who said I deserved to have it because of my bravery before the Senate. Who would have thought when my Aunt Gladys married and came to Rome that, one day, our whole family would be here. I still remember our conversation about the peace weavers—seems a hundred years ago. My Aunt Gladys is a peace weaver, and I suppose, in a way, I am one as well. When the emperor adopted me, it was not because he loved me as a daughter. He did it to seal an alliance. That makes me a peace weaver, too. I hope Emperor Claudius is happy with the result. For my part, I am content.

Life here is exciting. Sometimes, we go into the city, but for the most of the time, we stay at the villa. Always, we have amusements—exotic birds in wicker cages, musicians eager to entertain. People on the premises excel at playing the flute, the kithara, and the lute. They will perform at the slightest pretext.

I must admit that I am interested in the young senator. He holds himself aloof as all Roman men do. Women and domestic life are far beneath the notice of a member of the Roman senate. I do believe, though, he has noticed me. I have been instructed by his mother to sit modestly and quietly as men do not like to hear female chatter. I am not given to chatter, so he will certainly not be inconvenienced by me in that way. If I have an opportunity to speak directly to him, I shall make intelligent sounds. He may be surprised to discover that I can think and speak. At times, I realize I looking around a corner for him. Someday, he may look for me. When he does, he shall find a woman who is accomplished at many things—British royalty who has learned to be a fine Roman woman.

I am often absorbed by my own thoughts of him. "I wonder what he thinks of me? I wonder if he finds me beautiful? How must I appear to him? I wonder if he thinks me too much younger than he? He is muscular and manly with hair dark like his eyes. His face is pleasing, marked by a firm jaw line and noble brow. He and I are very different in appearance."

My sister, Ergain, came and sat beside me. She poked me in the ribs with her elbow. I frowned at her in annoyance.

"What was that about?"

She looked at me. "I know what you're thinking. You are thinking about the senator. When you look at him, you are like a calf looking at its mother."

"Hush, Ergain. I look nothing of the sort. I simply find him interesting."

"Interesting?" She snorted. "Nothing interests me that much!"

"There must be some young Roman you find interesting."

"No, sister Gladys. I am not content to settle down to Roman domesticity. I am going home to Siluria."

"Just how do you plan to do that?"

"I don't know yet. But I'm going." She stood and put her hands on her hips. "Don't you miss our home?"

"Do I miss Siluria? Sometimes I do. But our parents

and brothers are here. I'm beginning to feel at home in Rome. We've been here a year, Ergain. We must put down roots."

"My roots are in Siluria. Rome will never be home to me. One day, I'm going home."

I rose, gathering my scrolls. We walked together–my sister and I. She has a mind of her own, strong and proud and extremely opinionated. In some ways, she and I are alike. We British women can be formidable.

THEIRS IS THE KINGDOM

"Obstat, care Pudens, nostris sua turba libellis lectoremque frequens lassat et implet opus."
("Dear Pudens, their very number hampers my poems, and volume after volume wearies and sates the reader.")
Martial, *Epigrams* (248-251)

THE PLEDGE   53 *AD*   806 *AUC*

PUDENS SPEAKS:

 We will be married–a good union. We shall have sons. My future wife appears fragile, but she has her father's strength. Our marriage will unite two noble families. Rome will benefit from yet another tie to British royalty. It is time for me to be a married man, to assume the responsibilities of family life. The character of the princess Claudia is impeccable. We stroll the garden pathways and speak of our future. I delight in her. Her voice is soft, but she is never at a loss for words.

"Your land is beautiful. Such skies are never seen over Siluria. It is sometimes cold there, and damp." She looked at me with eyes as deep blue as a cloudless Roman sky.

"I remember the cold, but your land is beautiful, too. So green. The many trees."

"Yes, I love the trees. They tell me your armies were defeated as much by the trees as by our soldiers." She looked at me archly. Her eyes twinkled. I think she is teasing me. I cleared my throat.

"Let us not talk of defeat." I took her hand in mine. Her skin is soft. "I remember you. During the truce, when General Plautius was invited to your home, I came along as his aide. I was eighteen, and fancied myself quite the military man. I remember you and your sister and brothers."

"I was just a little girl then. I do remember my brother and you almost came to blows over some silly disagreement. But you remember me? What did you think of me?"

"I thought you were a sweet child. You hid behind the furniture or behind your mother's robes."

"I remember being in awe of the General–so intimidating. And then, as a part of the truce, he married my Aunt

Gladys and when I got to know him, I found him to be honorable and kind–dear Uncle Plautius."

"He is a great leader. I was proud to serve under his command. You have changed in these last years."

"I should hope so. Seventeen is very different from ten."

"Indeed." My eyes swept over her from head to toe. "You have changed."

She blushed.

"So, what do you do for amusement?" I asked.

"I read. I write. I love language. Sometimes I think my heart will burst before I can record what is in my heart."

"What do you write?"

"My thoughts. My dreams." She paused and ducked her head.

"What do you dream?" My eyes sought hers.

"Of a happy life."

"And you write this?"

"Yes." She turned to me. "My father says it is something I inherited–this hunger to write. My Grandfather took vellum from Rome into our country. Everyone in my family enjoys reading. Always copies of the works of your best authors are circulated and can be found in our centers of learning. My papa says we are a literary bunch."

"You must meet my friend, Martial."

"The poet? You know him?" Her eyes widened in astonishment.

"Yes. Are you familiar with his work?"

"Indeed. I find him witty, articulate, and often scandalous."

I smiled. "He comes to my villa to visit. He brings me poetry he has written for my perusal before he puts it out for public consumption. He asks me to correct his work, but doesn't always like my suggestions, nor does he always take them. I suppose you could say I am his editor."

Gladys laughed delightedly. "How fascinating." She looked at me with open admiration, the universal look that women give to men in whom they can find no flaw. It was as if she said the words (though, of course, she did not), "You are a wonderful man." I was flattered and strutted a bit–to impress her. Throwing out my chest, I struck a pose, and then felt silly. I am a Roman senator after all. I smiled. "Let me see if I can remember the epigram he wrote to me just recently. It goes like this: "A certain person, Rufus, lately looked me up and down carefully, just as if he were a purchaser of slaves or a trainer of gladiators, and when he had furtively observed me and pointed me out: 'Are you, are you,' he said, 'that Martial, whose naughty jests everyone knows who at least has not a barbarous ear?' 'I smiled quietly, and with a slight bow, did not deny I was the person mentioned. 'Why then,' said he, 'do you wear a bad cloak?' I replied, 'Because I am a bad poet.' That this may not happen too often to a poet, send me, Rufus, a good cloak.'

Gladys laughed in her charming way.

"And will you send him a good cloak?"

"Certainly–the least I can do for such a witty friend." I took both her slim hands in mine. "Ah, my dear, you shall be my wife. You shall give me strong sons. You are beautiful and you are bright."

She smiled. "For a woman?"

"For anyone, man or woman. I find you interesting. What is that you wear around your neck?"

"My mother gave it to me on my fifteenth birthday, the day I was initiated into our clan."

"What does it mean?"

"It can mean many things. If you trace it with your fingertip, you will eventually find your way back to where you started. With no set beginning and no end, it is like our lives with balance and flow, leaving and returning, with something eternal about it. It is passed down from mother to daughter. Perhaps, I shall have a daughter to give it to one day among all the sons." I nodded agreement.

We ambled slowly toward a fish pond and found a shady

place beneath a tree. We sat together on a stone bench and watched the orange and yellow fish dart through the water.

"I have a secret." She took a deep breath.

"Do you now?" I smiled at her.

"May I tell you?"

"Of course. I promise not to tell."

"You will be my husband. I feel I can tell you anything. I feel as if I have known you all my life. When I look into your eyes, I am like a ship that has found safe haven." Her words tumbled out in a great rush, as if she didn't say them immediately and all at once, she might never have another opportunity.

"You can trust me."

She paused and looked intently at me as if to take my measure, then spoke softly, almost in a whisper. "I fear that my family has put you in danger. You have been kind to us. If our secret is discovered, your household is at risk. I am a follower of The Way and all my family, except my father, are followers, too. Have you heard of it–The Way?"

I picked up a handful of pebbles and arranged them on the bench between us in a curved configuration.

She gasped. "*Ichthus.*" She blinked back tears. "You, too?"

I laid my fingertips upon her lips. "You are correct. It is not safe to speak it aloud. Our emperor has declared it a capital offense. But yes. I follow Him, too."

Gladys spoke: "He is risen."

I responded: "Risen, indeed."

In that confession, we entrusted our lives one to the other.

THE LECTURE: 53 *AD*   806 *AUC*

GWYNEDD SPEAKS:

Some months before my lady was married, the midwives were called in, a necessary precaution. No man wants to marry a woman who is unable to conceive. With the senator's family wealth, too much is at stake. My lady and the young senator are to produce a male heir as soon as possible. It is not enough for my lady to have a strong body. Other considerations remain. Marcella, the chief among the midwives, says there are certain signs of obvious female sterility, the worst of which is a protruding forehead. In my opinion, the lady Claudia has a beautifully flat brow. Lucky for her. Seven women sat in a circle to listen to Marcella's lecture. She turned to me and spoke sharply: "Gwynned, go fetch a bench for the lady." Marcella orders me around as if it is her right, which it is not, but that does not seem to matter to her. I do what she says. No one wants to be at odds with Marcella. So I brought the bench and placed it in the middle of the room. I said, "Yes, madam, yes, indeed." What I thought was another matter.

Marcella bade my lady to sit down on the bench and proceeded to measure her head. "Small heads are not good. Large heads are not good, either. The wife's head must be of a medium size and the features of the face must be in harmony. Eyes set too close together bode evil and will prevent conception. The nose must be straight and not too wide. Nor should it be too narrow. All in all, the features of the face must be in pleasant alignment, otherwise, there will be no heir."

Claudia listened raptly as Marcella lectured. Her voice was anxious as she asked,"What do you think? Is my head the right size? Do you think I shall be able to have children?"

"It seems so," Marcella responded. "But there are other tests we must perform before I can be certain. It is a good thing you are not fat. Fat tends to block the entrance to the womb and prevent conception. Stand up, my dear. Now, where did I put that incense?" She scrambled through her bag of midwifery tools. "Ah, here it is." She handed it to me.

"Gwynedd, light this." The order was imperious. I dutifully ran to the kitchen and begged the cook for a coal from the oven where the bread was baking. I carried the glowing coal back to the chamber and managed, after some difficulty, to light the incense. The smoke from it rose in a choking cloud. The odor was overpowering.

Marcella, ever in charge, spoke again to my lady: "Stand over the incense. Your cloak must cover it. Be careful not to burn yourself. If your breath smells of the incense, we will know that your body is hollow enough to receive seed and contain a child, and you will conceive."

Claudia dutifully stood over the incense, the hem of her garment encircling the bowl wherein it burned.

"Now exhale." My lady Claudia obeyed with a great 'whoosh.' Marcella stepped close to smell her breath. "Yes, I smell the incense. This is a sign that you are fertile. This time next year, you will be the mother of an heir to the senator's fortunes." Everyone smiled and clapped their hands delightedly at the good news. My lady was obviously relieved to hear that she would be able to fulfill her duty as a wife.

Marcella is very knowledgeable, even though I find her bossy in the extreme. The women, enraptured, sat in a circle on the floor as she lectured us: "Women are in great danger between the time of first bleeding and the time of their deflowering. To know a man's body is to open the entrance to the womb. That opening is what allows the blood to flow out. If this does not happen, the woman is in danger because the blood will back up into her lungs and heart. If that should happen, she will become licentious and she may suffer hallucinations."

We all gasped at the thought.

"The womb is eager to become pregnant. If it does not, it can wander around inside a woman's body causing all manner of ills. Women with heavy flow which lasts more than four days, are delicate and will produce delicate children. Women with light flow lasting two or three days are healthier and more robust, but they are often mannish in appearance and are not interested in having children."

"Oh, I'm very interested in having children, and I don't think I look mannish. I certainly hope not." Claudia looked imploringly at the midwife.

"Certainly not. You are a very feminine young woman. You don't drink heavily, do you?"

"Oh, no."

"Well, that's a good thing. Drunkenness has no place when you are attempting to conceive. You must be sober in the marriage bed with your husband. Otherwise, your soul might become a victim of strange fantasies. The child will always resemble the mother's soul. Yours is a great responsibility."

Claudia blushed and stammered, "How, exactly, is the child formed?"

Marcella spoke authoritatively. "Both the mother and the father produce seed. When the seed mingles in the mother's womb, the child is formed. If the father's seed is stronger, the child will have his characteristics. If the mother's seed is stronger, the child will take after her. If both parents produce strong seed, the child will be male. If both parents produce weak seed, the child will be female. To ensure strong seed, both the man and his wife should eat lightly before coming together in the marriage bed. Also a good massage will aid in conception. These are things that every woman should know before she stands before the marriage altar." We all nodded sagely. Marcella certainly knows a lot about babies. I have to give her that. She had one last bit of advice for my lady.

"Eat onions the day of your wedding. It strengthens the blood and aids in conception."

Thus fortified, my lady Claudia proceeded with her wedding plans. Every unmarried woman present at the lecture that day, left the chamber intent on measuring her own head, wondering if her body was sufficiently hollow to receive male seed, and pondering the efficacy of onions.

Theirs Is The Kingdom

Roberta M. Damon

Claudia, Rufe, meo nubit Peregrina Pudenti:
Macte esto taedis, O Hymenaee, tuis.
Tan bene rara suo miscentur cinnama nardo,
Massiea Theseis tam bene vina favis;
Nec melius teneris iunguntur vitibus ulmi,
Nec plus lotos aquas, litora myrtus amat.
Candid perpetuo reside, Concordia, lecto,
Tamque pari semper sit Venus acqua iugo.
Diligat illa senem quondam, sed ipsa marito
Tum quoque, cum fuerit, non videatur anus.

Claudia Peregrina weds Rufus, my own Pudens;
A blessing, O Hymenaeus, be upon thy torches!
So well does rare cinnamon blend with its own nard;
So well Massic wine with Attic combs.
Not closer are elms linked to tender vines,
Nor greater love hath the lotus for the waters,
The myrtle for the shore.
Fair Concord, rest thou unbroken on that bed,
And may Venus be ever kindly to a bond so equal knit!
May the wife love her husband when anon he is grey,
And she herself, even when she is old,
Seem not so to her spouse!
    Martial *Epigrams* IV xiii

THE WEDDING   53 *AD*   806 *AUC*

PUDENS SPEAKS:

Three days ago, the formal betrothal ceremony transpired. In the Roman fashion, Caractacus as father of the bride, and I as groom-to-be, exchanged the necessary vows and pledges. I offered my future father-in-law the bride purchase which he accepted. Although, in this case, the amount of money and property might have been considerable in view of the fact of the Pudentian family wealth, it was, in fact a mere token as has become the custom. The exchange is important, however, because it signifies the transfer of legal authority from Claudia's father to me. The dowry Caractacus paid to me was rather more munificent. We agreed that Claudia would marry *sine manu,* that is, she will retain membership in her father's family with all her inheritance rights intact. Everyone in the family was present as I faced my future father-in-law and asked,

"Do you promise to give your daughter to me to be my wedded wife?"

Caractacus gave the Roman response: "The gods bring luck! I betroth her."

I turned to Claudia and she to me. We kissed and I slipped an iron ring onto the fourth finger of her left hand. There is a vein that runs directly through the fourth finger of the left hand to the heart. Claudia blushed, smiled, and was conducted to her quarters by the women to await our wedding day three days hence. Caradoc and I went off together to drink wine.

For weeks, our villa has been alive with activity–cleaning, scouring, repairing, polishing, cooking, tasting, weaving, sewing, arranging, shopping, haggling–all because I was to be married to the Princess. Everyone important in Rome was invited to the nuptials. Around the villa, people hurried. Tempers flared, causing arguments with much gesticulating and arm waving mixed with bouts of convulsive laughter. I cannot think of my villa as anything but *Domus Pudens,* but since the arrival of my bride's family, people are beginning to call it the *Palladium Britanicum.* The servant population numbers right at four hundred, more or less equally divided between men and women. Even on ordinary days, the villa requires an extraordinary amount of labor just to keep the place running.

Our family has been most fortunate in our enjoyment of a measure of wealth. The house was built by my father. I was born here. I have always loved it. All high born Romans of means build their homes of masonry. Ours sits on an elevated hill east of the city–far enough away to avoid noise and congestion. My father designed the house to include many private rooms built around a large central courtyard. All the floors are of the finest Italian marble. Murals, mosaics and tapestries cover much of the wall space. My mother chose many of the pieces of art which adorn our home. Father ordered the construction of pools and fountains, but mother selected much of the statuary which stands in the courtyard and corridors. Adjacent to this property is an elaborately terraced and intricately connected system of baths which occupy more land than the property on which the main house stands. Outbuildings house the servant population. Their labor is unending.

For an occasion as auspicious as my wedding, I fear the work load has multiplied ten fold. The days of preparation before the wedding were filled with a cacophony of sounds–rumbling carts, squawking fowl, clanging hammers, tramping feet. Fragments of various conversations wafted simultaneously across the courtyard. I heard snatches of talk:

"Don't you bring that cart across my floor. I just finished polishing it. You'll leave tracks."

"How else do you suppose I'm going to get these figs to the kitchen? Move out of my way, you old cow."

"Don't you call me old cow. You might have been a young bull in your day, but from the looks of things now your stud days are over. Get on out of here."

"Buy my birds. They'll bring good luck to the young couple. Buy my birds."

"No birds. We don't want your birds. Move along."

"We're here to build the dais for the emperor. Where do you want us to put this lumber?"

"Ask the majordomo. He'll direct you."

The nuptials were something to behold. The emperor himself was a guest. He was, after all, my bride's self appointed adoptive father. Claudius sat regally, as befitted his office, on the specially prepared dais apart from the crowd, surrounded, of course, as he always was by Praetorian guards. From time to time, he summoned one or the other of the prominent guests and entered into private conversation. He seemed in a holiday mood this day, as indeed were all of the guests–with the possible exception of Agrippina, his fourth wife, who was also his niece– his own brother's daughter and the sister of Caligula. She sat beside him looking bored. What a scandal their marriage had caused! Shortly after those nuptials, the Roman Senate, in emergency session, was quickly called upon to quell the outrage of the populace by passing laws redefining incest.

"Claudius has not had much luck with his four wives. First there was Urgulanilla whom he married at his coming of age at sixteen. She was a troll–large and physically unattractive, sullen and given to fits of temper. At the end of her life, she was hugely obese–so obese that servants had to knock out a wall to remove her body from her bedchamber. She had committed murder on at least one occasion–not a pleasant person. Then there was Aelia, sister to Sejanus, the emperor's closest advisor. Claudius agreed to marry her when Sejanus offered her to him. It was a marriage in name only. Then he married Valeria Messalina when he was in his fifties and she was fourteen. In spite of the nobility of her family, she comported herself like a common whore, much given to wild parties with a multiplicity of men–many of whom died under strange circumstances after scorning her attempts at seduction. She made a public display of competing with a professional prostitute to see who could fell more men in a single day. Everyone knew about it except Claudius. He loved her and didn't want to know. None of his advisors had the courage to inform him. Messalina divorced Claudius while he was away in Ostia and married her paramour, Gaius Silius, at a drunken party. No one wanted to tell the emperor. Claudius' advisors got him drunk, it was said, and made him sign an order for her execution along with the groom and various of her followers. When Claudius sobered up the next day, he was devastated to discover that Messalina had already been executed at his command. Nasty bit of business. His present wife–the wife of his old age–was not much comfort to him, either. At least, that's the way things appeared to most of us. She was relentless in her promotion of her young son from her former marriage, Nero Claudius Drusus Germanicus–known to all as Nero. Claudius adopted him and favored him over, Britannicus, his own son by Messalina. Agrippina reveled in her power. Where her brother had been mad, she was merely hateful. Her ambition for Nero knew no limit. Three years previously, the Senate voted her the title "Augusta," the first imperial woman to hold the title since Livia, who was given the title only after the death of Augustus. Agrippina is excessively aggressive in her self promotion, receiving foreign dignitaries and appearing at public functions dressed in military garb. No, Claudius isn't greatly enthusiastic about his own marriages, but out of respect for our family, he accepted the invitation to my wedding, the second wedding of importance Claudius had attended within as many weeks. Nero, at sixteen, has just wed Claudius's daughter, Octavia. What a tangled, incestuous web. It's not easy to keep up with all the intrigue.

I am happy to report that our wedding is without taint of scandal or disapproval. Our wedding is cause for general celebration. The Roman Senate is in attendance. Everyone is here–from paunchy Marcus Plautius to young Andronicus Persis, the newest member of our exclusive club. For a wedding gift, the senators presented us with an intricately carved tri-fold screen inlaid with ivory and mother of pearl. I heard that the senators entered into long discussions about it, and that ultimately, most senators were happy with the choice. Claudia certainly seemed pleased.

Literary Rome is also out in force for our day. The writers will observe, gorge themselves on our food, drink our wine, and read their paeans of praise to the beauty of the bride and my virility and stalwartness. Chief among the writers is my friend, Martial–licentious as always. I am ever the recipient of Martial's literary efforts. Today, he will outdo himself by presenting his *epithalamion*–his wedding hymn–our wedding hymn, I should say–at the ceremonies. He has already shared it with me. It is replete with praises to the bride's beauty, and references to wedding torches, lotus blossoms, and nuptial wine. I suppose it is fairly standard fare, but Martial has thrown himself into it with his accustomed enthusiasm. It has special and particular meaning to us. One line I particularly remember has to do with the mixing of rare cinnamon sticks with nard. Our poet friend has a way of vividly calling an image to mind. Every wedding hymn, I am sure, seems unique to the two whose happiness is immortalized. He promises to write another hymn of praise at the birth of our first son. He smirked when he said it would be nine months and a half hour after our wedding festivities. We shall see about the timing.

Not every day are two such families joined–a senator and a princess. Never mind that her father is a prisoner in Rome. Caractacus commands respect as a man who held off the Roman legions for almost a decade–a warrior betrayed–never conquered. He has access, by the grace of the powers in Rome, to his Silurian wealth. Rome is ever impressed by wealth.

CLAUDIA SPEAKS:

 I slept. The women brought purifying potions for me to drink. I received relaxing massages. I soaked my hands and feet in scented oils, and gave myself up to the luxury of allowing the women to brush my hair until it lay heavy on my shoulders and shone like silk. Never have I felt so pampered. I received instructions from the women.

"You must be ready to receive your bridegroom, Princess Claudia. He will be eager to embrace you. You must be shy, but ardent." They taught me to lower my eyelids in modesty, but to arch my back and thrust my breasts upward in anticipation.

Our wedding day dawned clear and bright–a good omen. The women dressed me in my wedding garments. They all stood back in admiration. I am tall for a woman. I wanted to wear my hair loose to my shoulders, but the women seemed so scandalized that I allowed them to bind it up in the Roman fashion. I wanted it to cascade in waves and curls. Rufus loves my hair. The women said that all Roman brides wear the *tutulus*. With my groom's spear, they divided my hair into six parts and braided each section. They fastened each braid and then fashioned them into a cone on the top of my head. Everyone said that I looked like a proper Roman bride.

Priscilla came to me. "Before this day is gone, you will be my daughter-in-law. I want to welcome you, my dear child, to our family. You are beautiful and intelligent. Your eyes are blue as the Aegean. I am happy for Rufus. I have always dreamed of a good and kindhearted wife for him. I hope you give me many grandchildren."

"I hope so, too, my new and beautiful mother." She hugged me and smiled. I am happy that I have lived in the same house with her for a year. She and I have become friends.

I tried to concentrate on being serene. I could not help but compare myself to the Roman women. I am so different: slender rather than voluptuous–my coloring so different from their dark-eyes and raven-hair. Someone told me I appear fragile. I chuckled to myself. I look like my mother. We are apple blossom pink, but we are both sturdy and durable.

My wedding attire is simple and unadorned–a gauzy white billow tied at the waist with a cord of pure silk. There was much giggling and ribald commentary by the women who tied the knots of my sash which wound about my loins.

"The young master will have to await his pleasure tonight."

"He'll have a time untying all these knots, that's certain."

"He will be highly motivated."

My mother came to me and asked, "What jewelry do you wish to wear on this most important day?"

"Only my talisman, Mother. I want no other."

She smiled at me with tears in her eyes. "I wore it on my wedding day. It pleases me well that you choose to wear it today." My mother stepped back to look at me. "You are so beautiful. Never did I think my daughter would be a Roman bride."

And then, the women brought my veil–the *flammeum*– it means flame, and it is the color of fire, so sheer, it is

127

transparent. With my face uncovered, they pinned my veil, cloud-like under the braids in the back. They instructed me to say, "*Nubo*–I veil myself." The cloud reaches to my heels, and matches my shoes. The women arranged the wreath of flowers like a crown around my cone of braids and stood back to inspect me from head to foot. They made tiny adjustments in my attire and then sighed and declared me beautiful. I have never felt more beautiful in all my life. I was ready to meet my bridegroom.

PUDENS SPEAKS:

"Plautius, I think I am a little drunk–from prenuptial wine, yes, but also with the thoughts of my bride."

"Come, Rufus. Sit here on this bench. You are like every other man on his wedding day. You are not worried, are you?"

"No, of course not. But, she is so delicate."

"She may appear delicate, but I imagine her ardor will match yours. She is young and healthy."

"I'm no neophyte in these matters. I have experience, you know, though not proud of it. A man of my position is expected to be experienced. I have had women. A man serving in the Roman army understands that one of the rewards of conquest is sexual pleasure at the expense of the conquered. Rape and pillage are not new phenomena."

"Too true–and a sad commentary. We Roman men divide women into categories: maidens, matrons, matriarchs, and mistresses. Keep them straight." Plautius clapped me on the shoulder.

"I'm no child. I grew up in Rome. I can't remember when I did not know of Tiberius' cruelty or the madness of Caligula. Intrigue of every stripe–deceit, poisonings, false accusations, murder–it is all a part of the history I have lived. For sport I have seen men hack each other to death. I've seen wild animals kill prisoners. I have witnessed, on the public stage, sexual acts performed as entertainment."

Plautius nodded. "Sexual license makes Roman court life a pig sty. Every abomination is readily available. But, in the best of families, there is a sense of honor."

"Certainly, in my family, we were taught honor. I am proud of my father's service to Rome. He was an exemplary man. I have tried to emulate him. I miss him and wish he could have lived to see me married. I swore allegiance to Rome long ago. Recently, I swore allegiance to a new God. Plautius, I know you follow the Nazarene. Today is a good day to tell you that I, as well, am a secret follower of The Way. I find honor in this new religion. It teaches a new ethic. I want to be a true husband to my wife. I will treat her with the respect she deserves and be faithful to her. The excesses of Roman court life sicken me. I want a family."

"I applaud you, my young friend. Don't worry about tonight. Respect reigns between you and Claudia. You will have a good life. I hope this time next year, you will have a son." We rose and saluted each other in the Roman way, a hand on each other's shoulder.

I chose Aulus Plautius, my old general and mentor as my best man, fittingly, because we had been together in Britain when I first saw Gladys, and because Plautius married Claudia's Aunt Gladys Pomponia. They have a good marriage. Pomponia is Claudia's matron of honor. She helped me explain to Claudia and her family the differences between Roman and Silurian weddings. Here, the best man pronounces the legal formula that seals the marriage in the eyes of Rome.

The wedding party gathered around. Plautius looked at us with great affection. "*Nuptius consensus non concubitus facit.* Consent, not sexual relations, make a marriage. Do you, Gladys Claudia, daughter of Caradoc Caractacus, King of Siluria, of your own free will take as your husband Rufus Pudens Pudentia, and will you be under his legal authority promising to be faithful to him to the death?"

"I take him to be my husband, and I will be a faithful wife to the death."

"Do you, Rufus Pudens Pudentia, take Gladys Claudia, Princess of Siluria, to be your wedded wife? And do you promise to provide for her and to assume legal responsibility for her until your death?"

"I do assume legal responsibility for her, and I take her to be my wedded wife until death."

Claudia's Aunt Gladys placed my bride's hand in mine.

Plautius concluded: "You are now under Roman law, husband and wife." We were married.

The wedding guests shouted and cheered. We turned to face the crowd, and I conducted my bride to the wedding feast. Our guests pelted us with walnuts, a tried and true fertility symbol. There was much good-natured jostling and irreverent comment. The wedding feast was plentiful and joyous. Gifts were lavished upon us. The wedding guests cheered. The wine flowed freely. Toasts were offered to our future happiness and fecundity. I promised to do my part to insure the Pudens name be carried forth. My bride was radiant. I could not have been more filled with pride. At the end of the day, we were escorted around the villa by the light of many torches. We arrived at the colonnaded garden opening to the bedchambers. As she had been instructed to do, Claudia rubbed fat and oil on the doorway of our bedchamber and wreathed it with wool. She poured water into a bowl and lit a lamp, all symbols of her assumption of the wifely domestic role. She set the lamp beside the lavishly decorated replica of our marriage bed just outside the door. As the crowd cheered, wedding hymns were sung. I untied every knot in her wedding sash. Martial read his poem. Other poetry was read, as well. Everyone wished us well. This night, instead of going our way to separate bedrooms, I picked up my bride in fine Roman fashion, and carried her across the threshold into our bedchamber. I then stepped out while the *pronuba*—the faithful wife of a living husband–undressed my bride, took Claudia's jewelry–just the simple gold circlet–and put it away. She then put Claudia in our bed, and pronounced a blessing on our marriage. When she stepped out of the room, I, finally, entered the bedchamber and closed the door behind me. I understand that our wedding guests enjoyed a splendid celebration with much drinking and feasting. They told me later that the party lasted all night. I wouldn't know. Claudia and I had a celebration of our own.

CLAUDIA SPEAKS:

 I am delighted with domestic life. My husband is satisfactory in every way. I am also highly amused at my sister. In spite of her protestations about marriage in general, she will soon be wed to the Lord of Caer Salog, a Roman patrician, also a follower of The Way. He seems smitten with my sister. I don't suppose, however, that Salog will be making plans to leave his holdings in Rome. Ergain still maintains that she will be returning to Siluria. I can not imagine her being in any way submissive. I also can not imagine a Roman male taking orders from his wife. We shall all be watching with great interest as the events unfold. Meanwhile, I can heartily recommend married life to her.

"The houses of the rich contained great masonry hearths on which was laid a bed of coals. Here, pots, pans and grills could be in use all at the same time to cook the countless courses of a dinner."

Eugenis Ricotti, *Dining as a Roman Emperor* (6)

THE MOTHERS 53 *AD* 806 A*UC*

PRISCILLA SPEAKS:

 Queen Ergain and I settled with our needle-work on benches in the atrium.

"I want to know how your cooks make that delicious pear dessert," she said to me.

"That's an old family recipe. My mother-in-law made that for special occasions when Quintus was a boy. You peel and core about a dozen nice ripe pears and boil them. Mash them and mix in pepper, cumin, honey, *passum* and a bit of oil. You add six eggs and put it in a casserole. Bake it and serve it with pepper sprinkled on top."

"How do you make *passum*?"

"Oh, that's easy. Take wine or grape juice and boil off half the liquid. We use it in so many of our recipes. Mostly, we use it as a base for sauces."

"You have foods that we have never seen in Siluria. Eating is quite an adventure. I did not think I could be content here, but I find myself enjoying your country."

I rummaged through my sewing basket to find the blue wool. "Well, you know, Rome has not always been home to me, although it has been home to Rufus all his life. I was born in Tarsus."

"So, how is it that you came to Rome?" Ergain pulled a scarlet thread through her tapestry.

"That's quite a story." I thought a moment about the events which brought me here with Quintus. "It still seems strange to me that I am the lady of *Domus Pudens*. I am living my second life, you know. I sometimes can not believe I am in Rome. How it came to be is wonder."

"The story sounds intriguing." Ergain looked at me over her tapestry, her hands still at work with the silken threads.

133

"When I was a girl of fifteen, I married Aaron. We lived the life of pious Jews in Tarsus. My husband was a scholar, held in high esteem by everyone who knew him. He was also a Roman citizen, as was my father. Both Aaron's father and mine were men of means and highly respected. I was proud to be my father's daughter, and proud to be married to Aaron."

"Sounds like a life of privilege."

"Yes, in a way, it was, though my life with Aaron was simple. I bore him two children: Saul, who was fiercely independent, even as a child, and grew to be, I say quite without modesty, a brilliant intellectual. His mind absorbed knowledge as a sea sponge absorbs water. And two years after Saul's birth, a daughter was born–Rebekah, a precious child. When the children were still quite young, their father died–my Aaron. I was left to rear two children alone."

"That must have been difficult for you." We chatted comfortably. I felt a kinship with Ergain. She was a queen. She could have been imperious, but she made no demands on me or my servants.

"It was a dreadful time. We went back to my father's house, the children and I. They missed their father. I longed for my husband." For a brief moment, I felt the old grief clutch at my throat. "The years passed. The children were growing up. The family decided that Saul needed more intellectual stimulation than Tarsus could afford. When my Rebekah married and settled into a good life, I took Saul to Jerusalem so that he could take up his rabbinical studies with a famous teacher. I made a life for myself and would have stayed in Jerusalem indefinitely. By the time Rebekah married, both my parents had died. Since I had no brothers, I inherited my father's wealth. Money was no problem. Most widows in my country remarry as soon as possible in order to have a means of support and a protector. I felt quite safe, though, with

Saul in the house. I found myself enjoying my independence. With my son studying under a prestigious rabbi, I had the time and opportunity to cultivate friendship with some of the more prominent people in the city. I was content with my life. I sometimes missed Aaron with an overwhelming grief. I suppose I shall never recover completely from that loss, but I learned to be content with my life as I established it."

"I can't imagine what life would be without my husband. I am devoted to him. I'm sure it was a painful time for you." Ergain nodded sympathetically.

"Yes, very difficult." Priscilla paused a moment, remembering. "But, I decided I would make a life for myself. When Pilate was made procurator, his family moved to Jerusalem with him, of course. Pilate's wife, Claudia Procula, became a friend to me–or rather, I was a friend to her. By that time, I knew Jerusalem well–the streets, markets, social life. I was happy to act as her guide. Procula seemed lonely and somewhat overwhelmed by the move. We talked together of husbands and children. Ironically, it was Procula who, quite inadvertently, introduced me to my second life." A servant brought us a ewer of water and sweet cakes. I paused, thinking of how lovely for us to pass an afternoon in this way. "Quintus went from Rome to Jerusalem on some business with Pilate. The two men were deep in conversation as they walked down a corridor in the procurator's residence, when I, quite literally, ran into them. Perhaps, I should say I ran them down. I was laden with a huge stack of fabric samples I had brought for Procula's consideration. I could not see over or around the stuff I was carrying. I was in a hurry, my arms felt as though they were breaking with the weight of my burden. I suppose I was not really watching where I was going when the encounter–the clash–the wreck–whatever you want to call it–occurred. I caught both men from behind. My fabric samples slipped and slid out of my grasp into a slithering pile of silk and linen. Pilate stumbled and Quintus went sprawling. I was totally humiliated. Just picture it. My veil slid down my back. My hair was disheveled. I stammered out an apology. 'Oh, please forgive me.' I stooped to retrieve the fabrics, which now seemed to cover a large portion of the floor. My face felt hot. It must have been crimson. I don't know what I expected from them–fifty lashes or banishment from court life at the very least, I'm sure. To my great relief, they laughed and helped me pick up the drapery material."

Pilate said, "Well, Priscilla, if you wanted to meet this handsome fellow, I could have introduced you in a more dignified manner." He looked at me with great merriment as he helped his guest to his feet.

Procula appeared on the scene at that moment and joined the teasing. "My, Priscilla. You certainly know how to make a lasting impression on a man. I have heard of women flaunting themselves, but this is a remarkable ploy."

As I hurriedly stacked the material, I said, "Please, could we forget about this."

"Forget?" Pilate laughed. "This is the most entertaining thing that has happened in some time." He turned to his guest. "Senator Pudens, may I present to you my wife's friend, Priscilla, late from Tarsus, who has been most gracious to us since we have moved to Jerusalem. Priscilla, this is Senator Quintus Cornelius Pudens, of Rome."

He looked at me with merriment in his eyes. As he rearranged his toga, he laughed. Then, he put his hand over his heart, bowed low, and said. "It is a great pleasure to meet you. Never have I been attacked from the rear by such a charming lady."

"Of course, we all laughed. It was an inauspicious beginning, I must say. And that was how my second life began. A year later, Quintus and I married. I had always thought I would never remarry, because I was content with my life. I was a thirty-two-year-old widow, but certainly not on the marriage market. Growing older did not frighten me because I was well-situated financially. I told Quintus as much. He had not married. Although he could have had any young woman he wanted, he wanted me. He chose me."

"What a lovely story." Ergain smiled. "And so you married again and came to Rome."

"Yes. Quintus brought me to this villa–to *Domus Pudens.* And a year after that, our Rufus was born. Having a child at mid-life is very different from bearing children when one is young. Rufus was a dear little boy–so curious. And he grew up to be a soldier and an engineer. I am so proud of him. When Rufus was away in Britain, the Lord's Apostle, Peter, came to our home from Jerusalem. Quintus and I first heard the gospel story from him, and we became followers of The Way. Rufus became a believer after his service in the military. He has been the joy of my old age. He is the same age as my daughter's children–strange to have a child the age of my grandchildren, but he fills me with joy. They are all grown, now."

"And do you see your other children?"

"Not often enough. Rebekah is busy with her life in Tarsus. Saul writes me. He is a world traveler. He has changed his name to Paul."

"Really? Why did he do that?"

"Oh, that's a story for another day. I must get to the kitchen to see that the cooks have begun their work."

"You certainly have had an interesting life, Priscilla."

"You are right. I have."

ROBERTA M. DAMON

THE PREGNANCY   54 *AD*   807 *AUC*

CLAUDIA'S JOURNAL:

Kalend of May:
I am almost sure I am with child. I feel different–sleepy much of the time and nauseated. The thought of food, or the smell of cooking, makes me sick. My breasts are tender and heavier. I am beginning to feel that I inhabit a stranger's body. This morning at my morning meal I gagged over the porridge. My mother and Priscilla exchanged knowing looks and decided that it was time to call in Marcella.

The women–my mother, Priscilla, Gwynedd, and as many of the other servant women as could–gathered in the atrium to hear Marcella. The first thing she did was to question me: "Do you shiver after you and your husband have come together?"

"Sometimes, I do."

"Are your breasts swollen?"

"And has the flow of blood stopped?"

"Yes, for two months now."

"Do your limbs feel heavy?"

"Yes. And I'm tired much of the time."

"I am certain that you are with child." At her words, I felt a thrill of hope and joy. Marcella continued. "You are in the first phase of the process. You must concentrate on keeping the seed within your womb. You must not allow strong emotion to affect you–no anger, no sorrow, no fear, no surprise, no extreme joy."

I tried not to be too joyful. I took a deep breath and held it.

"You must be serene at all times. We do not want the seed to escape your womb. No, do not hold your breath.

You must make no sudden movements. Try not to cough or sneeze. Do not lift anything heavier than a feather. Do not leap into the air. Do not sit in the bath. Do not sit on hard chairs or sedan seats. Do not get drunk. See that you do not have a nosebleed, as that is a sign that the child will not survive."

I tried to remember everything she was saying. What if I sneezed? Or coughed. I don't have to worry about leaping into the air, not something I customarily do, but sneezing and coughing might come upon me when I least expect it. I must remember what I am not to do.

I looked around and noticed that every woman in the group was listening intently to Marcella's words and her instructive lectures. "During this seed preservation phase, we will anoint you with freshly pressed oil from unripe olives. You must go to bed for two days–alone. Your husband must leave the marriage bed for a time to give the uterus time to rest."

All the women nodded agreement. Everyone knows the marital activity must be suspended to avoid weakening the seed. Husbands are at liberty to seek consolation elsewhere for these months of waiting. Some women are relieved that, during pregnancy, they are not expected, indeed they are forbidden, to fulfill their marital duty.

Marcella felt my breasts and my belly. She nodded sagely. "I believe you are already entering into the second stage. It will last about four months. I am going to instruct you to eat lightly. You will be nauseated and have an upset stomach. You may have a fever from time to time or feel dizzy. And, you may have the need to eat strange things like earth, charcoal, and unripe fruit. You must not give in to these cravings."

The whole thing seems very unpleasant to me, but the women who had children were in universal agreement with Marcella's warnings.

Kalend of Sextillis:

This is my fifth month. Marcella taught us about the *pica* stage: a one day fast will ease the stomach and prevent sickness. Oil rubdowns must be given daily. The diet will include small portions of easily digestible food–porridge, soft boiled eggs, cold water. If the stomach should become upset, astringents should be applied. These include rose oil, myrtle, or unripe olive oil. I am to wear a tightly wrapped woolen girdle for support.

About the sixth month, my food intake will be increased, I will sleep, and I will begin a regimen of exercise to augment my strength for labor and delivery. During the seventh month, physical exertion will slow because of the greater weight of the baby. Then, I shall wear linen support bandages. I shall have wine and sweet-water baths to calm my mind. My belly will be rubbed with oil to prevent marks that remain after birthing. The birth canal will be injected with softening oils and goose fat.

Kalend of October:

Marcella brought her birthing stool to show us. She gave her lecture in the atrium: "This birthing stool has seen many a child well born. It has a crescent shape. The bars across the front are for the mother to hold on to while she strains to push the baby out. The arms of the chair are strong because they must withstand heavy pressure during the birthing. The back of the chair is likewise strong. The mother pushes her hips and buttocks against it at the time of maximum effort. The stool has an opening cut in the middle for the baby to drop through. To the lower parts of the stool we affix an axle which has a windlass on each side. In difficult labor, we often extract the child by wrapping ropes around the arms or other parts of the baby's body. We can attach the ends of the ropes to the knob and extract the child by rotation. The front of the stool is left open. I sit in front of the mother in order to give her encouragement. The child is delivered while the mother is in the upright position."

I tried to concentrate. I trust Marcella and her experience in these matters. She gives me great comfort.

Kalend of November:

The months drag by. I feel as though I have been expecting this child all my life. It will soon be over. I'm ready. Hurry, little baby. Your mother wants to look upon your face.

THEIRS IS THE KINGDOM

ROBERTA M. DAMON

"Claudia caeruleis cum sit Rugina Britannus edita, quam Latiae pectora gentis habet! Qual decus formae! Romanam credere matres. Italides possunt, Atthides esse suam. Dibene quod sancto peperit fecund marito, quod sperat generos quodque puella nurus. Sic placeat superis ut conige guadeat uno et semper natis gaudeat illa tribus." ('Though Claudia Rufina has sprung from the woodstained Britons, how she possesses the feelings of the Latin race! What grace of form has she! Mothers of Italy may deem her Roman, those of Attica their own. May the gods bless her, in that she, a fertile wife, has borne children to her constant spouse, in that she hopes, though youthful still, for sons-and daughters-in-law. So may it please the gods above she should joy in one mate alone and joy ever in her sons and daughters.")

Martial, *Epigrams* Vol. 2 (277)

THE BIRTHING: 55 *AD*   808 *AUC*

CLAUDIA SPEAKS:

 I felt the first birth pangs before sunrise and thought of calling Gwynedd, but as the pain subsided I decided to lie still and wait for the next one. Before the day is over, I shall know what it means to give birth. I am curious about the process. This birthing I want to experience silently and alone before the alarm is sounded throughout the villa. Now, I lie still, my belly grossly distended. Putting my hands on my belly, I speak to my child who will be born:

"We have work to do, little one. I will try to be gentle with you."

I feel a need to control my breathing. I close my eyes and see, behind my eyelids, a waterfall of vivid colors–red, orange, gold, yellow. I envision myself on a great, long swing anchored to the crescent moon. Back and forth I go, my legs pumping, my hands holding on to the ropes of the swing, higher and higher until I stop pumping and I float above the world. I look down from a great height and see in my homeland, my house, my room, my childhood bed. I see the crones gathered about me anointing my breasts, my belly. How dear they are, how wise. The pain intensifies.

"Gwynedd, it is time to call the midwives. I am in pain."

She is immediately wide awake. Out of the bedchamber and into the courtyard she runs. "Call the midwives! Her time has come!"

A kitchen servant races quickly toward the bedchamber where the midwives sleep. She pounds on the door. They were summoned days ago to make everything ready for the birth. They have been waiting.

Now, I hear feet drumming and the sound of fists pounding on a door. I hear the shout, "The mistress is experiencing birth pains." The household is immediately awake. I hear Marcella's voice from down the hallway.

"Very well. Don't cause a panic. First babies have a way of taking their time." I hear her talking to the other midwives. "Come. The lady is about to deliver the first child ever born in the whole world."

Laughing, the other three rouse themselves from slumber, gather up their oils, wines, unguents, herbs, bandages, towels, basins, the birthing rope, a pillow to put the baby on, the knife, and the birthing stool, and proceed solemnly toward my bedchamber–Marcella, Antonia, Julia, and Talia.

"Hurry. She's in pain." Gwynedd, white faced and urgent, greets the women.

"And how fares my wife?" I hear Rufus' voice outside the doorway.

"Good morning, Senator Pudens." I hear Marcella, instruct my husband. "You must find something to keep you occupied throughout this day. You must not come near this bedchamber. We shall surely keep you notified of all that is happening. Go find food and some men to keep you company. The gods will smile on this birthing and you will have a fine son before the day is through."

"May I see my wife?"

"You may come in to comfort her, and then you must leave."

Rufus enters my bedchamber. I am sweating and writhing in pain. I try to be brave, but I am in distress.

"I pray all will be well with you and the child."

I try to smile. My face contorts with pain. "Go away, husband. I shall be busy this day." He backs out of our room. I hear, as from a distance, Marcella giving orders.

"Antonia, wrap her hands in bands of linen. She will be pulling hard against the ropes. Talia, wash her down with sweet oil. It will refresh her spirits. Julia, secure the ends of the rope. She has to help this child into the world."

Marcella directs the activities. Expertly, she places her instruments on a clean linen towel. After she washes her hands in wine and in water and dips them in clean olive oil, she places goose fat in the birth canal to help the baby's passage. I am determined not to scream. As the hours pass, the pains grow more frequent and in intensity. Finally, I scream whether I want to or not. Patiently, the midwives rub my feet, legs, and belly. They encourage me to push and they speak words of comfort.

"Come, little mother. Pull on the ropes. Harder, harder still. Good. Good. The baby will soon be here." For hours, I labor.

Finally, they help me onto the birthing stool. Antonia kneels behind to catch the baby. Marcella readies the knife. If the doorway will not open, she is ready to cut. "Push, little mother. We can see the top of his head. Push. Let us see if this child has marbles or not. Push."

"I can't push anymore." I am limp with exhaustion.

"Yes, you can," Marcella insists. "Push! Talia, cut the lemon and put it under her nose. It will revive her."

With one mighty wrenching effort, I push the baby into the world. He is a fat, squalling boy. I faint momentarily from pain. Talia presses wine to my lips. Julia hands the knife to Marcella who cuts the cord. I reach for the baby, but Antonia takes him, wraps him in a warm towel, and carries him to a basin where she washes him, pats him dry, and slathers him with oil. Talia and Julia attend to me, massaging my belly to encourage contractions, and Marcella opens the bedroom door and calls for the Senator.

"You have a son—a big, healthy boy." To a servant girl she says, "Call the wet nurse. The baby is born."

Rufus rushes into the room. "Where is my son?" Marcella carries the baby to me. "You did well, little mother," she said. "Here is your boy." Rufus and I look at our newborn child. Our son. We murmur words every parent has spoken. "He's perfect. He's beautiful. Look at his hair. Look at his hands. Count his fingers and his toes. He looks just like his father." The wet nurse comes into the room. She is a slave who gave birth two weeks before. Her breasts are engorged with milk.

"And what will you call him?" Marcella asks.

We answer together with the name we had chosen: "Timotheus."

They put the baby to the breast. Marcella explains, "He will not suckle until tomorrow or the next day as is the custom with newborns." The child soon tires and sleeps. I, too, shall rest. I am depleted from my labors and the hours of striving. The wine works its narcotic effect, easing my discomfort and making me sleepy. Before I sleep, I hear the *gallicinium*–the "rooster's crow"–that blast of the bugle that signals the changing of the guard at the fourth watch–three in the morning. I have labored in childbirth all day. My husband keeps watch. In my dreams, I swing on the crescent moon and float high, high above the world.

For the occasion of the birth of our first child, Martial, ever faithful friend, penned an ode. He made a remark to Rufus that I did not quite understand. He said, "Your timing is just as I had predicted." The two men laughed. The poem was a hymn to the fertility of this blue-eyed Briton, and the glory of Roman motherhood.

I was eighteen when our first child was born. In the next three years, I gave birth to three more children, another boy and two girls. I kept Marcella and her band of midwives well occupied in those years. At twenty-one, I was the mother of four–Timotheus, Novatus, Praxedes, and Pudentiana. I bear the marks in my body. These children are dearer than life to me.

PAUL TO RUFUS PUDENS FROM MACEDONIA
55 AD   *808 AUC*

From Macedonia, I, Paul, an apostle of Jesus Christ write unto you, Rufus, my brother in the flesh and in the Spirit. Grace be to you and peace which is in our Lord Jesus Christ. I thank my God whenever I think of you and hear of your faith and your good works toward all those in the household of faith. I have great joy when I remember you and I am encouraged and strengthened by your love. I have heard of your suffering. We strive against principalities and powers of darkness. Be strong. Keep the faith. Pray always and the Lord will give you strength to face peril, even unto death, whether by fire, wild beasts, tearing of limbs, or a cross. God is for us, my dear brother. I have suffered deprivation, beatings, shipwreck, and dangers of every sort. I count it all joy to be able to suffer for his name, inasmuch as he suffered death for us, even death on a cross. I write to you to beseech you to care for our mother as you have in the past. Let every good work adorn you in the Lord. Greet Claudia, my sister, and the dear child, Timotheus. May your unfeigned faith dwell in him also. I send this letter by the hand of our brother Eubulus. I adjure you by the grace of our Lord to offer him hospitality that he may strengthen the church that is in your house. Grace, mercy and peace from God the Father and Christ Jesus, our Lord.

PAUL'S LETTER TO PUDENS FROM GREECE
56 *AD*   809 *AUC*

I, Paul, an Apostle of Christ Jesus, write unto you, my dear brother. I send greetings to all who are in your household. I pray that you will receive Phebe, my sister and helper in the Lord, into your house. She is a deacon of the church at Cenchrea. I have put into her hands my letter to the church in Rome. She will be faithful to deliver it into the hands of Hermas. It is profitable for your instruction. Stand firm in the faith. I shall do my best to come to you in the Spring. Greet my sister, Claudia, and the dear children. Walk in love, for in so doing you will be able to dispel the powers of darkness. Grace and peace be to you in our Lord Jesus Christ. Amen.

THEIRS IS THE KINGDOM

"Saint Paul was sent to Rome in the second year of Nero [56*AD*] and remained a prisoner at large for two years."
Jerome *Annales Ecclesias,* in *Notis* ad 19 *Maii,* as quoted in Andrew Gray, *The Origin and Early History of Christianity in Britain* (19). With this date, Bede agrees.

THE APOSTLE   56 *AD*   809 *AUC*

PUDENS SPEAKS:

 Paul is here with us. He is under arrest, but not in chains. He is allowed the freedom to walk the streets of the city and has arranged for a house of his own, but for the present he is at the villa. We are known by many names: *Domus Pudens, Paladium Britanicum, The Apostolorum, The Titulus, Pastor.* It is good to have Paul with us. He will preach on the next Lord's Day to the church in our house. The soldiers are here guarding him. Our villa seems to expand as the need arises to provide room for relatives, friends, and strangers. People are drawn to this place. Claudia's family is still with us, though it will not be many months before Caractacus will have served his sentence. I had a conversation with my father-in-law a month before Paul's arrival in Rome. I hope that Paul might be able to persuade Caractacus to become a follower.

"Paul will be coming to Rome soon, " I said to him. "My half brother is a world traveler. I have read you parts of his letters to me, and now I want you to know him. If the authorities will allow it, he will be staying here at *Domus Pudens*."

"Tell me again. How is he your half brother?"

"He and I have the same mother, but different fathers. He is eighteen years older than I. You have heard my mother's story. She married when she was fifteen to a man of high rank and had a son, Saul. Then, she had a daughter, Rebekah. When the children were still young, she was widowed. She went to live in Jerusalem for Paul's schooling where she met my father who was on a state visit to Pontius Pilate. When she married my father, he was already established as a Senator. She must have been

153

about thirty years old at the time of their marriage. I was born the next year. Saul was already a rabbinical student when I was born. He has changed his name along the way. The family history is pretty complicated. Anyway, most people know him as Paul."

"Why did he change his name?" Caractacus listened intently.

"It had to do with his religious conversion."

"Ah, yes. It is true, is it not, that believers often take new names? So, what kind of fellow is he?"

"He is brilliant–highly educated, an avid writer. He speaks several languages fluently–Hebrew, Latin, Greek, Aramaic. He preaches and establishes communities of believers all over the world. Mostly, he gets himself into trouble with the authorities. Paul has more energy than any other ten men I know. By choice, he has not married, saying a family would hinder him in his work. To tell you the truth, I don't think a wife would tolerate his ways. Anyway, I'm not much of a judge on the matter, but I don't think Paul is very attractive to women. He is small of stature and he has weak eyes. I guess he got all the brains and I got all the good looks." I said it as a joke.

"It takes intelligence to be a Roman senator and a civil engineer." Caractacus sought to console me.

"Oh, I know, but my brother is extraordinary. You would have to know him to understand fully what I am saying. A Pharisee, highly educated in the Jewish law, he followed his rabbinical studies with the best scholars. His personality is–how shall I describe him to you? Intense. Yes, that's the word. I think you will find him intense and interesting."

"I am sure I will. Are you anything like him, Rufus?"

"Not at all. I would describe myself as solid, steady, adequate, content to stay in Rome. Well, you will have ample opportunity to talk with him."

"I look forward to it."

The day Paul's ship arrived, a group of us were there to meet him. Hermas, Andronicus, and Persis, from our household, and Aquila and Herodion from the church of the circumcision. It is a three day journey from Rome to Puteoli where Paul's ship docked. We met Paul at Forum Appii at the post station, the usual halt at the end of a day's journey from Rome. We traveled the Appian Way built three hundred years ago. I wonder how many feet have trod that road? The old Romans did good work.

"There he is." Persis saw him first. We cheered as he approached, accompanied by two guards. All of us ran to meet him. I was the first to embrace him.

"Brother Paul! Thank God you have arrived safely. It is good to see you." Paul was greeted and embraced by all our company. He turned and introduced his two traveling companions, Luke, a Greek physician, and Aristarchus, a Macedonian, from Thessalonica. The soldiers stood aside, alert and watchful.

"How was your journey?" I asked.

"We should never have sailed. I told them it was too dangerous and I was right. We came fourteen days through the worst storm you can imagine. God sent his angel to me to tell me we would all be saved. I never doubted it. Our ship broke up, finally, on the Isle of Melita. I am grateful to be on land again. We are all very tired. I will tell you the entire story as we walk toward Rome. I have longed to see my family. How is our mother? And how are Claudia and the children?"

"They are eagerly awaiting your arrival as are the others in the villa. The children are eager to see you. The women have been in the kitchen for a week getting ready for you. They will attend to your needs–a clean bed and all the food you can eat."

"The authorities will keep me under guard. Being at your home is a very pleasant prospect. I have learned to be content with little, but I shall be happy and grateful for much. God has supplied all my needs to this day. I am confident that He will continue to care for me."

"Paul, we are hoping those in power will allow you to be with us at *Domus Pudens*. If you must have guards with you, we can provide for them as well."

"That's a generous offer. We shall see what Caesar will allow. Perhaps because you are a senator, the emperor will listen to a request from you, however, I do not want to put you in danger."

"No matter. We are grateful to God for sparing your life." Paul nodded at me.

"Yes," he responded thoughtfully. "Let us hope Caesar will be as generous."

We set off for Rome, talking, laughing, and singing. At times our party filled the breadth of the road. Once, we stopped to sleep awhile under the trees. Then, refreshed, we continued our trek toward the capital. Paul told us the details of his journey from Caesarea, and we marveled that anyone survived. I am amazed at my brother's stamina. He is smaller in stature than I am, and despite the fact of his more advanced age, he is muscular and taut and physically, very strong.

We walked through plains dotted with houses and gardens and great villas. Then we passed the Aquaduct Claudius completed a few years ago. Built on high columns, it brings water to the city from fresh springs far away. One of the many wonders of the city, that project was completed while I was serving in Britain. Leaving the sheltering pines, we caught sight of the hills of Rome. We were almost home.

THEIRS IS THE KINGDOM

"Pomponia Graecina insignis femina, A. Plautio, quem ovasse de Britannis rettuli, nupta ac superstitionis externae rea, mariti iudicio permissa. Isque prisco instituto propinquis coram de capite famaque coniugis cognovil et insontem nuntiavit." ("Pomponia Graecina, a distinguished lady, wife of Plautius who returned from Britain with an ovation, was accused of some foreign superstition and handed over to her husband's judicial decision. Following ancient precedent, he heard his wife's cause in the presence of kinsfolk, involving as it did, her legal status and character, and he reported that she was innocent. This Pomponia lived a long life. She escaped unpunished, and it was afterwards counted a glory to her."

Tacitus, *Annals* (*lib* xiii), McHenry (25-34)

THE EMPEROR   57*AD*   *810 AUC*

PUDENS SPEAKS:

 We are sick to death of Nero and we are terrified. Britannicus is dead. Rumor has it that he was poisoned by our exalted emperor and his dear mother, Agrippina. With Britannicus goes the last hope of the return of the Republic. His father, Claudius, with his dying breath, wanted his son to flee to Britain, hide there, and eventually raise an army. It was the desire of Claudius that Britannicus would come back to Rome, overthrow Nero, and reestablish the Republic. I suppose that Claudius was the last to wish the Republic reinstated. When Britannicus refused his father's plan, he sealed his own fate. Britannicus lived on borrowed time from the death of the old emperor. Well, Nero and Agrippina have finally eliminated that threat to their power.

It seems Rome will forever pay homage to an emperor. We in the senate do not have the power we once possessed. All power in Rome resides in one man who believes himself to be a god. Nero is a madman and a fool. He continues to be self absorbed, over indulged, and feared. He flaunts his mistress. From what I know of Poppea, she and Nero deserve each other. In this one aspect of her son's life, Agrippina disapproves. Agrippina, herself, is evil walking. Rome's palaces harbor nests of vipers.

Nero is determined to stamp out any religion that does not recognize him as divine. The Way is in danger of annihilation. We at the villa are horrified and grief-stricken at the arrest and death of so many of our number. Our Aunt Gladys–Pomponia Graecina, was arrested and charged with adherence to a pernicious foreign superstition. She was imprisoned for ten days and then, following ancient tradition, she was handed over for trial to her own husband. In times past, these kinds of proceedings proved a perfect way for a disgruntled husband to rid himself of a harridan. Not in this case, of course. Never have I known a husband and wife more devoted to each other than Aunt Gladys and Uncle Plautius. At her trial, Plautius, played his part to the maximum effect. Solemnly, he called her from her prison cell and examined her before us all. He then pronounced her innocent of all charges. He stated firmly, for added emphasis, that she is a lady of the highest character. All of us attended her mock trial and then came home afterward for a celebration. We give thanks to God that what would have been a great grief has turned into great joy. Pomponia should never have been subjected to arrest and imprisonment. She and Plautius are growing old. We hope they will close their villa and come to live with us. Times are so turbulent. But they are stubborn in their independence.

So many of our number are called upon to face death with courage. They sing hymns of praise to the Christ, which drives the oppressors to a fury. And it breaks our hearts. We do not know when we shall be called upon to follow the example of those who have been martyred before us. When my time comes, I pray to God that I shall be as brave as my brothers and sisters in Christ. We live in the hope of eternal glory.

We in our household of faith have reason to rejoice. Through Paul's preaching, Caractacus has come to know the Lord. Last week he entered into the baptismal bath. I was present at the ritual. As he came up out of the water, Linus pronounced the blessing. He said that we are buried with Christ in baptism, and we are raised to a new life. He held the new white robe, and as he placed it around his father and said, "Now put on Christ. Old things are passed away. Behold, all things are become new." In spite of persecution, we persevere. Claudia was overcome with joy at her father's profession of his faith. While we mourn our losses, we rejoice at our gains.

"Nothing served so much to recommend Christianity and extend it in Britain as its persecution by Rome. Common oppression drove the two religions into each other's arms, and finally united them in so indissoluble a union, that we cannot now separate in British Christianity the Druidic from the Christian element."
Williams Morgan, *Saint Paul in Britain* (92)

THE DEPARTURE   58*AD*   811 *AUC*

PUDENS SPEAKS:

We sat in the *caldarium*. The servants attended to the heating of the water. Steam rose as we eased ourselves into the bath with a sigh.

"I can hardly believe it, but I will have served my sentence come this summer." Caractacus settled lower into the hot water and looked across at me. "I can't believe I have been in Rome for seven years."

"Impossible! It seems like yesterday that you and Gladys stood before Claudius, and she became his adopted daughter. Seven years. The world moves so fast." I smiled at my father-in-law. "I'm talking like an old man. Seven years is time enough, though, for Claudia and me to marry and have four children. They have been good years."

"They have been good years for me, too. My time in Rome has not been onerous, thanks to you. I have enjoyed your hospitality. I have been with my family. My days of battle are over. I can look back and say that I served my country well. The worst of my suffering has come of not being able to leave this city. I was never in chains after Claudius pronounced my sentence, but I was never free either. Well," the old warrior shifted his weight so that water splashed out onto the tiled floor, "I have kept my word and served my time." He paused. "I want to go home to Siluria."

I looked at him. The two of us had always been respectful of each other. "Won't you stay? After all, your grandchildren are here. They are Roman."

"It will be not be easy to leave them, but I leave them in good hands. You are a good man, Rufus. My daughter and the children are well provided for. No, I shall go back to my home, finally. I have a deep desire to see my country again. I want to draw my last breath there and be buried beside my ancestors."

"Don't say that. You have good years ahead of you."

"Come, Rufus. Don't try to pretend I won't die someday."

"But no time soon, I'm sure." I reached for a towel and wiped the sweat from my face. "Tell me, Caractacus, do you have some plan to wreak vengeance on your betrayer?"

"Vengeance is for younger men. No, I am tired, and I just want to go home. I leave Aregwedd to her own conscience, if she has one. I have heard that she has cast her husband aside for his armor bearer and that her people are supporting the husband against her. The British do not approve of adultery in their royals, but honor was never a part of Arregwedd's character. No, I shall not seek vengeance. Evil has a way of destroying itself–at least, I hope so. That would apply to Roman emperors as well as British traitors." Servants poured boiling water into the pool. The steam rose around us. Caractacus accepted a drink of cold water from the hand of a servant. He looked thoughtful. "I feel a deep need to leave Rome. Rome is home to you. It will never be home to me. Our peoples are very different, you know."

"Yes, we are different, but we all do what must be done. We are given our life circumstances, and we deal with them. Is that not true?"

He smiled and shrugged. "Too true. For instance, I never aspired to be a warrior."

"You were a superb warrior. You must admit that without false modesty. What a tactician you were–and are, I suppose." I have always admired my father-in-law for his military service.

"Yes, but that is not what I wanted in life. I was to be king, certainly, but being king of Siluria is a gentle occupation for the most part. We Britons may fight among ourselves, but it is usually over some minor land dispute. We do not invade beyond our island. Rome wants to conquer the whole world and will practice all manner of evil in order to do it. All we wanted was to live in peace, raise our crops and our children, learn about the earth and the stars, and worship the Supreme God. We had no desire for world conquest. We do not love war. We certainly have proved we know how to defend ourselves, but conquest–we leave that to you. You Romans! You want it all–the whole world."

"You must admit, Caractacus, that during the days of Augustus, Rome was the whole world. *Urbs Roma orbs humana*–Mauretania, Numidia, Gaul, Hispania, Germania, Italy, and Asia to the Euphrates. You also must admit that there was peace and prosperity. The *pax Romana* extended to the four corners of the earth. The army fought no wars during that time and was put to work building roads. Magnificent! The empire extended far enough to support a hundred and twenty million people. There had to be peace in order to concentrate on such matters."

"Yes, but what you call 'peace,' I call subjection. Where Caesar rules, there is no freedom. I am not antagonistic to Roman culture. My grandfather, Lear, was educated in Rome. He lived in the palace with the nephews of Augustus. The emperor, himself, was their teacher and mentor. Britain has a history of diplomatic negotiations with Rome. Our nobles lived in Rome and often worshiped at her shrines. We have always carried on a lively trade with Rome. But with all that, you must remember that Britain remains stubbornly unconquered–the only free land of this civilization. When Claudius invaded us, I'm sure he was well aware that when Julius Caesar tried it a hundred years before, even he did not fare well across the channel."

During the seven years of his captivity, Caractacus and I enjoyed intellectual sparring. We are divided in culture. We were opponents in battle. We are, nonetheless, joined by family and love of freedom. My father-in-law continued. "Our God smiles on our way of life."   "Rome has her gods, too." I sipped cold water.

"Yes, and what an aggressive lot they are: Mars, Jupiter, Neptune, Pluto–warriors all. In their name, look at what has happened. Every sort of bestiality, every indignity, every murderous intrigue is practiced as a matter of course. The populace is drugged on blood and bread. Imperial Rome is greedy and rotten. In Druidism, we are concerned with truth, beauty, goodness, fecundity, love."

"Not all of Rome's gods are what you describe. Rome has her gentle gods and goddesses, too. Do you know Picumnus and Pilumnus–the brother gods who protect infants and pregnant women?"

"Of course, I don't know them. That's precisely my point. Your truly important gods are the gods of power, not the ones concerned with birth. I want to go home where life is more important than death. I want to live out my life in that green and gentle land. You are a Christian. You speak of love and of a gentle spirit. Your faith informs your behavior. You are very much like us, Pudens. Druidism and Christianity are the two religions Rome seeks to destroy. Whereas Britain extends religious toleration, Rome permits no religion but its own. Look at what happened to Pomponia. What possible harm could that dear lady have done to Rome? Following her belief, she did no evil. She extended herself to the poor. She taught children. She was guided by nothing but love and goodness. Her arrest was a barbaric act and a disgrace to an empire that calls itself civilized. Rome would have executed her but for an error. And look how many innocents have been slaughtered. No, Pudens, Rome will kill us all because she can."

"Dear God, Caractacus. I fear you may be right." I grunted as I shifted my weight. "And yet, not all is done in the name of power. There is the Roman sense of honor to be considered."

"Ah, yes. Honor. A most exalted concept." Caractacus signaled for a servant to bring towels. We emerged from

our bath, clean, relaxed, and dripping. We wrapped ourselves in warm towels of coarse linen.   Clean clothes were
laid out for us. We dried ourselves and dressed. Together
we walked to the *triclinium*.

"Eubulus was one of the 70 disciples, and a follower of St. Paul the Apostle, along with whom he preached the gospel to the whole world, and ministered to him. He was chosen by St. Paul to be the missionary bishop to the land of Britain, inhabited by a very warlike and fiery race. By them he was often scourged, and repeatedly dragged as a criminal through their towns, yet he converted many of them to Christianity. He was there martyred, after he had built churches, and ordained deacons and priests for the island."

> *The Greek Menologies* ad 15 March as quoted in Morgan, *Saint Paul in Britain* (81)

"Ergain is commemorated as the first female saint of the Isle of Britain."

> *Genealogies of the Saints of Britain* as quoted in Morgan, *Saint Paul in Britain* (85)

THE VENTURE   58 *AD*   811 *AUC*

ERGAIN SPEAKS:

 My dear husband and I are going on a missionary journey. My grandfather, King Bran, will go, as well as dear old Eubulus and several other younger believers. We are going back home to Siluria. Our plan is to establish a college. From the beginning of our marriage, I have talked with my husband of going home. Salog has caught the vision of a work in my homeland. I did not dream that any man, much less a man of great means, would forsake a life in Rome for the rural quiet of my country. I believe with all my being that God has worked in my husband's heart and has whispered in his ear the vision of what Christ's gospel can accomplish there. Soon, my father will have served his sentence imposed by the Emperor Claudius. My parents will go back to spend their last years at home. My father says that he wants to die looking on the green hills of Siluria. My sister is content to live in Rome. Not I. Not ever. From the day we were marched into this city in shame and disgrace, I have vowed I would not stay.

Not only do I want to live my life in Siluria, but also I want to have a part in making Britain Christian. I have long dreamed of establishing a center of learning where young evangelists can be trained, where priests, deacons, and bishops can be ordained and educated in the faith. I envision a college from which missionaries can go out to all of Britain and other countries, as well. Is it not a worthy vision?

Claudia sat, combing the tangles from Pudentiana's hair.

"When shall you go?" She stopped to wipe tears from her eyes.

"As soon as we can make provision for our travels. Don't

cry, sister. God is in our plans."

"I know. I simply cannot imagine life in Rome without you. We have never been separated in all our lives. And after you leave, mama and papa will be going back to Siluria, too. I will be very lonely without my family around me."

"Gladys-Claudia, you are surrounded by family here–Rufus, four children, Linus, Paul, all your brothers and sisters in the Lord. Be happy for me. God has work for me to do. I cannot stay in this city and accomplish God's task for me."

"I know. I do understand, but I am already feeling lonely without you. What shall you do?"

"As British princesses, we own lands, you know. I am thinking of going to Llandaff where grandfather established a little group of followers when he became a believer. I think that core of folk could be the beginning of my college. I'll give the land and the resources to build a school. Oh, Gladys, it will be a place of prayer and serious study. Think what God can do with such a place! Eubulus can be our bishop. He will be our spiritual leader and the example for all to emulate. I will teach the women. Salog and Eubulus can teach the men. We will set about the establishment of churches. It will be such an adventure."

Gladys looked at me with love in her eyes.

"Oh, Ergain. How can I be selfish and try to keep you here, when God has touched your heart with such a vision? God go with you, my sister. May God keep you close to his heart."

I smiled at her.

"You wouldn't like to join us, would you–you and Rufus?"

"There is no way I will leave Rome. Rufus' life revolves around this city and the Senate. Besides, God has work for us to do here."

"I worry that your lives are in danger in Rome."

"I know." Gladys looked thoughtful. "I feel safe here at the villa. I feel safe with Rufus."

A few days after the conversation with my sister, our little band of missionaries set sail for Siluria. I am going home at last.

ROBERTA M. DAMON

THE SAILING   58 *AD*   811 *AUC*

CLAUDIA SPEAKS:

The Ides of July, my parents were to leave Rome for Siluria. The day before their sailing, I walked in the garden with my father one last time. It was typical of him to instruct me. "I don't think you are in danger at the villa. Your husband is a good man and competent. He will take care of you as he always has." My father put his arm around my shoulders. "It is hard for you to say good-bye to your mother. It is hard for her. She will miss you and the children. You must come back to Siluria to see us. Pudens can easily pay the price of your passage."

The thought of saying good-bye to my parents brought tears to my eyes.

"Papa, I know you feel you are doing the right thing. I, too, know the longing to return home. From the time I married Rufus, my home has been in Rome, but I never had to give you up. I have had my parents, my husband and my children under this roof. With all of that, I have never stopped longing for Siluria's gentle hills. I envy you the sight of our homeland."

"For these seven years, I have wanted nothing so much as to get back to it."

"It is in our blood, Papa. I have married Rome and my children are Roman, but I shall die a Briton. When you get back to Siluria, kiss its soil once for me."

"I shall do it. My dear daughter, you were Gladys before you were Claudia. And I was your father long before Claudius adopted you. You never were truly his daughter. You were always mine. His adoption of you was not in my hands. I hated being a prisoner and will never be at home here. I have no regrets about leaving Rome, only sorrow

173

at leaving you and the children."

I tried to smile. "I shall be brave, Papa. I am your daughter, after all. The royal family of Siluria possesses both courage and pride. Honor is mine in being your daughter." I ducked my head. "I hope you are proud of me."

"Dear daughter, from the time you were a baby and I carried you on my shoulders, you have given me reason to be proud. I shall always remember your bravery when I stood before Claudius and the Roman Senate pleading for my life. You were just a girl, then. Now, you have grown into womanhood. The day you stood beside me in the Senate, I thought, 'These Romans will get a good look at what we Britons are made of.' They did that day."

"I shall miss you, Papa."

"And I you, dear one. But if we should not meet again on this earth, we shall meet again in that land more beautiful even than Siluria."

I leaned on my father's shoulder and wept. "God go with you, Papa." He held me close. I have always felt safe, held by my father's strength.

"Be careful, Gladys. Teach the children to be careful. Rome is full of treachery. Be safe. May God protect you." With that, he kissed me and I thought my heart would break.

Before dawn the next day, we went down to the docks amid all the ongoing construction, to wish the travelers godspeed. Our little sons were delighted to see the ships and to watch the workmen at their tasks. Timotheus and Novatus are old enough that they will miss their grandparents. The girls are so little, they won't remember. My children didn't understand my tears, but they all cried when I did. We waved until they were out of sight.

THEIRS IS THE KINGDOM

"The royal family of Britain was ardently attached to both Greek and Latin literature."

Williams Morgan in *Saint Paul in Britain* (?)

"Had the large collection of British Archives and MSS. Deposited at Verulam as late as 860 AD descended to our times, invaluable light would have been thrown on many subjects of interest. Amongst these works were the Poems and Hymns of Claudia."

Vide Matthew of Westminster, William of Malmesbury as quoted in Morgan, *Saint Paul in Britain* (118)

THE SOLON   59 *AD*   812 *AUC*

CLAUDIA SPEAKS:

 I couldn't believe it when I received word that the emperor's mother wants to see me. I can not imagine what she wants. I don't know her well, although I am often invited to social events because my husband is a senator. At those events, Agrippina is present, of course. What does she want of me?

I must say that court life in Rome terrifies me. We are aware, here in our villa, of the things that take place in Nero's palace. Senators must be well informed for their own safety. Some of them participate in the parties, the banquets, the orgies. My husband begs off from most social contact. He claims business concerns preclude his participation. We live cautiously. Our way of life is vastly different from life at court. We are careful to be cordial to and supportive of the imperial family. We must be circumspect in all things. Rufus has made himself indispensable to the emperor. To find an engineer of my husband's skill and experience is a rare occurrence. But, one falls from favor so easily in Rome. Even skillful men are executed on Nero's whim. His caprice has cost the life of many of our friends. Nero is a despot and completely mad. He scandalizes Rome's elite by horse racing and driving his chariot in the circus, like an insane child at play, but his play is deadly. We know that he castrated a male slave and then "married" him. He goes out at night and stabs citizens who are unfortunate or foolish enough to be in the streets. Nero murders for entertainment and throws the bodies of his victims into the sewers of Rome. We pray to God for protection from evil, of which, in this city, there is an abundance. Rome feeds and thrives on violence. Followers of

177

The Way are the most vulnerable of all.

"What shall you wear?" Priscilla questioned me.

"I am less concerned about my clothes than I am with the invitation itself." I frowned as I tried to imagine what Agrippina would say to me.

"Coming from the imperial family, an invitation is a command." Priscilla is right. Agrippina never makes a request. She only makes demands.

Priscilla lowered her voice. She looked around as if she thought someone might be listening. "Britannicus should have succeeded his father. How could Claudius have named Nero his successor? How could Claudius have allowed his own daughter to marry that slug? Well, I know how. Mama Agrippina gets her way. And Octavia's marriage to Nero sealed that bargain." Priscilla spat out the words as an epithet. "Nero is a fat, indulged, overgrown, self-serving child who is guided by his mama. He is no husband to Octavia. He flaunts his mistress before the citizenry. Poppaea is as evil as his mother. She traded her husband for Nero's power. How many people have been put to death? How many more will die before he is gone?"

"Priscilla, hush. You must not say these things. I'm frightened to even discuss it. I believe we can trust everyone in our household, but if Nero should hear of that kind of talk, Rufus would be in danger and all of our family including the children." I took a deep breath. "Perhaps we should speak of other things."

"Perhaps," Priscilla agreed. " Do you ever think of Siluria?"

"Of course I do. There will always be a longing in my heart for my childhood home. If Rome were not so violent, I could be content here. My loyalty is to Rufus. Our children are, after all, Roman. The day Claudius granted our father clemency and adopted me as his daughter, I decided to be true to Rome. I suppose it is the same with you. Do you ever miss Tarsus?"

"Oh, my dear. Tarsus seems like a dream, another life.

A life before Rome I can barely remember. I have to believe it was God's hand that led me to Quintus and life in this house. I wish you could know Simon Peter. He came here to this house, you know. He baptized both Quintus and me. What a dear man. He preached love and forgiveness—a. message contrary to anything Rome knew—or knows." Priscilla picked up my comb. "Let me comb your hair." She worked the tangles out and made two simple braids which she wound around my head. "There. It's not elaborate, but it is elegant." She adjusted the cloak around my shoulders and inspected me from every angle. "There now. You are ready to meet the emperor's mother. Be brave. I shall pray for you." We embraced and I went out to my sedan.

All the way into the city, I wondered about the purpose behind this meeting. It is wise to be inconspicuous in Rome. What have I done to catch Agrippina's attention? I would know soon enough. Just after midday, I arrived at the royal residence and was conducted by a servant into the atrium to await the arrival of Agrippina. Offered fruit and water, I declined both and wondered if I offended in doing so. In an effort to calm myself, I breathed deeply. With every breath I prayed, "Lord, be with me this day. Strengthen me and help me. A summons to the palace can often be a one-way trip."

"Well, so you are here." Agrippina swept into the room, her entourage of servants following. With a dismissing wave of her hand, they backed out of the room and left us alone.

"I am here, Augusta." I gave a slight bow. "I hope you are well. So many in the city have been ill."

"I don't believe in getting sick. I simply won't do it." She looked a tower of strength. Her hair was curled and braided in a complicated fashion and piled high on her head. She dressed in military garb. Her use of artifice was excessive, her face white with lead paste, and her cheeks red with too much ochre. Her eyes and brows were evil

179

looking with kohl. Beside her I am excessively pale. Agrippina is never without large showy pieces of jewelry. She raised her head, squared her shoulders, and declared in her most commanding tones, "I choose not to be ill."

I nodded, without knowing exactly how to respond. This woman is extremely aggressive. It is rumored that she was the *de facto* emperor during the last days of Claudius when he was falling into senility. Rome whispered that it was she who poisoned our late emperor. Her ambition for her son is without limit.

"And how is the Emperor Nero?"

"My son is well. He will do greater things than Claudius ever did. He has plans for more gardens and monuments. Rome will love Nero's buildings more than they love Claudius' aquaducts."

"Claudius did wonders for Rome. I'm sure Nero will surpass him in glory."

"Yes, he will. I shall see to that." She looked at me with one eyebrow raised. " I remember your wedding day. But more importantly, I remember the day you stood before the senate–the day Claudius adopted you to seal the alliance between Rome and Britain. You were a strong young woman then. Are you still?"

"Let me say that I take after my father–a very strong man." I had no idea where this conversation would end.

"Good. I have no use for weaklings. Women who pretend they are too fragile to think for themselves deserve what they get. We strong women don't mind pushing to get what we want, don't you agree?"

I murmured something inconsequential which she must have interpreted as agreement. I have long noticed that aggressive people assume others will agree with their viewpoint even when it may not be so.

"So, you were a daughter to Claudius. That makes you a sister to Britannicus. So sad about his untimely death, was it not? He was so young and virile. I was delighted when Claudius adopted my son to be his own, but I always thought it somewhat strange that Claudius favored Nero over Britannicus. I do believe Claudius always considered Nero more of a son than his own blood. How strange that is. It may have to do with the fact that Britannicus was Messalina's child. Well, that's history. And now Nero is emperor. It is interesting how these things happen." She smiled with her mouth. Her eyes glittered like a serpent's. I tried not to shudder. Agrippina looked at me.

"So, you are a foreigner, yet you have risen high."

"I was born high. I am the daughter of a British king, though I have sworn allegiance to Rome."

"Yes." She seemed to take my measure. "What is the trinket you wear around your neck? Is it a talisman? Does it ward off evil?"

"No. It was a gift from my mother on the occasion of my fifteenth birthday."

"Curious. It looks old."

"It has been in my family for many generations."

"I hear you hold court among the literati." Agrippina was blunt. If something caught her attention, she spent as much time as it took to satisfy her curiosity, and then she quickly moved on to another subject. Briefly, I pondered my response.

"I would not call what I do 'holding court.' That is for the emperor and his advisors. I do preside over a literary salon."

"When do you meet?"

"The second day after the kalend of the month."

"So you meet ten times a year?"

"Yes."

"Who attends?"

"We are a group of writers who meet to share the fruits of our labors."

"Does the poet Martial attend?"

"As often as he is able."

"Are you a writer?"

"Yes."

"What do you write?"

"Odes, hymns, epigrams."

"The Emperor Nero is both literary and musical. He plays the lyre you know. He writes superlative poetry. Perhaps he might come to your villa to perform."

My heart contracted sharply.

"As he desires, my lady. The audience would not be large." Agrippina looked thoughtful.

"No, I suppose not, but it would be made up of the finest literary figures. Perhaps I shall encourage him to join your little group. It might inspire him to even greater heights. Of course, he might summon all of you to the palace. Your husband is an engineer, is he not?" The mention of my husband startled me. I am always careful not to mention his name or call attention to my children.

"Yes. That is correct." I kept my face impassive. I will give no more information than is necessary.

"Nero is thinking of having a large monument erected in my honor. I know just what I want–an equestrian statue with me in full military regalia, surrounded by great fountains. I shall require your husband's services. I'll inform him soon. You are dismissed." She clapped her hands and servants entered. Agrippina spoke in her most acerbic voice. "Show the Lady Claudia out."

I was conducted from the august presence. My thoughts were tumbling.

"What if Nero did decide to come to the salon? He would expect to be the center of all attention. He would go into one of his interminable concerts and expect everyone to pay homage. I don't want him there, but I can't refuse. Maybe Agrippina will change her mind about suggesting that he attend. What if Nero calls all of us to his palace? We would be in mortal danger. What have any of us written that would displease him? If we write verses superior to Nero's, what might he do? What will Agrippina require of my husband? She holds as much power over us as does her son. Oh, dear God, help."

I stumbled into the front door of our *domus* greatly relieved to be home. My husband would soon return from the Senate. Priscilla met me in the atrium.

"Well? What did she want?" Her voice was anxious.

I burst into tears.

ROBERTA M. DAMON

"Afflicti suppliciis Chraistiani genus hominum superstitionis novae ac maleficae." ("Punishment was inflicted on the Christians, a class of men given to a new and mischievous superstition."

Seutonius, *Lives of the Twelve Caesars* (111-112)

THE HUSBAND   59 *AD*   812 *AUC*

CLAUDIA SPEAKS:

 For ten days, I worried about my visit to Agrippina. I cried and prayed and prayed and cried. I could not eat. Food stuck in my throat. My husband was driven to distraction.

"Claudia, you must stop this. You will be ill."

"I can not help it. I am afraid of those people. What if Nero comes to my salon? What if he summons all my writers to his palace? What if Agrippina calls on you to help design that detestable monument?"

"And what if she does not? We have not heard one word about it since the day of your visit. Agrippina may have forgotten about the whole thing. She may have decided not to invite Nero to your salon. Or, she may have invited him, and he refused. She may not have mentioned it to him, or if she did, he may have dismissed it."

"What if he doesn't refuse an invitation to come here? What if the emperor of Rome comes to our house and some horrible thing happens?"

"He won't come."

"How do you know?"

"I do not know." My husband put his head in his hands. "I am just trying to comfort you. You know that whatever happens, God is with us."

"I know that in my heart. Of course, you are right. I am so scared–frightened for all of us, but most of all for the children." My husband did what he always does. He stood before me, pulled me to my feet, wrapped his arms around me, and whispered love. His strength never fails to give me courage. Sometimes, I grow tired of being strong, the daughter of a British king. Sometimes, I am just a woman.

185

Sometimes, I am a little girl lost in the tall grasses, running from some evil thing. Rufus, dear Rufus, leads me safely home again. My husband is a man of courage and faith. He loves me, and I love him. Courage and love and faith are strange and wonderful. I was comforted.

The next day, the messenger came. In Rome, we never know what the news will be. Sometimes, there is a crisis in the Senate. Sometimes, there is a problem that requires the engineering skills of my husband. Sometimes, there is an invitation to celebrate the dedication of some monument or arch or garden. Today, the messenger brought news of Agrippina. Rufus unrolled the notice and read silently.

"Oh, great God, what does this mean?" He looked suddenly pale.

"What is it? What?"

"Agrippina is dead. She has been executed."

"Executed? By order of her son?"

"It would seem so."

"But why?"

"Everyone knows Agrippina bullied Nero. I suppose he tired of it. Claudia, I'm going to the Senate to find out more about this. I'll be home tonight with more information."

I hugged him close. "Be careful."

"I will. Keep the children in today."

"Yes."

I spent the afternoon with Gwynedd, the children, and their grandmothers. Timotheus, at five, is very bright, and grows more and more difficult to keep entertained. Whatever Timotheus does, Novatus is close behind. The girls are easily distracted. Gwynedd brought clay. The children molded little pots and lamps and small animals. They arranged them in the atrium in the sun to dry, so proud of their handiwork. Even little Pudentiana showed me something that looked like a lump, but she said it was a sheep. They made such a mess. Clay was everywhere–on the floor, all over the children, in their hair. Ordinarily, I would not have tolerated the activity inside, but today I found my-self unable to be away from them. And they seemed content not to be out of doors. Afterward, we all went to the baths and had a wonderful time splashing in the warm water. We dried ourselves, and dressed. I readied the children for sleep.

I left the children in the care of their nurses while I stopped by the kitchen to see about our evening meal. I did not know when Rufus would be home, but I could think of little else. Agrippina is dead. Nero ordered her death. What does it mean for Rome? For all of us?

The sun was setting when Rufus arrived.

"What news?" I asked him.

"She is dead. He ordered her execution. Where are the children?"

"Eating their supper. They are ready for bed."

"I will go to them. After they are asleep, I will tell you the details."

I nodded agreement, still deep in thought as I heard the children's squeals of delight when their papa peeked into their room.

"What did you do today?"

He was met by a chorus of voices. "We made animals and pots with clay. We made a mess."

"Oh, did you?"

"Pudentiana made a sheep, but it doesn't look like a sheep." I heard Rufus laugh.

I turned to the nurse and instructed her to put the children to bed. They will never go to sleep as long as their father gives them his attention. Besides, I was eager to hear the news. When the household had settled into silence, Rufus came to me, and we dismissed the servants. He spoke in a whisper.

"Do you remember when Agrippina almost drowned? That was Nero's first attempt on her life. Today, he sent his men for her. They said he was literally frothing at the mouth with rage when he ordered his guards to kill her. She was hacked to death and her body cut into small pieces."

"How horrible." I shivered as I imagined the scene. "But why?"

"Nero was enraged with her. She constantly harped on her disapproval of his mistress. He obviously had enough of it and made no secret of his desire to see his mother dead. Often, he said that his greatest fantasy was to watch in glee as his guards hacked her to bits, that he dreamed of urging the guards to cut her up in smaller pieces, that he wanted to take off his sandals and dance in her blood until he was red to the knees. He is completely mad. Everyone is terrified, and no one can predict what he will do next. I don't know how much longer Rome can endure his reign."

"He is so young. He may reign for years."

"We must not speak of this again, my dear. We must not speak treason."

"Well, one thing is certain." I felt a sudden sense of relief.

"And what is that?" My husband pulled me onto his lap.

"It is unlikely that you will be asked by Nero to build a monument to his mother." My husband looked at me blankly. Slowly, understanding dawned on his face. The, he leaned back, shoulders shaking with laughter.

LETTER TO CLAUDIA FROM ERGAIN
59 *AD* 812 *AUC*

From Ergain to Claudia Rufina, greetings. I long to see you, my dear sister, and all that dwell in your house. We are in Glanmorganshire. I have given land for our school to establish a center of learning where followers of The Way may prepare themselves to preach more effectively the gospel of the Lord Jesus. We have lost our dear brother, Eubulus. He was often persecuted by wild tribes while preaching the word of the Lord. Yesterday he was dragged through the streets and killed. He lived a life dedicated to the spread of Christ's gospel to the ends of the earth, beginning when the Lord sent him out as one of the seventy. I desire that those who took his life might find eternal life through the shed blood of our Savior. Eubulus is the first of Christ's martyrs in Britain. He has received the crown of life laid up for him. Embrace your dear children. Greetings to Pudens. May the grace of our Lord Jesus Christ be poured out on you in abundance.

ROBERTA M. DAMON

"And what are the deacons but imitators of the angelic powers, fulfilling a pure and blameless ministry unto him as the holy Stephen did to the blessed James, Timothy and Linus to Paul."
> Ignatius, *The AnteNicene Fathers* vol. 1 (69)

"The report is true which I heard of thee whilst thou wast at Rome with the blessed father Linus."
> Ignatius to Mary at Neapolis, *The AnteNicene Fathers* vol 1 (122)

"Sanctissimus Linus, frater Claudiae." ("Holiest Linus, brother of Claudia.")
> Clement of Rome, as quoted in Andrew Gray, *The Origin and Early History of Christianity in Britain* (31)

"Concerning those Bishops who have been ordained in our lifetime, we make known to you that they are these: Of Antioch, Eudius, ordained by me, Peter; Of the church of Rome; Linus, brother of Claudia, first ordained by Paul; and after Linus' death, Clemens, the second ordained by me, Peter."
> *The Apostolic Constitutions* (Book I, Chapter 46)

"The Apostles having founded and built up the church at Rome, committed the ministry of its supervision to Linus. This is the Linus mentioned by Paul in his Epistle to Timothy."
> Irenaeus, Bishop of Lyons AD 180 *Opera*, Lib. Iii., c. I., as quoted in Andrew Gray, *The Origin and Early History of Christianity in Britain* (31)

THE ORDINATION   60*AD*   813 *AUC*

TIMOTHEUS SPEAKS:

"My Uncle Linus is a bishop. He was not a bishop yesterday, but he is today. My Uncle Paul said some words and did some things with oil and water and bread and wine, and now Uncle Linus is a bishop. We are not supposed to tell. I am not sure what a bishop is, but my Uncle Linus is one. It has something to do with the people who meet at our house to sing and pray. Brother Hermas is our pastor. He is a good man. When all the people meet to pray, it is not anything bad, but we are not supposed to tell, anyway. I think we would be in trouble if we tell.

I have a big family. My Uncle Paul and my Uncle Linus are not brothers. Can you guess how they are both my uncles when they are not brothers? It is a riddle. How can that be? Well, I will tell you the right answer. My Uncle Linus is my mother's brother. My Uncle Paul is my father's brother, except you would not guess it. My father is really old, but my Uncle Paul is really, really old—maybe even half a hundred. My mother is old, too. So I guess all grown up people are old. You have to be old before you can be a bishop.

Some of the people in our family are young. My brother is Novatus. I am older than he is. I am the oldest in my family, except for the grown-ups. I have two sisters named Praxedes and Pudentiana. Pudentiana is still little. She can walk and talk some, so we do not have to be careful around her if we have a secret we don't want anyone to know about because, even if she wanted to tell, she couldn't because she does not talk much yet. Praxedes will tell secrets, so we have to be more careful, because she knows how to talk, and she does not know how to keep a secret. If we want to surprise our mother or our father, we don't tell Praxedes because she can not keep a secret, and she knows how to talk.

Our Uncle Paul has been everywhere there is to go in the whole world. He tells us children stories. He told us once about when he was on a ship, and there were more than a hundred other men on the ship, and there was a big storm that came up, and the ship crashed, and everyone had to jump off, and the waves were really big, and they had to grab onto pieces of wood, and other things that float, and they were all saved, but they thought that they would all drown and be dead. Uncle Paul said that God took care of all of the people on the ship.

On certain days everyone meets at our house to sing and pray and hear Pastor Hermas preach. Sometimes, when Uncle Paul is here, he preaches. Sometimes, my Uncle Linus preaches. They all say the same thing. They all preach about Jesus. Jesus is the Son of God. My Uncle Paul told me. Today, they all decided that Uncle Linus should be a bishop and our mother and father decided that all of us four children should be there when Uncle Linus got to be one. They said it was really important and would be the first time that Rome would have a bishop.

I do not know what Rome will do with a bishop. I think being a bishop is important, and that a bishop is a really important person, because everyone seems to think it is important for a bishop to be in charge of things and be the one to tell other people what to do. My father said that I have it all backwards, and that a bishop is not the most important person, but that a bishop is really the one who is like a servant to everybody, and that if someone is in trouble or needs food to eat or clothes to wear or something like that it will be the bishop who helps out. My Uncle Linus would be good at that, because he is a man who is kind and will help anyone who comes to our house looking for something to eat or a place to sleep. One time, Uncle Linus came into the house without his sandals, and we thought he had just left them at the door like always so the floor of our house wouldn't get dirty, but he gave his sandals to a man in the city who didn't have sandals to wear, so I think he will be a good bishop.

 "St. Paul lived, according to all evidence, when he was in Rome, whether in custody at large (*libera custodia*) or free, in the bosom of the Claudian family. There is no dispute that Claudia herself was purely British, and the British character of the family, as well as the close domestic ties of affection between this family and St. Paul, are manifest."

Andrew Gray, *The Origin and Early History of Christianity in Britain* (31)

"When Saint Paul claimed Roman citizenship, he was claiming the full protection of Roman law over the local law of the province of Judaea; and his cry 'I appeal to Caesar' was the cry of a provincial who knew himself to be especially favored and protected by the emperor. He claimed the right to be tried by the emperor or by a judge responsible to the emperor, and his person was inviolate until the trial had taken place."

Robert Payne, *Ancient Rome* (187)

"The children of Claudia and Pudens were brought up at the knees of St. Paul."

Roman Martyrologies, as quoted in Morgan, *Saint Paul in Britain* (113)

THE UNCLE 60 *AD* 813 *AUC*

CLAUDIA SPEAKS:

 I happened upon a sweet scene today. Paul was seated on the floor of the atrium, and all four of my children were draped over and around him. Pudentiana was in his lap, sound asleep. Praxedes was under his left arm, cuddled as close as she could get. Novatus was on his uncle's right side, also snuggled in. Timotheus was sitting directly in front of Paul, his eyes as big as the full moon. His uncle was telling him an adventure story. I motioned to Paul that I would take the baby, but he shook his head and continued his narrative. He does not seem to mind being besieged by my little ones. I brought my needle work and settled down close by. I must confess, I like to hear Paul's stories, too. He makes them sound exciting, beyond the imagination.

He shifted the baby slightly and continued, "So, one day, I was telling some people about Jesus. Sometimes when I tell the story, people listen, and they believe what I say. That day, I was talking to people who did not know Jesus and did not believe what I said. They were so angry that they called the soldiers to come to get me. When the soldiers came in, they grabbed me and tied me with leather straps. They were ready to whip me, so I stood up and said, 'You better watch out. What you are doing is against the law. I am a Roman, and the Roman law says that you can't whip me.' Well, I tell you, they were afraid to beat me after that. The people were still angry with me, and they meant to do me harm, but, that night, something wonderful happened. Can you guess what it was?"

Timotheus said, "You ran away."

"No, that's not it. Can you guess again?"

"You whipped the guard."

"No. I will tell you what happened. Jesus came and stood by me. He said to me, 'Do not worry, Paul. You told people in Jerusalem about me. Now, go tell people in Rome.' I knew, from then on, that Jesus is always with me, no matter what bad things might happen. Well, those angry people decided they would kill me–forty men who decided they would not eat anything or drink anything until I was killed. But someone heard them make their plans."

"Who?" Timotheus asked breathlessly.

"It was your cousin, Aaron. He is the grown up son of your Aunt Rebekah. Aaron ran to the chief captain and he said, 'Chief Captain, you need to know that there are forty men who have decided they will not eat or drink anything until they have killed Paul.' The chief captain believed him, and do you know what he did?"

"What? What?"

"The chief captain called two centurions. Centurions are captains in charge of a hundred soldiers. So they called two hundred soldiers and seventy horsemen, and two hundred spearmen. 'At the third hour of the night,' he said, 'Go get Paul and put him on a horse and ride to the governor's house. And that's what happened. So I did not get killed. Do you know who took care of me that night?"

"The chief captain?"

"Yes, and do you know who else?"

"The soldiers."

"Yes, and do you know who else?"

"Jesus."

"That's right. And Jesus will take care of you, too. The next time, I will tell you about the night of the storm when the ship I was on broke all to pieces."

"Tell me now, Uncle Paul." Timotheus was enthralled with the stories. I smiled at Paul. "You have won the hearts of my children, Brother Paul, but I think, now, you and they need some rest."

"Ah, Claudia, they lift my heart and refresh my spirit. They are not only beautiful, but see how bright they are. These boys will be great soldiers of the cross. These girls will bring joy to the heart of God." I lifted Pudentiana from Paul's lap and handed her, still heavy with sleep, to her nurse. I gathered up the other three and took them away to feed and bathe them. Timotheus and Novatus ran across the lawn to gather small branches.

"Look, mama, we are soldiers. These are our swords. We are soldiers of the cross."

"Be careful with those. Do not hit anyone and be careful not to poke an eye." They swished their 'swords.' They twirled and whirled, around and around, laughing, falling down, and rolling on the ground.

"Look at me, mama, look."

I look at my children with such hope and such love. My thoughts are invariably ambivalent. My precious little ones. I want them to grow up strong and good. But, oh, sometimes when I see them frolic like new lambs, I do wish they could stay young and safe and innocent forever.

"Claudia was the authoress of a volume of epigrams, a volume of elegies, and a volume of sacred poems or hymns. Copies of these were preserved in the library at Verulam at late as the thirteenth century."

Williams Morgan, *Saint Paul in Britain* (121)

THE STRANGER   62 *AD*   815 *AUC*

THE SLAVE SPEAKS:

 "I saw what you did." He grabbed me by the shoulder. "I saw you steal that bread."

"Do not report me. Please, I will make it up, somehow." I cowered, expecting to be struck. "I am strong. I can work." I am sure I did not look strong. I must have looked half-starved. I was filthy–dirty from travel and sleeping out of doors. He grabbed my hand, turned it over, and saw the brand on the palm. He saw that I am a slave. He probably guessed I am a runaway.

"Come with me." He marched me back through the streets of the marketplace past the stalls of fishmongers, shoemakers, dealers in grain, potters, and weavers. Straight to the baker's stall we went. He spoke to the baker in a low voice.

"My name is Cassius, servant to Senator Pudens. This man stole bread from you. I am here to make restitution. I shall pay you four times what he owes you. Do not speak to the authorities about this matter." The baker nodded agreement, eager to be paid more than his bread was worth. My benefactor produced several coins from his leather pouch. The bargain was sealed.

"What are you going to do with me?" I was stunned that the debt had been paid by this stranger. I am cynical enough to know that no one does that without exacting a price.

"What do you want from me?" Leery of his intentions, I expected to be used in some despicable way. If this is freedom, it is, so far, no better than slavery.

"I am taking you home to my lady. She will decide what will be done with you." Cassius led me through the streets

199

of the market place and on to the main road. As we walked, he asked me, "Where do you come from? How did you get to Rome?"

"My home is far away. I came here by ship–to Rome because that's where the ship was going."

"Do not be insolent with me. I am taking you home with me. I will clean you up before I take you to meet the lady." On we walked, eastward, the sun hot on our backs. At last, we approached the entrance to a huge villa with servants everywhere. Within the hour, Cassius had arranged for me to have a bath, clean clothes, and a substantial meal.

"Well, you look better. You smell better, too. Come with me." Cassius walked toward the salon off the open courtyard. Warily, I walked behind him. As we approached, I saw a beautiful lady, evidently laboring over a bit of writing.

"I hesitate to interrupt you, my lady. I have a matter to discuss with you."

She looked up from her work. "Yes, Cassius. Come in. I don't mind an interruption. Who is your young friend?" She nodded and smiled. We entered.

"I brought him home from the market. I caught him stealing bread. He looked hungry, so I brought him here."

"And have you had something to eat?" She looked at me. I was dazzled and embarrassed by her beauty. Her hair was the color of the sun, her eyes, the color of the sea. Around her neck she wore a small gold disc. Instinctively, I thought about stealing it.

"Food. Did you have food?"

"Yes, thank you." I felt my face go hot. I did not expect to be greeted by such a lady. She has kind eyes. I looked down at the sandals I was given. Suddenly, I was ashamed, and I did not know why.

She smiled. When she spoke her voice was soft and warm. "My name is Claudia Rufina. I am the mistress of this house. Do you have a name?"

I continued to study my own toes. "Onesimus, my lady. My name is Onesimus." It sounded strange to my own ears. For months, I had not spoken my name aloud, nor had I heard it spoken by anyone else.

"And from where do you come, Onesimus?" The question was asked politely, gently. It sounded to me as if she might be truly interested.

"I'm from Colossae, my lady."

"You will stay here tonight. Cassius will see to it that you have food to eat and a place to sleep. In the morning, we shall visit my husband's brother. He has friends in your city. Cassius, please see to the comfort of our young friend." Cassius nodded.

I looked into her face. I saw kindness there. I was emboldened to speak. "Thank you, my lady. I have never met anyone like you. I am in your debt." My heart sang. I would gladly be her slave. She nodded. We were dismissed.

Cassius led me to a bedchamber. He gave me bedclothes and a basin of water for washing. We talked long into the night. "So, Onesimus, tell me about your life in Colossae."

"There is not much to tell. My master is a good man, but I did not like being a slave. I have tried to run away before, but I was always caught."

"Sometimes I think of traveling around the world. I have never been on a ship. You have stowed away on several, I suppose. How did you do that without getting caught. And what is it like to be out on the open sea?"

"I have been on some ships. Once, I sneaked on ship before dawn and was able to hide under some sacks of corn. Another time, I walked right on board and told the captain I was there to make sure the ropes were secure. As for being out on the open sea, there is nothing in this world like it. To look over the bow of a ship and see nothing but water as far as you can look is a little frightening. When the wind is up and the sails are full and the ship is moving, it is a thrill. I can see why some men make a life of sailing. I do not know about life in Rome."

"Life in this house is good. The master of the house is a Senator. The lady Claudia is accustomed to feeding the strangers that members of her household bring in. No one knows how many people have found refuge here. This house is a place where sick folk are brought to receive the care they need. A number of rescued children live on the property. In Rome, if women have babies they do not want or can not care for, they leave them on the hillsides to die. The lady Claudia will never turn one of those babies away. People bring them to her. The hungry find food here. Poor people find sandals and clothes and a meal. The villa is beginning to be known as a haven for those in need."

"It is that for me. I thank you, Cassius, for bringing me here."

"You are fortunate. The streets of Rome are not safe for a runaway."

It has been a long time since I have slept under the roof of a fine house. Tonight I sleep under a senator's roof. Imagine that! What a great improvement it is over sleeping in the street. Cassius responded, but as he spoke, exhaustion overtook me. Cassius was still talking when I drifted into a deep and restful sleep.

The morning dawned bright and clear. We quickly washed and dressed. The lady Claudia called for Cassius.

"Meet me in the kitchen with your runaway within the hour. I must prepare food for Paul." She hurried to the kitchen. We waited outside. Soon she emerged, carrying a large basket lined with a clean towel and filled with food from the night before–bread, meat, fruit.

Cassius took the heavy basket and helped her into the conveyance. She settled in. Cassius and I walked behind the sedan. Through the countryside and into the outlying district we traveled, straight into the center of Rome. Down long, narrow streets we went, until we came to the prison. I became uneasy. Where are they taking me? They said they were taking me to visit her husband's brother. That sounds a little strange. Perhaps, they are going to report me after all. Perhaps the kindness they showed me was just a ruse to get me to remain calm, but then, why would they go to all the trouble to take me to their home and feed me and give me clean clothes? If they were going to throw me into prison, this Cassius fellow, could have done that when he caught me stealing bread. My thoughts raced. Why were we stopping? Where is her husband's brother anyway?

We stood before the gates of the prison with its customary contingent of guards on duty. Cassius alighted and walked boldly to the closest guard.

"This is the lady Claudia bringing a basket of food to the prisoner, Paul. She is the wife of Senator Pudens."

"I must inspect the basket." The guard took the heavy container and quickly rifled through it. He smiled at Claudia. "Caesar's tax on this basket is two figs." He took the ripe fruit, tossed one fig to his colleague, and popped the other into his own mouth.

Claudia smiled back. "I don't mind paying that kind of tax to Caesar. Next time, I will bring you a meat pie."

"We look forward to your visits, my lady." He ordered the gate to be opened.

Down steep steps and through dark, narrow, corridors we went until we came to the grate that covered the pit where Paul and his friend were imprisoned. Claudia knelt and called through the grate.

"Brother Paul," she called. "I brought you something from our kitchen."

"Dear sister." Paul stepped to the center of his prison and looked up to the light coming from the grate above.

Claudia ordered the guards, "Remove the grate." With great clanking, the two men on duty strained to lift the heavy grate and set it aside. Claudia tried to lower the basket of food down to the prisoners.

Paul observed from below. "The basket will not fit. You'll have to pass the food down a bit at a time. How good of you to come. I prayed for you this morning. Praise and glory to our Lord. You are his emissary. What riches you bring to me, not only this food, but your own sweet presence."

Claudia passed the food through the opening which was just large enough for a man's body to be lowered from above. That done, she lay down on the cold stones and put her hand through the opening, reaching down toward her brother-in-law. Paul reached up and took her hand. She heard him murmur a prayer. Then, the other man, took her hand.

"Sister Claudia. Thank you for coming. You are a blessing."

"As you are to us, Brother Luke. I have brought a young man to see Paul. Please, speak to him, Brother Paul. He is from Colossae and a stranger here."

Paul stood looking up from the pit. "Pray, Claudia, as I talk to him."

"Yes, I shall pray for him."

"What is your name, my son?"

"Onesimus."

"Onesimus. Your name means 'Useful.' Give me your hand." I lay down on my belly and thrust my hand into the opening. The preacher took it between his own two hands. He saw the brand on my right palm.

"You are a slave?"

"Yes."

"I, too am a slave. Who is your master in Colossae?"

"A man named Philemon."

"I know him. A good man. Your master is honorable.

"Did you say you are a slave?" I asked.

"Yes. I am a bondslave to the Lord Christ. My desire is that all men should know Him as I do. My Master is the Son of the living God. He died on a Roman cross and rose again the third day as He said He would. If you believe in Him, you will be forgiven of your sins and you will have abundant life and life eternal. Have you sinned, my son?"

"I have run away from my master, stolen things, robbed

people. I have been dishonest, and I have hurt people. Yes, I have sinned, and I carry it like a burden on my back. Sometimes, I think I will die beneath the weight of it."

"You will die beneath it. It is too heavy for you. I am, of all men, chief of sinners. I consented to the death of a good man named Steven. Then, I gathered up the followers of Jesus and threw them into prison. Many of them died. I met Jesus one day when I was on my way to Damascus and was struck blind by a light far brighter than the sun. My heart became a stone in me because I had been the enemy of his followers. When I believed, He healed me of all my transgressions, forgave me, and made me new. I no longer had to bear the weight of all my sins. Christ carried my burden as He carried His cross. He will carry your sins. Do you believe this?"

His words overwhelmed me and filled me with longing to be free, free within, and free of my burden. "I believe. Help me. What shall I do?"

"Confess Christ. I wish you could stay with me. I could more fully teach you about spiritual matters. And you could be of great help to me. You could live up to your name. But you must go back to Colossae, back to Philemon. Tell him you have found new life. Ask his forgiveness. God forgives you. Philemon will forgive you, too."

"What if he doesn't? My penalty would be death."

"Yes. I know. Do not be afraid, Onesimus. I will write a letter to him you can take it with you. He will forgive you for my sake." Let me talk to the lady Claudia once more."

Claudia knelt at the opening above.

"Sister, when you come back, bring me writing materials. Mine are almost depleted. This time tomorrow, I will have a letter ready for our young friend–my new son in my bonds. Will you do that for me? "

"Of course, I will. What else can I bring you?"

"More figs, please. And your own sweet spirit. You refresh my heart." Claudia passed Paul a hymn she had written. She whispered, "He is risen."

Paul responded in a firm voice. "He is risen, indeed."

As we left, we heard Paul singing the hymn she had written:

Glory and praise to God,
The creator of heaven and earth.
Glory to Jesus, the crucified One,
Who gave us new birth, Who gave us new birth.
Praise and glory to Him
Who gave us new birth.

THEIRS IS THE KINGDOM

"It is delivered to us by the firm tradition of our forefathers that the house of Pudens was the first that entertained Saints Peter and Paul, and that there the Christians assembling formed the Church, and that of all our Churches at Rome the oldest is that which is called after the name of Pudens."

> Gildas Baronius, *Annales Ecclesias* in *Notis ad 19 maii*,
> as quoted in Morgan, *Saint Paul in Britain* (59)

"Claudia was the first hostess or harbourer of St. Peter and St. Paul at the time of their coming to Rome."

> Robert Parsons, *Three Conversions of England* vol. I
> (16), as quoted in Andrew Gray, *The Origin and*
> *Early History of Christianity in Britain* (19)

THE LORD'S DAY 62 *AD* 815 *AUC*

HERMAS SPEAKS:

 I stood before the community of believers at the villa the morning of the first day of the week. "Let us praise God," I said to the fifty people crowded into the courtyard for the time of worship and prayer. We love the community of believers who meet in the atrium. The fellowship is sweet. Claudia says it reminds her of her days as a child in Siluria where all worship was conducted open to the sky above. We are safe, so far. Because he is a senator, Rufus enjoys influence among the powers in Rome. We do not believe that he is yet suspected of being a follower of The Way. No accusations have been lodged against him. We are thankful that *Domus Pudens* is far enough from the center of the city that we can gather here. Many of our brothers and sisters worship in the catacombs. We do conduct worship clandestinely, because Nero is slaughtering our people. Hundreds have been killed for no reason except that they profess Christ. Claudius decreed Christianity a capital offence. Nero carries out the decree on a massive scale. Every person who worships at *Domus Pudens* has suffered the loss of a family member or a friend. Some have endured multiple losses. Others have barely escaped with their lives, having their homes and goods confiscated. Many have sought asylum here with us.

"Let us sing a psalm." I begin: "O give thanks unto the Lord, for he is good."

The response was sure, voices rising like a strong wind and carried to the heart of the God who hears: "For his mercy endures forever."

"O give thanks unto the God of gods."

"For his mercy endures forever."

"To him who alone does great wonders."

"For his mercy endures forever."

"Who remembered us in our low estate."

"For his mercy endures forever."

"And has redeemed us from our enemies."

Heads held high, the believers responded: "For his mercy endures forever."

I lifted my eyes to heaven. "Oh Lord of all lords, we praise your name for, indeed, your great mercy endures forever. Heaven and earth may pass away, but your love will sustain us through peril. Help us in our time of distress. Comfort those who have lost family members. Strengthen those who are in prison because they speak your name. We remember our brothers, Paul and Luke. Keep them safe from harm. Help us to rejoice when our enemies persecute us. In the name of Jesus, our Lord, Amen."

I read portions of the letter our brother Paul wrote to us when he was in Corinth. We have read it many times since it was delivered to us by our sister Phebe, because it is rich in comfort and Paul has much to teach us through it. He writes: "The sufferings of this present time are not worthy to be compared with the glory to come. If God be for us, who can be against us? Who shall separate us from the love of Christ? Shall tribulation, or distress, or persecution, or famine, or nakedness, or peril, or sword? As it is written, 'For thy sake we are killed all the day long; we are accounted as sheep for the slaughter.' No, in all these things we are more than conquerors, through him who loved us."

"Paul writes to us that we should not be afraid," I told them. "He writes of his firm belief that God will prevail, that nothing can take away our faith. Nothing! No power on this earth! Listen to Paul's words. 'For I am confident that neither death, nor life, nor angels nor principalities, nor powers, nor things present, nor things to come, nor height, nor, depth, nor any other created thing shall be able to separate us from the love of God which is in Christ Jesus our Lord. Amen. So be it.' Now it is time for you to speak." I sat down and waited for the Spirit of God to move. The gathering grew silent. One by one, people rose to tell great things God has done.

"My daughter was sick with a fever. We prayed, anointed her head with oil and laid hands on her. She was restored to health."

"My father has come to know the Lord. He will be baptized, soon."

"Jesus came to me in a vision. He told me not to be afraid. Every member of my family–my mother, my father, my wife, my three children, were taken to the arena. They were mercilessly put to the sword. In my vision, I saw my children in the arms of Jesus. One day I shall be with them."

From the worshipers there were murmured words of encouragement:

"Praise God."

"Yes, brother."

"We shall pray for you."

"God be with you."

In the very back of the crowd, a young man stood. No one knew him. We were all curious. We looked at him. Many had to turn their bodies to see and hear him better. He spoke with an accent we could not place.

"My name is Onesimus. I am a slave of Philemon of the city of Colosse. I ran away from my master and made my way here. For six months I ran, hiding in barns, stealing food, or going hungry. I slept in the woods–stowed away on two different ships. My life was often threatened. Finally, by the time I came to Rome, I was in rags, so I stole clothes from some women who were washing the family laundry in the river. I stole food from the open market. My hands are swift. I did not get caught–until day before yesterday. Someone saw me–Cassius, from this household. He brought me to your lady, Claudia. She gave me food, let me sleep here in this house, and yesterday, she, herself, took me to the prison to visit the preacher. His friend was with him. They told me about Jesus. My master at home is a follower of The Way. I had often seen him pray, but I never understood what it meant until the preacher in prison explained it all to me. I am on my way back to Colosse. I have in my hand a letter the preacher wrote for me to deliver into the hands of my master. The preacher told me the letter is for my good. The preacher knows my master. I do not know how to read. I pray that someone here would read it for me."

I rose to my feet. Cassius led Onesimus to the front of the gathering and stood beside him, his hand upon his shoulder. The runaway slave handed the letter to me. I read these words:

"Paul, a prisoner of Jesus Christ, unto Philemon, our brother. I beseech you for my son, Onesimus, whom I have begotten in my bonds, which was formerly useless to you, but now is useful. Receive him as you would receive me. I would have kept him with me, but could not without your permission. Receive him now, not as a slave, but as a loved brother. If he has wronged you, or if he owes you anything, I will pay." There was more. By the time I had read it all, everyone was moved to tears by the sweetness of God's forgiveness and His power to transform and liberate lives.

All the believers surrounded Onesimus and we laid our hands on him in blessing. We prayed for him. We embraced him. We took up an offering and received enough to pay his passage back to Colosse. We show our love in practical ways.

"We shall pray for you every day."

"You are our brother in the Lord."

"May God bless you and keep you safe."

"Go, tell what great and wonderful things the Lord has done for you."

We broke bread and rejoiced together, sang a hymn, and went out with a benediction ringing in our hearts. The words were Paul's: "The grace of our Lord Jesus Christ be with your spirit. Amen."

"The blessed Simon Peter, on seeing his wife led to her death, rejoiced at her call and of her conveyance home, and called very encouragingly and comfortingly, addressing her by name, 'Remember thou the Lord.' Such was the marriage of the blessed and their perfect disposition toward those dearest to them."

> Clement of Alexandria, *The AnteNicene Fathers*, vol. 2 (541)

"Have we not power to lead about a sister, a wife, as well as other apostles, and as the brethren of the Lord, and Cephas (Peter)?"

> I Corinthians 9:5

THE BROTHERS   62*AD*   815 *AUC*

PUDENS SPEAKS:

 I visited the *carcer*. Because I am a member of the Senate, the guards allow me to speak to Paul face-to-face. I walk the streets of Rome a free man. My brother is the one in chains. How strange that I draw strength from him. It should be the other way around. Paul does not falter or faint. He serves as a great inspiration to all the believers in Rome. Our people are under the heaviest persecution. Many of them have already been slaughtered. They go singing to their death. Urbane was thrown to the wild beasts. Stachys was crucified. Apelles also died on a cross. Others are marked for death. Tryphena has been charged with sedition. She awaits trial. Patrobas also has been convicted and awaits his death. Simon Peter's wife, Perpetua, Eubulus' daughter, was led away to be slain along with a dozen others. Persis was burned alive at one of Nero's garden parties. Who among us will come through this great tribulation?

"I do not fear for my own life. It may be that I shall be spared because of my service to Rome. Engineers are ever in demand. Perhaps my skill will protect me from Nero's caprice. No, I do not fear for my own life. I fear for my wife and for my children." I kept my voice low as I talked to Paul. "For so long we felt we were protected at the villa. We are on the edge of the city, far enough away that we were not in any danger. But they are coming now for our number. I cannot bear to think of losing my own children."

"My little brother, do not fear. What glory awaits us. They can only kill this body. They cannot kill us. I have faced death so many times. I have come to believe with all my being that I shall live this life for Christ as long as it

215

is granted to me, and when I die I shall come into my reward. What can they do to me that is worse than what they have already done? They can kill me. What is that to me? I shall look upon the face of my Lord. Whatever I suffered here in this life will be as nothing compared with the glory that is to come." Paul's eyes burned with the conviction of his words.

"I also believe, but I know how cruel Rome is. Nero is mad. Until we are rid of him, this madness will not stop." Paul put his hand on my arm.

"No, Rufus. When Nero is dead, there will be another madman and another and another. There is no end to evil in this world. Only in God's kingdom do we find peace. I know what persecution is. This is not the first time that I have experienced it." He pulled his robe off his shoulder. I gasped when I saw the scars on his back. "How many stripes have been laid on my back? I have lost count. I bear in my body the marks of the Lord Christ. I count it joy to suffer for his name. No one knows what a debt I owe Him. I am now persecuted. You must remember, Rufus, that I was a persecutor. I did to followers of the Way what is now being done to me. I am forgiven by His grace. Is that not wonderful to think that I am forgiven of my great sin?

"Yes, wonderful." I took Paul's hands in mine. I felt him flinch with pain. His hands are gnarled and stiff, the joints swollen and red. My eyes filled with tears. "I hate to see you here. I wish I could take you out of this place. We live in plenty while you suffer here."

"Do not trouble yourself about me. God is good. I am content. You come to see me. Claudia brings me food. I pray here–sing, write, preach. Sometimes, far into the night, I preach loud enough for prisoners and guards to hear me. Some have come to know the Lord even in this place. Listen well, Rufus. If I die, I die to His glory. If I live, I live for His glory. All is in God's hands. I do not fear. You must not fear either. God will give you the grace to bear whatever comes. Be strong."

"I have no trouble with fidelity. I will be faithful unto death. I hope I find the courage and strength of our martyred brothers and sisters."

"God will give you the strength you need. I have said it before and I will say it to you, here in this fetid prison. God's grace is sufficient for me and sufficient for you."

"I believe that, Paul, but I am not like you are. I do not have the kind of mind you have. I am quiet and private by nature. I have an engineer's mind. I struggle to understand what you seem to know without effort."

"Not without effort, Rufus! I, too, have struggled, but I am fueled by my memory of who I was before I traveled the Road to Damascus and what happened to me that day. I was blind and now I see. I lived in darkness and I saw a great light. I was wrong and I am made right. I heard his voice. He called my name and He gave me work to do. Do not fear, Rufus. The Lord himself is with you wherever you go. And the kingdom of God dwells within you."

We embraced. I came away comforted.

"Blessed are you when men shall revile you, and persecute you, and shall say all manner of evil against you falsely, for my sake. Rejoice, and be exceeding glad, for great is your reward in heaven, for so persecuted they the prophets which were before you."

Matthew 5:11

"And I looked, and behold a pale horse: and his name that sat on him was Death, and Hell followed with him. And power was given unto them over the fourth part of the earth, to kill with sword, and with hunger, and with death, and with the beasts of the earth."

Revelation 6:8

THE FIRE 64 *AD* 817 *AUC*

CLAUDIA SPEAKS:

 From the hill, we could look out over the city. We first saw smoke rise as a small cloud, and then we saw flames. Someone yelled, "Fire!" and the entire villa came alive with running men, urgent in preparation. My heart was pounding. I heard Rufus urgently shouting orders.

"Marcellus, take ten men and find as many vessels as you can. Take them to the baths. Form a brigade. We will need every able bodied man. Divide them into teams. Keep one team working and one resting. Soak everything in sight–the lawns, the gardens. Soak the outbuildings and the main house. Keep the water flowing. We don't know what these winds will do." He ran to find us. The children were clustered around me.

"Claudia, keep the children safe. Tell the women to form a kitchen brigade to cook, make bread. Keep the ovens going. These men must keep up their strength."

"Will it reach us?" I instinctively turned to Rufus. Sweat was pouring down his face. Urgency was written in his every expression and gesture, but his hands were steady.

"I do not know. We will do everything we can to prevent it. Keep the children inside. I don't know how bad the smoke will be." Rufus was obviously thinking fast. "Take what you will need and go to the bath house with the children. Take their teacher with you. The bath house is the safest place on our property. We may need to evacuate, but perhaps we can wait it out."

The men began to fill receptacles with water and passed them along the line to be thrown on the main house and outbuildings. They soaked blankets in water and laid them over walls and on roofs. The operation took on a rhythm, dipping buckets or basins into the pools, passing them up the line–hands and arms swinging, releasing, receiving, throwing the water in cascades, and returning the empty vessels to be filled again and again.

I held our girls close. Timotheus and Novatus now nine and ten years old beseeched their father. "Let us help, father. We can help in the brigade."

"No. I want you to stay out of the way of the men." When he saw their faces fall, Rufus took them by the shoulder. "I give you the most important job of all. You two are my special deputies. You must guard your mother and your sisters. Do not fail me."

"Yes, father." They squared their shoulders, proud of the adult responsibility. In a lower voice, Rufus spoke to me privately. "Go. Take the children, their teacher, and their nurses. Keep them safe. Marcellus and Antonius will direct the operations here at the villa." He shouted orders: "Cassius, pack up my books and papers and get them away from here."

"Where shall I take them, Senator?"

"I don't care–just away from here. I don't want them soaked–or burned. I hold you responsible for them." Cassius nodded and left to find servants who could help him load the carts.

"How bad is it?" I have always trusted my husband's judgement.

"We can't tell yet, but it seems to be coming from the center of the city. It is dry as tinder in there, and it could burn for days. I'm going into the city to see what I can find out."

Cassius stepped forward. "I'm going with you, Senator. The men will take care of your papers. Lady Claudia, I pray that you and the children will be safe. Rufus hastily embraced me and the children.

"God go before you. Be careful." My hand automatically rose to my throat and to the talisman I had so long worn. I found comfort in this small gesture as I fought back a feeling of dread. As we spoke, the chariot driver led two horses across the lawn. He handed the reins to Rufus and Cassius. The two men leaped upon their rearing mounts and rode at a gallop down the villa road and on to the Vicus Patricius that led straight to the center of Rome. Their horses, eyes rolling, mouths foaming, snorted in fear as they caught scent of the smoke.

I watched as my husband rode toward danger. Suddenly, I had a memory of my father as he rode away to war when I was a little girl. I looked at Praxedes and Pudentiana and realized that my two daughters were just about the age now that I was then. Instinctively, I knew how my children were feeling as I remembered how frightened everyone was at my father's going. As long as my father was at home, I felt secure. As the sound of the horses' hooves faded from my hearing, I gave way to tears. When the children began to cry in response, I quickly regained my composure. For a few moments, I held my children close.

"Don't worry, mother." Timotheus planted his square little body before me. "I won't let anything bad happen to you and my sisters. Novatus and I will take care of you."

"Thank you, my son. You are brave." I smiled into four pairs of brown eyes so like their father's. "You are right. All will be well. Let us pray for your father and Cassius, that they will come home safe and soon." They bowed their heads and prayed. How beautiful they are! And how dear!

I am well aware that my husband is in many ways like my father. Neither is content to stand by and observe. They are in the thick of the battle—no matter what the cause. As frightened as I was, I had to smile a little. How like my husband to go charging off into the night straight into the jaws of death. If something requires a solution, he can solve it. If something needs building, he can build it. If there is a battle to be fought, he will fight to the death. I am fortunate to be married to a man who is steady in a crisis. I thought about courage in a precarious world. Men were not the only heroes. Women, too, faced peril, but of a different sort. Oh, some of them had shown themselves to be as intrepid as men on the battlefields. Consider Boadacea. Every Briton had thrilled to hear of her exploits at the head of a British army of a hundred and twenty thousand men. Nowhere in the history of Greece or Rome was her equal. It would never enter my mind to lead an army into battle. Yet, I remember what Rufus told me after the birth of our babies. He said he had never seen such bravery even on the battlefield. We are so different, Rufus and I. My people love peace, but faced adversity with unflinching courage. These Romans are a different breed–full of intrigue. Not Rufus, of course, but so many of the noblemen. Until my family was brought captive to Rome, I believed in the essential goodness of people. Now, I am convinced otherwise.

The new emperor is quite mad. The old emperor, though personally kind to me, was, nonetheless, a cruel and ruthless man. He had declared it a capital offense to profess Christ. No wonder Rufus laid his fingertips on my lips in his garden that day when I wanted to speak of my faith. Even back then, it was too dangerous to speak it. Well, Claudius died by treachery. Rumor had it that Agrippina killed him with a poisoned mushroom. She obviously had not used enough poison, because Claudius lingered and had to be poisoned a second time. He finally died in October. Will ever there be an emperor of Rome who will die of old age in his bed? The Emperor Nero is worse than Claudius ever thought of being. When he ascended the throne at age seventeen, all Rome trembled. Nero is a poison that seeps out, killing all it touches. The stories about him are true. Everyone in Rome knows how he illuminates his garden parties. Christians, forced to wear tunics soaked in wax, are tied to poles and ignited as his guests arrive. Everyone knows that Christians are hung high along the roadways, covered with pitch, and set on fire to provide light for the nocturnal processions. Everyone knows that Christians are sewn inside the skins of wild animals and are thrown to vicious dogs to be mauled to death. Everyone knows, and everyone is terrified. Nero may look like a young fool with his emerald monocle in his eye, the better to see the gore of the arena, but he is no fool. He is a monster who slaughters the innocent without compunction. He massacred the Druids on the Isle of Mon at Anglesey, butchered twenty men at one time, poisoned his own brother, and, finally, more shocking than anything else he had ever done, ordered his soldiers to hack his mother into small pieces. In killing Agrippina, Nero killed the one person who was, possibly, more evil than he.

I looked at my children with love and concern and drew them close to me. Suddenly, I thought, "What am I doing? There is work to be done." I stood, spurred into action. Gwynedd stood by.

"What shall I do, my lady?"

"Pack up the children's clothes. We are going to spend the night in the bath house." I left Gwynedd and the nurses to tend to the children and get them settled for the night. That would not be easy. Everyone was wide awake with excitement. I ran to the kitchen to make sure the women were baking bread and found the place an ant hill of activity, bread already in the oven and stew boiling over the fire. "Good," I nodded to the cooks. "No one is going to get much sleep this night–not the firefighters and none of the kitchen workers."

I stepped out to watch the fire. The flames rose high now, casting eerie orange light over the city. Our villa lies outside the city, east of Rome, far enough away from the conflagration that we were not in immediate danger. But the blaze illuminated the night sky, and we could smell the smoke and feel the heat. The bucket brigade never stopped. Through the long hours, the men worked to keep the buildings soaked with water.

Cassius and Rufus came home black with soot and utterly exhausted. Their mounts trembled with fatigue.

"Are you well?" I felt I was looking into the mouth of hell.

"We are. And you and the children?"

"Safe."

"Thank God."

Servants ran to help the two men dismount and take the horses to the stables.

"What news of the fire?"

"No one knows how it started. Someone said that it was set in one of the shops near the Great Circus beneath the Palatine. The rickety buildings between the Viminal and Esquiline went up like tinder. Right now, it is an inferno. They say that it will have to burn itself out. There is no way of controlling it. No one knows how many hundreds or thousands of people were caught in it. It looks like Nero will get his wish to rebuild Rome." Sweat poured down Rufus' face. He and Cassius were weary to the bone. They stumbled toward the bath house. I ordered food to be laid out for them in the *triclinium*. After they bathed, they embraced the children.

"Timotheus, Novatus," Rufus knelt beside his sons. "We are safe. And so is everyone here."

The boys stood at attention before their father. "We took care of our mother and the girls. We did all you told us to do." Timotheus spoke, his head held high.

"We were not afraid, father." Novatus spoke in a light, piping little voice, but he stood straight and tall beside his older brother.

"Good. You are brave. You did well. You can be trusted. I am very proud of you. You are good sons. You bring honor to our house." Rufus smiled at his sons. The warmth of accomplishment filled their hearts.

The two men ate ravenously, and then, at last, they lay

down to sleep for the first time in three days. For nine days and nights Rome burned, as if hell itself had engulfed the city and incinerated everything in its path. Almost the entire city was destroyed. Then the rains came. Torrential storms swept over the city. High winds flung the heavy rains into the cauldron that was Rome. For days, steam rose like mist from a lake. The fires were finally extinguished. Nothing was left but smoking ruins. Everything in the path of the fire was demolished beyond recognition. The acrid stench was choking. Everything was blanketed with ash. The rains turned what was left into a viscous black slop. Thousands of people died, their bodies cremated in the ovens of their own homes. Animals lay dead, their carcasses half burned. What was left was covered with flies. Ten of Rome's fourteen districts were utterly destroyed.

Nero played the part of a hero. He opened public buildings to the homeless and made an ostentatious display of the sacrifices he offered to the god, Vulcan. Unfortunately, he neglected to do it before the fire. We are cynical. We knew Nero would not assume the responsibility for so grievous an event. And, it did not take long for the news to reach us. The official word was out. Christians set the fire. We are arsonists. According to Nero, we also cause earthquakes, floods, and plagues. The Roman gods are obviously furious and seeking revenge. The official word is that the Christians are to blame for all of Rome's misery. Believers are to be immediately rounded up and killed—not an easy task. Multitudes in Rome, now, are followers of Christ. When Claudius expelled the Jewish converts to Christianity, there were some forty thousand of them. I wonder how many of us there are now. Nero must be crazy with rage. He will not rest until all the followers of The Way are eliminated. He wants to restore Rome to her pantheon of gods as a part of his own legacy. Paul is particularly vulnerable because he is seen by the authorities as an agitator.

I am frightened. I looked at Rufus. "What shall we do?"

Rufus embraced me. He spoke words of comfort. "We shall live our lives as we always have. This villa is known far and wide as the *Paladium Britanicum*. We shall continue to worship here. We shall receive our Christian brothers and sisters here. We shall receive the apostles and the preachers. Hermas will continue to teach and preach to our household and to be our pastor. This place shall continue to be a haven for all who need shelter, and that certainly includes my brother. Even before I knew the Lord, my father received Simon Peter into this house. This is not new. We live in dangerous times, but we have always lived in dangerous times. Twenty years ago, the Emperor Claudius persecuted believers. Now it is Nero who seeks to kill us."

"Is there no end to it? Can they not leave us in peace?"

He held me closer. "You know what Paul says: 'Be strong in the Lord and in the power of his might.'"

I pressed my face into my husband's chest. He is so solid, so strong. I bit my lip. "I shall be brave. God is for us."

"Then who or what shall be against us?" Rufus took out his kerchief and wiped the tears from my face. "That's my brave girl." He held me closer.

Days later the rumor reached us that the Emperor Nero entertained himself by playing his lyre while watching the flames consume the city. The official word was, of course, a denial. Nero, they said, was not even in Rome at the time. How could anyone think that he would burn his own city? After all, the emperor would have to be insane to do something like that.

"In his farewell charge to Timothy, he sends him the greetings of 'Pudens and Linus and Claudia.' These, with that of Eubulus, are the only names of the Christian band mentioned by him; these ministered to him on the eve of his martyrdom, and these attended him when he was on the block of the state *lictor*, a little distance out of Rome, and these consigned his remains with their own hands to the Pudentinian family tomb on the Ostian Road. St. Gregory I, Bishop of Rome, specified the '*Aquas Salvias*,' now called '*le tre Fontane*,' on the *Via Ostiensis*, as the site of his martyrdom. The *Chiesa di S. Paola alle tre Fontane*, preserves the memory of the site."

Andrew Gray, *The Origin and Early History of Christianity in Britain* (34)

"To leave the examples of antiquity, and to come to the most recent, let us take the noble examples of our own times. Let us place before our eyes the good apostles. Peter, through unjust odium, underwent not one or two, but many sufferings, and having undergone his martyrdom, he went to the place of glory to which he was entitled. Paul, also, having seven times worn chains, and been hunted and stoned, received the prize of such endurance. For he was the herald of the Gospel in the West as well as in the East, and enjoyed the illustrious reputation of the faith in teaching the whole world to be righteous. And after he had been to the extremity of the West, he suffered martyrdom before the sovereigns of mankind; and thus delivered from this world, he went to his holy place, the most brilliant example of steadfastness that we possess."

Clement of Rome, *Epistola Corinthios* c. 5 *The AnteNicene Fathers* vol. viii (218)

"I am now ready to be offered, and the time of my departure is at hand. I have fought a good fight. I have finished my course. I have kept the faith. Henceforth there is laid up for me a crown of righteousness, which the Lord, the righteous judge shall give me at that day; and not to me only, but unto all them also that love his appearing."

II Timothy 4:6-8

THE PERSECUTION   64 *AD*   817 *AUC*

HERMAS SPEAKS:

 Paul is dead. The detail of soldiers, under orders, took him yesterday, bound, to the block on the Ostian Way and beheaded him. There was no great light. There was no voice from heaven–just the quick flash of a razor sharp sword and the grisly aftermath. Thank God it was a quick and merciful death. Because he was a Roman citizen, he was spared crucifixion. Paul showed no fear. He would give no quarter to the enemies of Christ. It drives the Romans to fury that believers die with a smile. How many of us now have gone singing to our death?

I remember old Simon Peter calling to his wife as they carried her away to die–that old man and that old woman– together for so many years. When the Lord chose Simon, he called him from his boat and his fishing. His wife went with him from Galilee, and she stayed, too, even when her husband denied the Lord. Well, Peter was forgiven, and he became the rock. When the soldiers took his wife to her death, Simon called after her: "Perpetua, remember thou the Lord." His voice was tender with pain and love. One day, they will come for Peter. Death is no stranger to any of us. And yesterday, it was Paul's turn. Death has been Paul's companion for years. There were more brushes with death for him than any of us can count. Paul meant it when he said that for him to die was gain. 'To live is Christ,' he said. He knew no other after the vision.

His family was around him. Rufus and Claudia, their children, Cassius, and I followed the detail on the half day's journey in the heat and dust to the place of execution. The soldiers allowed him to kneel in prayer before the moment of his death. I heard his last words: "Even so, come

229

Lord Jesus."

I saw the flash of metal and heard the swish as it whirred in the air. I saw the severed head roll on the ground. I saw the blood pour out. My first thought was of Paul's great mind–all that learning–all that insight–all that logic–all that intensity–now reduced to blood, and bone, the eyes dulled in death.

As male next of kin, Rufus asked the captain of the guard for permission to carry Paul's remains back to our villa. Permission was granted, very likely because Rufus is a member of the Senate. Claudia and the girls washed his body and wrapped him in a linen shroud. The church gathered. With tears, we sang Paul to his glorious home. He always said that his body was mortal but the day would come when he would put on immortality. This is his day to receive the crown that awaited him. At last, Paul looks upon the face of Jesus who poured out his life in obedience to death on a cross. Paul was faithful to the end. He ran a good race. We laid him to rest in the family tombs.

We are left with questions. Why does evil rule? Why should Paul's great intellect be obliterated with one stroke of the sword? How long must we suffer? How long can we endure this crushing weight? Who will be the great evangelist now? Who will see after Paul's churches? Who will pick up the fallen banner? We must have faith that God will raise up leaders. All of us will be faithful to do the work God has given us. And our children after us. The seed is planted–watered with the blood and tears of the martyrs. God will give the increase. We are left to weep, but not as those who have no hope. So many of our number have died for the faith–beginning with those Paul, himself, persecuted before he was a believer. I am not sure he ever got beyond that shame. Paul proclaimed that he lived a debtor to grace.

So. We go on. We run with patience the race that is set before us. Sometimes, though, I think I do not have the patience or the strength to put one foot in front of the other. We have all depended on Paul for guidance, for assurance, for comfort. Today, I returned alone to pray at the tomb where we interred his body. My prayers were for eternal light to shine upon him–just as it did on the Damascus Road so long ago.

LETTER FROM CLAUDIA TO ERGAIN 64*AD* 817*AUC*

 To my beloved sister, greetings. You have heard of our great fire. Much of the city was destroyed, and many people perished. *Domus Pudens* was spared. Our men worked unceasingly to protect all of us. We did not imagine or think that the persecution we suffer here could be increased, but followers of The Way stand accused of starting the conflagration. Many of our number have gone to their death in retribution. Four days ago, we followed the soldiers as they took Paul to the block. We weep at his death, but we rejoice in the Lord always. Paul has received the crown of life laid up for him, and he sits with Christ in heavenly places. How many times did we hear him say that to live is Christ and to die is gain. Rejoice, dear sister, and again I say rejoice. You are in my prayers. I pray that he who has begun a good work in you will complete it to the day of Christ Jesus. Grace be to you and to the household of faith.

Non in alia re tamen damnosoir quam in aedificando domum a Palatio Esquilias usque fecit, quam primo transitorium, mox incendio absumptum restitutamque auream nominavit. (There was nothing in which he was more ruinously prodigal than in building. He made a palace extending all the way from the Palatine to the Esquiline. At first he called it the House of Passage, but when it was burned and rebuilt, he called it the Golden House.

Suetonius, *The Lives of the Caesars* (135)

"Known as the Domus Aurea because of its rich decorations, it was an immense complex centering about a vestibule lofty enough to house a gilded bronze statue of Nero himself, one hundred twenty feet high, and surrounded by parks, artificial lakes, and colonnades, one of which was reportedly a full mile in length. One of its banqueting halls was circular and equipped with a revolving ceiling; its rooms were richly painted and set with jewels and mother-of-pearl; the ceilings of ivory were pierced with pipes that sprayed perfume upon the banqueter."

Robert Payne, *Ancient Rome* (171)

"Alas, what an artist is dying in me."

Nero of himself, quoted www.bible-history.com/ neroNERONeros_Character.htm

THE END 68 *AD* 824 *AUC*

PUDENS SPEAKS:

 After the great fire which had cleared huge spaces where the *insulae* had stood, Nero ordered construction of the *domus aurea*– his new palace surrounded by elaborate gardens. Most offensive to the populace was the massive statue–the colossus–depicting him in god-like pose that rose above us all. There was more than one plot to rid Rome of this despot. In retribution, Nero ordered many of his former supporters put to death, among them Seneca, his tutor, and Poppaea–his former mistress and now his wife, pregnant with their unborn child. A network of spies grew up in our city to discover those who were "not with Nero." No one was safe.

Nero was mistrustful of everyone. He saw plotters behind every garden wall. At last, he left Rome in disguise in fear for his life. The armies defected. The Senate declared him an enemy of the state and stipulated that when he was arrested he would be punished in ancient style–stripped naked, his head thrust into a wooden fork, and flogged to death with sticks. When Nero learned of this, he ordered his men to dig a grave and to fetch wood and water for the disposal of his corpse. We heard that Nero was a coward to the end. He asked that those around him commit suicide first to give him courage. He required his scribe to help him to die. Finally, when he heard soldiers approaching, he drove a blade into his throat. They put him on the funeral pyre dressed in the gold-embroidered robes he wore in January. The funeral cost two thousand gold pieces. His death marked the end of the Julio-Claudian dynasty.

A week after his suicide, Nero's reign was officially

stricken from the record and he was declared *damnatio memoriae* by order of the Senate. I was gratified to cast my vote. The senators were, for once, unanimous in their decision. Whatever one may think of Claudius, when he was murdered, we pronounced him *divus*. Not so with Nero. He died an ignominious death. Everyone wonders what Rome will be under the new emperor—and who that might be. Nero has no blood relatives to succeed him. In his megalomania, he killed every member of his own family who might have any claim to power. Already there is uprising among the armies in Germany. Civil war surely will follow.

LETTER FROM CLAUDIA TO ERGAIN 70 *AD* 823 *AUC*

Greetings, dear sister, in the name of our Lord. I pray God's blessings on you as you labor in Siluria to the Glory of His name. We continue here at the *apostolorum*, in spite of our losses, to give praise daily to Him who loved us and redeemed us from our sins. Rufus is well, but under considerable strain. Our new emperor has called upon him with other engineers to render aid in designing a huge amphitheater which will be built over the excesses of Nero's palace on the Palatine. He continues his duties with the Senate. I have married a man in demand by those in governmental authority. God gives him strength and wisdom. My children are well. I give thanks that they are followers of The Way. Members of our household of faith are distressed to hear of the sacking of Jerusalem. We have news that the city has fallen to Rome. I should rejoice since I have pledged loyalty to Rome, but our brothers and sisters who have come to Christ out of Judaism are grief-stricken. All of the power and excesses of Rome do not touch us here. The Kingdom of God is within us, and we carry in our hearts the love and peace of God. May you be blessed with God's peace that is beyond our human understanding.

"Iudaeos impulsore Chresto assidue tumultuantis Roma expulit." (Since the Jews constantly made disturbances at the instigation of Chrestus, he expelled them from Rome."
Suetonius, *Vita Claudius* (52-53)

"Located at the highest point of the Via Sacra which leads to the Roman Forum, this triumphal arch commemorates Titus'conquest of Judea which ended the Jewish Wars (66-70). . . . The arch was erected posthumously, after Titus had already become a 'god.'"
Mary Ann Sullivan, sullivanm@bluffton.edu
8/16/2003

THE TRIUMPH   70 AD   823 AUC

PRISCILLA SPEAKS:

 Jerusalem has fallen. The legions marched triumphantly through the streets of Rome. Titus is hailed as the hero of the hour. The populace was out in great numbers to shout approval. Women threw flowers and men got drunk in celebration. They say that Titus leveled everything in the old city. The soldiers entered the holy temple and stripped it of every valuable thing, including the ark and the golden menorah from off the altar. Before the temple walls fell, they say that bodies slid down the steps in a river of blood. The temple was then reduced to dust and ashes. That beautiful structure–forty years in the building–destroyed utterly. Only four years ago, Rome perpetrated a wholesale massacre there. We heard then that there was an orgy of fire and bloodshed, and that forty thousand Jews had been killed. They said there were crosses without number lining the street with dying men impaled helplessly in the pitiless sun. Titus finished what Nero started. Hail Caesar.

So many years have passed since I walked Jerusalem's streets. I can not imagine what the city must be now. My heart breaks to think of it. I remember my life there fondly: after Aaron's death, when I took Saul there for his rabbinical studies. He was only sixteen at the time. As a young widow, I needed to reestablish my life. I remember the city as welcoming to me. I had many friends there. I remember Procula with great affection.

The Jerusalem I knew was alive with commerce, the market places full of noisy, haggling customers and shop keepers. I remember the temple crowded with worshipers. There, in the temple complex, the air was alive with the sound of rabbis reading scripture, the sound of debate of interpretation against dissenting interpretation. My Aaron used to say if you put three Jews in a room, you would get four opinions. I remember the temple with the sounds of bleating sheep in the holding pens and the sound of squawking birds. I think of the money changers and the great trumpet-shaped receptacles where people cast in their offerings. Often, I sat with other women in the court set aside for us. How many prayers ascended to God from that place? It is unthinkable that the huge pillars are fallen, the veil of the temple burned to ashes, the holy of holies violated.

I wonder how many people our soldiers killed this time. How many widows and orphans are left to weep? Six years ago, Rome killed my son. I will never forget him or how he died. I could not make myself witness his death. Rufus, Claudia, and the others followed the soldiers out to the place of execution, but I stayed home and wept that day. I felt as though the sword which killed him pierced my heart. Six years. . . seems like yesterday. The day before they killed him, Rufus took me to the *carcer* to see Saul. Oh, I know everyone called him Paul, but I named him first, and he will always be my Saul. His name means "asked for." I prayed to God for a son. How delighted we were when he was born–and how we delighted in him as he grew. He was a bright light in the darkest of worlds, a world now darker without him.

And the darkness is deeper now with Jerusalem leveled. In Pilate's palace, I met Quintus. The holy city was a part of my life. It's all gone now. Jerusalem, oh Jerusalem. The Master wept for you. I also weep.

THE GIFTS 71 *AD* 824 *AUC*

CLAUDIA SPEAKS:

 I called Rufus and the children into the atrium yesterday. The sun warmed our courtyard, its light playing in our fountains, participating in our day of celebration.

"I have gathered you children around me because Pudentiana is fifteen today. If you had been born in Britain, this would have been the day that our last child would be initiated into the clan. On your fifteenth birthdays, all of you would have had a celebration. You are Roman. I know you are proud of that, but I want you to remember that you are also of royal British blood. I remember well the day I was ushered into the clan. I wore a white robe with gold trim and stood with other young people under the open sky in our place of worship while the bards recited our family histories back through nine generations. That was the day your grandmother Ergain gave me the gift of the talisman which has been passed down through the family from mother to last daughter for generations. So now, Pudentiana, I give it to you with every hope for God's blessing on you. Wear it, and remember all the strong women who have worn it before you."

I took the talisman from around my neck and put it around the neck of my younger daughter. "Oh, mother, I do thank you." She ran her finger around the design, gazing at it with misty eyes. "I shall take such good care of it. I have loved it all my life." She kissed my hands.

"The talisman has many meanings, my dear. I do not know its beginning, but I know that it has taken on new meaning for all the women who have worn it–the stages of life, the balance and flow, the life force. Now, I pray that you see new meaning as you wear it"

"I see *ichthus*. I see three. I see continuity, and therefore, hope."

"Yes. It has a way of speaking to each woman in her language and in her day." I turned to my sons and to Praxedes. "I have gifts for you, dear ones, as well. Novatus, I want you to have my father's shield. He carried it into battle against the Romans, as the brave warrior he was, always proud of never having been defeated. General Ostorius Scapula took this shield from my father at his capture. He gave it to his predecessor, General Aulus Plautius. When Uncle Plautius married my Aunt Gladys, he gave it to me. Keep it and honor the memory of your grandfather. Let it remind you, as your Uncle Paul wrote, to put on the armor of God."

Novatus took the shield. "Thank you, mother. This is my shield of faith." We embraced.

I smiled at Timotheus. "My dear son, I give to you this collection of pens, the ones your Uncle Paul used to write letters in prison. They are worn and not valuable, but I wanted you to have them in remembrance of one who loved you and whom you loved as a little boy. I remember your sitting cross legged on the floor while Paul told you great adventure stories. I wanted you to have something of his. You loved him so."

Timotheus received the gift with tears. "Scarcely a day passes that I do not remember that dear man–some word, some gesture, an attitude. I loved to hear his stories. I am so grateful. This is better than gold." He kissed me on the cheek. My sweet son–my first born.

I turned to Praxedes. "My dear daughter," she stood before me. "I give you this iron ring. The metal is not precious, but the ring itself is worth more than gems. Your father placed it on my finger the day of our betrothal. My treasure all these years, I have always known that one day I wanted my eldest daughter to have it. Keep it safe, my dear. It is a circle of love."

"No gift would I rather have. Thank you, mother." She kissed me and embraced me.

I turned to the four most treasured people in my life after Rufus. "Your gift to me is your love and respect for me and your father and for each other. Let nothing break that bond as long as life shall last."

We stood and held hands forming a circle. "We promise," they responded. Rufus came and stood behind me, his arms encircling me. I leaned on him. Together, we have produced these children, stalwart in the faith.

"May the wife love her husband when anon, he is grey, and she herself, even when she is old, seem not so to her spouse!"
    Martial *Epigrams* vol vi (xiii)

"Walk circumspectly, not as fools, but as wise, redeeming the time, because the days are evil."
    Ephesians 5:15-16

"Be ye kind one to another, tenderhearted, forgiving one another, even as God for Christ's sake hath forgiven you. Be followers of God, as dear children, and walk in love, as Christ also hath loved us and hath given himself for us."
    Ephesians 4:32-5:1

"For I reckon that the sufferings of this present time are not worthy to be compared with the glory which shall be revealed in us."
    Romans 8:18

THE SHELTER 86*AD* 839*AUC*

CLAUDIA SPEAKS:

 Within these walls our world is safe. We close out the violence and the bloodshed. We reject the greed and the power of Rome. We, ourselves, are Romans, but our first allegiance is to Christ. This is treason according-ing to the secular authorities. Paul taught us that we walk a narrow path between our dedication to God and our responsibility toward our government. After all, my husband is a part of the Roman Senate, so we live dangerously. We are always at risk. But inside this house–inside this house–we are safe. Here, we live what Jesus taught. Here, we are governed by love.

My husband and I often sit in the evening in our garden. I am restored, always, by the sight of our garden and the trees and hills that surround this city. Last evening we talked at length about the things that concern us. Rufus ordered a tray of sweet wine and cakes.

"Here, dear one." He handed me a cup of wine. "Let us sit and sip and talk awhile."

"You are most kind, sir," I answered with a teasing tone. I took the goblet and made room for him on the bench beside me. "Rufus, this year I am an old woman."

"Never. You will always be the girl who walked with me in the garden."

"I remember it as clearly as if it were yesterday. Ah, dear. As I look back on it all, I am amazed at what has happened in our lives. Our children are grown and good people. Think of that! It seems only days ago that they were tumbling around my feet. They follow our Lord. I hope I have not failed them."

"There is no better wife and mother in all of Rome. Our

children are a credit to your dedication to them." He smiled at me. "I have something for you."

"A gift? For me?" Rufus reached into the folds of his toga and brought out a small blue glass vase.

"Oh, it is exquisite."

"I hope you like it. A shipment of glass came in today from Tyre. The color made me think of your eyes."

"You lavish me with gifts. Yes, I love it. Thank you. How dear you are. I shall put it in our bedchamber."

"You deserve every good thing." Rufus held out his wine cup for me to refill. I poured it half full. "The grapes are good this year. I hope the wine we make in the autumn will be as good as this we drink tonight."

"Yes. It will be a good harvest." He paused and thought a moment. "Claudia, do you ever regret this life I have given you? You might have lived out your life in Britain as a royal princess."

"No regrets, Rufus." I took his big square hand between my hands. "In the garden, that day by the fish pool, we pledged ourselves to each other and to the Savior. How can I regret that promise? I am sometimes sad, but I do not regret."

"What makes you sad, my dear?"

"I have often longed for the company of my parents and Ergain. They were such a light in my life, so precious to me. I still weep when I remember Paul. What a tower of strength he was to us all. When I allow myself to think of all those we have lost because of our faith, I cannot help but grieve. Does that mean I am weak?"

"You have a tender heart–one of the things I have always loved about you. I used to watch you with the children years ago. You were like them in some ways–innocent, loving, playful–tender with our children. For that, I owe you my gratitude."

"You gave them to me, Rufus–our children. They have always been dearer than life to me. And you, Rufus. God brought you to me. You are strong. You have always been brave. You are the *paterfamilias* of this house, but you have never misused your authority. I married a wise and good man."

"I want to honor my Master. You know, I have found that following Him is the easiest thing I have ever done. I do not mean to say it is not dangerous as Rome considers danger. I mean, rather, I have found that He transforms us into people who think of others before thinking of ourselves. We are often rewarded by Rome because even they find us honest, trustworthy, and lovers of peace. We live in a world where most people are concerned with reprisal, vengeance and vendetta. None of that appeals to me. So, we followers of Christ are a strange lot in their eyes."

"Sometimes, I want to climb to the top of the highest hill in Rome and shout: 'I am a follower of The Way. You poor, hungry, burdened people, come to Him and He will give you rest.' That sounds so foolish, and I won't do it because I don't want to endanger this house, but my heart breaks for Rome."

"Claudia, in your own quiet way, you have reached a large portion of the populace. Who can know how many people you have taken in, fed, clothed, taught? How many babies have been brought to you from off the mountain? How many poor people have you helped? How many children have you taught? How many hymns have you written? Perhaps that is more effective than shouting." My husband smiled at me in the twilight. I put my head on his shoulder. He stroked my hair. I am proud to be his wife. He is known across the city as an excellent engineer, an effective senator, and a faithful husband. He is known inside the walls of this house as a man who has the strength of a lion and the gentleness of a lamb. Inside this house—inside this house—we are safe.

"*Barbara pyramidum sileat miracula Memphis, Assyrius iactet nec Babylona labor; nee Triviae templo molles laudentur Iones. Dissimulet Delon cornibus ara frequens; aere nec vacuo pendentia Mausolea laudibus inmodicis Cares in astra ferant. Omnis Caesareo cedit labor Amphitheatro; unum pro cunctis fama loquetur opus.*" ("Let barbarous Memphis speak no more of the wonder of her pyramids, nor Assyrian toil boast of Babylon; nor let the soft Ionians be extolled for Trivia's temple; let the altar of many horns say naught of Delos; nor let the Carians exalt to the skies with extravagant praises the Mausoleum poised in empty air. All labor yields to Caesar's Amphitheater. Fame shall tell of one work in lieu of all.")

Martial, *Spectacles* (2)

"*Hic ubi sidereus propius videt astra colossus et crescunt media pegmata celsa via, invidiosa feri radiabunt atria regis unaque iam tota stabat in urbe domus. Hic ubi conspicui venerabilis Amphitheatri erigitur moles, stagna Neronis erant.*" ("Where the starry Colossus sees the constellations at close range and lofty scaffolding rises in the middle of the road, once gleamed the odious halls of a cruel monarch and in all Rome there stood a single house where rises before our eyes the August pile of the Amphitheater, was once Nero's lake. Where we admire the warm baths, a speedy gift, a haughty tract of land had robbed the poor of their dwellings. Where the Claudian colonnade unfolds its wide-spread shade, was the outermost part of the palace's end. Rome has been restored to herself, and under your rule, Caesar, the pleasures that belonged to a master now belong to the people.")

Martial, *Spectacles* (2)

"These are they which came out of great tribulation, and have washed their robes, and made them white in the blood of the Lamb."
Revelation 7:14

"The first to suffer for the Church was Jesus Himself—not a martyr, of course, but the inspiration and source of all martyrdom."
John Foxe, *The New Foxe's Book of Marytyrs* (4)

Must I be carried to the skies on flowery beds of ease,
While others fought to win the prize and sailed through bloody seas?"
Isaac Watts, "Am I a Soldier of the Cross," Hymn

THE WORK   90 *AD*   843 *AUC*

PUDENTIANA SPEAKS:

 It was dark night. The city was asleep. At the third watch, Praxedes and I slipped out of a doorway and moved silently in the shelter of the shadows toward the arena, our black cloaks covering us from head to foot.

"Do you have the talisman?" Praxedes never failed to ask me.

"Yes. It is concealed in the folds of my robe. Do you have the ring?"

"I never go out at night without it. I feel the power of our parents' love with it on my finger." She showed me the iron betrothal ring my father had placed on our mother's hand so long ago. We carried a large basket lined with linen. The basket was empty except for the two metal scoops wrapped in cloth against any alerting noise. We did not talk, but went about our task as if nothing in the world was more important than this. The truth is, we were doing God's work.

Because of our endurance from having walked the distance so frequently, we arrived in a short time at the guard post and waited. Aulus Silvanus was on duty. We knew him from previous encounters. Silvanus walked his post, alert for our arrival. When he caught a glimpse of movement in the shadows, he unobtrusively dropped a large metal key onto the pavement stones and walked on. I broke away from the concealing wall into the moonlight, quickly retrieved the key, and beckoned to my sister. Together, we picked up the large basket and walked silently down the dark maze of corridors to the door that led to the *amphitheathrum Caesareum*. Our footsteps were muted by the rags we had tied around our feet to muffle any sound. We stopped to listen. There. There it was again. I felt a prickle at the nape of my neck. We held our breath as we strained to hear. Then we saw the cat looking at us from atop the wall. Relieved, we moved on down the corridor toward our task. We arrived at the gate to the large open space of the arena. With the heavy key, we gained entrance. In the moonlight, we could see what had to be done.

Earlier in the day, in this place, the populace had thrilled to a bloody circus of death. In a mockery of Christ's passion, fourteen Christians were crucified. The drama was played out complete with a mock trial, flogging, reviling, spitting, mocking, and a placing of a crown of thorns on each victim's head. Each Christian, to great applause, was nailed to a cross. Finally, in a show of well-choreographed synchronization, fourteen spears were thrust simultaneously into fourteen writhing bodies. The crowd went wild. Then, because crucifixion is such a leisurely spectacle, the victims were doused with pitch and set aflame. The audience watched until nothing was left but ashes, amusing themselves all the while eating and drinking and conversing.

"That one died first. I guess he's gone to meet the Nazarene. We do these people a favor, you know. They all want to die so they can be with their god."

"Their god is weak. Why doesn't he come down to save them?"

"Their god is not weak. He is strong–just no match for the Emperor Domitian."

The raucous laughter, the jeers, and the catcalls now had ceased, but they lingered in the air like a malevolent cloud.

Our work waited, and time was short. If we were discovered, we would be the next main feature at the games. Pulling out the tools, we unwrapped them and worked quickly and quietly, scooping up ashes and dumping them into the basket. We prayed silently as we labored. Sometimes, as we would this night, we took our basket home filled with ashes. Sometimes, it was filled with crushed or bloody bones. Human remains take as many forms as the diversity of tortures the Romans can devise.

This night we left the arena, closed and locked the door behind us, and went back to the guard tower bearing the heavy load between us. We put the key on the pavement where we had picked it up and left as quickly and as quietly as we had come, slipping back into our own gate just before dawn. Hermas met us as we came through the door. We nodded silently to him.

"Interment at the usual time."

It had become a ritual.

Now, I cannot remember a time when we did not go out to gather the dear remains of martyred believers. We were still children when we first began. At ten and eleven, we helped inter the remains of our uncle Paul, beheaded on the *Aquae Salviae* in the *Ostian* Road. We have vivid memories of him. When we were children, Uncle Paul would come to our home. He lived with us before he had his house and was imprisoned for the faith. Even though his guards were always with him, he brought us little surprises, so we were always happy to see him. He was indulgent with us and funny. I do not think we really understood his death. Certainly, we were too young to understand the political implications of it. Uncle Paul left a magnificent legacy. We have heard that someone is collecting his writings. He spent his entire life traveling around the world, preaching and teaching. I have no idea how many people came to believe in Christ because of his work. Such a scholar and linguist. All that brilliance snuffed out with one flash of a Roman sword. Dear God, it is impossible to understand.

Our Uncle Linus was executed only a few months ago. We knew and loved him all our lives. We feel lost without him. How many thousands have been executed! Martyrs all. Uncle Linus was killed because he was the Bishop of

Rome, ordained at the blessed hands of our Uncle Paul. Uncle Linus became a follower of The Way in Siluria when he was just a boy. He came as a young man captive from Britain when our grandfather, King Caradoc, was brought to trial. Our Uncle Linus lived with our family at the villa and studied at the university before any of us children were born. After he completed his studies, he stayed. He was always a part of our household. We delighted to hear our mother tell the story of their capture and the trip to Rome. Before they were marched into the city, Uncle Linus vowed to protect the women of the family. Later he laughed at the absurdity of a solitary youth pitting himself against the might of Rome. The cruelty of his death is not what he deserved. He should have died in his own bed of old age. Christ's followers in Rome are not often allowed that luxury.

I read an inscription on a grave marker not long ago at the tomb of a young woman. The inscription read: "She had married at eleven, bore six children and died at twenty-seven." If one is a follower of The Way, one can expect to die for the faith. If one is a married woman, one can expect to die in childbirth. If one is in politics, one can expect to die early. In Rome, life is most often brief. We spring up like grass and we are soon cut down.

LETTER FROM ERGAIN TO CLAUDIA 94 *AD* 847 *AUC*

To my sister in the flesh and in the spirit, greetings. Word of the great persecutions in Rome reaches us here. May God keep you and your household safe from evil. We continue the work here in Glanmorganshire and build churches to the glory of our Savior. Cor Ergain has become a known center of learning. We send missionaries out to other lands from this college. Our church here at Llan-ilid grows in grace and in numbers. From this consecrated place, we lift daily prayers for all those who suffer for our Lord's sake. Our dear father has received the rewards promised to him through the shed blood of Christ. He died in the faith three days ago. His last words were the words of our dear Paul: "Even so, come Lord Jesus." I watched at his bedside for many days and nights. He recalled the early days of his captivity and repeated over and over again how proud he was of you, dear sister, the day you stood beside him in the Roman Senate. At times, in his mind, he was a boy again, roaming the hills of Siluria. At times, he was a young father carrying one of us children on his back through the woods. He had an easy death and a gentle crossing. Do not weep as those who have no hope. We shall behold him standing beside our Savior when we cross over to be with them and with all who have named the name of Jesus and have suffered martyrdom.

"And when he had opened the fifth seal, I saw under the altar the souls of them that were slain for the word of God, and for the testimony which they held."
Revelation 6:9

"No Christian brought before the Tribunal shall be exempted from death and torture without renouncing his religion."
Domitian in Foxe, *Book of Martyrs* (12)

"I exhort you all therefore, to yield obedience to the word of righteousness and to exercise all patience such as ye have seen before your eyes–not only in the case of the blessed Ignatius and Zosimus and Rufus, but also in other among yourselves and in Paul himself and the rest of the apostles. This do in assurance that all these have not run in vain, but in faith and righteousness, and they are now in their due place in the presence of the Lord with whom they also suffered. For they loved not this present world, but Him who died for us and for our sakes was raised again by God from the dead."
Polycarp to the Philippians, *AnteNicene Fathers* vol 1 (35)

"Fear none of those things which thou shalt suffer: behold, the devil shall cast some of you into prison, that ye may be tried; and ye shall have tribulation ten days. Be thou faithful unto death, and I will give thee a crown of life."
Revelation 2:10

"Propterea igitur publici hostes Christiani, quia imperatoribus neque vanos neque mentientes neque termerarios honores." ("That is why Christians are public enemies–because they will not give the Emperors vain, false, and rash honors.")

Tertullian, *Apology* (158-159)

THE TRIBUNAL   96 AD   849 AUC

NOVATUS SPEAKS:

 I was standing in the courtyard of the Senate when Cassius ran to me. He was clearly overwrought. "They have just arrested your father."

Terror clutched me. "Where is he?"

"They are taking him to the *Curia* to bring formal charges against him."

"What are the charges? He has done nothing against the law."

"They are charging him with foreign superstition under Domitian's order. They will give him an opportunity to renounce his religion."

"He will not renounce his faith."

"Perhaps he will renounce it in order to live."

"Not even if it means death. You know my father. He is old and stubborn."

"I have served your father all my adult life. No one has done more for Rome. How can they do this?"

"My grandfather said once, 'Rome will kill us all because she can.' They arrest my father because they can. Cassius, go to the villa. Tell my brother what has happened. Don't tell my mother or my sisters. Tell Timotheus to meet me at the *Curia*." He nodded. I ran through the back streets of Rome, dodging carts and throngs of people. I arrived at the Senate in time to see my father, bound, taken inside. I pushed my way through the crowd. A Praetorian barred my way.

"Please. They have my father. My father is Senator Pudens. Let me pass."

"I have orders. No one goes beyond these doors." He was adamant. I sat on the steps, put my head in my hands and prayed. "Who would want to harm my father? He has served Rome all of his life. Who stands to gain from his death? I know of no enemies that would seek to do him harm. Oh, God, spare his life." As I sat, praying, I felt an arm around my shoulder. I looked into my brother's face. I always take courage when Timotheus is near.

"I'm going to see what they are doing." I watched him walk up the steps and speak to the guard on duty. The guard opened the door and Timotheus disappeared inside. I am amazed at my brother's ability to talk his way into or out of any situation. I waited. When the sun was high, the doors opened and my father, still bound, was conducted, under heavy guard, in the direction of the *carcer*. Timotheus ran to me.

"They charged him with foreign superstition and told him to renounce his faith. Of course, he would not. They have sentenced him to death. I don't know when the execution will be carried out. You should have seen him, Novatus. That old man stood with his back straight and his head held high. He said to the assembly, 'You can kill this body, but you will never kill my spirit. I have given my life to Rome, but my first allegiance is to the Christ who gave his life for me. I shall never die.' He has such courage. He saw me and smiled. I have never been so proud of anyone in my life."

"Come, Timotheus. We must go to the villa and tell our mother and our sisters."

THE VIGIL   97 *AD*   850 *AUC*

PUDENTIANA SPEAKS:

 "She is resting quietly. We need to sleep while we can, Sister." Praxedes stood beside our mother's bed. "I will sit with her awhile. Go rest. You have not slept in days. I do not think I can sleep just yet." I pulled the blanket up under mother's chin. "If we are tired, she is more so. Thank God the fever has subsided."

Our mother's thinning skin in the flickering lamplight is the color of old parchment. Her eyelids are translucent, closed over eyes too tired to see or know. She is wrinkled and frail. Blue veins are visible on her hands and at her temples. Her body is thin beneath the covers. I can not think of her as old. My memories of her are the memories of my childhood. To us, her children, she was the most beautiful woman who ever walked the earth. I have always known that she could not forever look as she did when I was a little girl, but I think of her as my mother—never young, but ageless and always there—like air and food. Her security was not something we questioned. She was simply a gentle presence, a quiet voice, a reassuring touch. I picture her now as she was—at her writing table with stylus in hand, or frolicking with us on the sun drenched hillside, or bathed and freshly dressed to greet our father when he came home from the Senate—her hair golden in sunlight or lamplight—her laughter lilting, her eyes sparkling. What a blessing to have her for our mother.

Timotheus stepped inside the bedchamber. His face was lined and drawn. He stood in the shadows and looked at this dying woman who had given us life.

"How is she?"

"About the same. She is sleeping. The fever seems to

have abated, but her breathing is difficult. Let her rest while she can. We labor to come into this world, and we labor going out." I took my brother's hand in mine and rested my cheek in his palm "We have seen so much death, but this one is breaking my heart."

"She is our mother. We are losing our mother. Has Novatus returned from *Ostia*?

"He is on his way home. Praxedes and I have not left her since she fell ill."

Timotheus sat beside her bed. "She has not been herself since father's death. I can not believe he has been gone a year. I think mother decided when he died that she did not want to live in this world without him. What a grand reunion they will have. They will see the Lord."

"Yes, and Uncle Paul and mother's Aunt Gladys and all those who have gone before."

Praxedes, who looks like a ministering angel, stepped back into the room with a bowl, a pitcher of water and a damp cloth. She smiled at us and went to work, pouring warm water into the bowl and dipping the cloth to wet it. Gently, she wiped mother's face and neck and washed mother's thin, small body. Tenderly, my sister anointed mother's face, hands, and feet with warm, perfumed oil. Having completed the ritual, she slipped clean linen beneath her. As I watched, I could not help but think of my mother's willing hands which had ministered to so many needy people–to the old and the dying, to the poor, to all the neglected infants, to us—her children. My sister is so like mother. There are no kinder words I can speak.

It was past the third watch when Novatus arrived. We embraced him and comforted each other.

THEIRS IS THE KINGDOM

"For love's sake I beseech thee, being such an one as Paul the aged, and now also a prisoner of Jesus Christ. I beseech thee for my son, Onesimus, whom I have begotten in my bonds."
Philemon 1:9-10

THE BISHOP   112 *AD*   865 *AUC*

ONESIMUS SPEAKS:

 If I have one thing to say it is that I was a slave and now I am free. I was a thief and now I am forgiven. When I came back to Colossae from Rome so many years ago, I went to the home of my master with fear and trembling. The scene is burned into my brain.

"So, you have returned." Philemon stood over me as I knelt at his feet.

"Yes, Master." My voice shook. My hands were unsteady as I reached for Paul's letter.

"Why are you here? You ran away. You stole money from me. I expected never to see you again." His voice was stern.

"What is this?" He reached for the letter, the single sheet of papyrus which I carried next to my skin all the long journey from Rome. My life depended on it. Philemon opened it and read. To my astonishment and vast relief, he took my hand and pulled me to my feet. He then embraced me. I will never forget his words: "My brother." I wept in his arms.

The next Lord's day, to the church that is in his house, Philemon read the letter, and all of the believers embraced me. Philemon returned Paul's letter to me to keep as a reminder of God's great transforming power. That happened many years ago. Paul wrote in that letter: "I have confidence in your obedience. I write this letter to you knowing that you will do even more than I say." Indeed he did. Philemon more than lived up to Paul's expectation of him. I served Philemon from that day with a heart grateful for his forgiveness. In Christ, we are brothers. In Christ, I am free. Philemon taught me to read and instructed me in the ways of the Lord. I was with him when he died.

"Useful" is my name. I was useful–profitable–to Philemon, as he was to me. I pray daily that I shall be useful to the Lord. People tell me I am. I was ordained years ago to serve as Bishop in Ephesus. Not long ago, when our brother Ignatius was on his way to Rome to face the wild beasts in the coliseum arena, the *Amphitheatrum Caesereum*, he wrote from Smyrna to the church here. He called me "Useful" in that letter, just as Paul had done when I was young.

We are now engaged in a great endeavor to collect all of Paul's letters. Useful work, I would say. Even now, the letters are being circulated and read in the churches. There is one especially tattered and worn. I have treasured it all these years–that little letter the great apostle to the gentiles wrote in his own hand that day so long ago amid the filth and stench of a Roman prison to Philemon, pleading for my life. Some of the brothers believe it is too short and too personal to be included with Paul's great long doctrinal letters, but I insist on its inclusion. As brief as it is, it means everything to me. It tells my story of God's redeeming grace.

Theirs Is The Kingdom

"Pope Pius I, by the request of the blessed Praxedes, dedicated a church in the baths of Novatus in the *Vicus Patricius* to the honor of her sister, the holy Pudentiana, where also he offered many gifts and frequently he ministered, offering sacrifice to the Lord. Moreover, he erected a font of baptism and with his own hand he blessed and dedicated it and many who gathered to the faith he baptized in the name of the Trinity."

Liber Pontificalis, Eleventh Century Entry

THE CHURCH   143 *AD*   896 *AUC*

THE BUILDER SPEAKS:

Kalend of March
"Your Grace, I have here the plans for the church. We shall leave the original house walls in place wherever they can support the weight of the new structure. Part of the wall must be fortified. We will extend the new building to cover the baths and incorporate the baptismal font into the main part of the hall."

The blessed father nodded. "This holy place shall be sanctified to the memory of the family of martyrs who lived in this house. The blessed Praxedes, before her martyrdom, requested that the church be dedicated to the memory of her sister. Now that Praxedes and her brothers have joined Saint Pudentiana in their heavenly place, we shall dedicate this house of prayer to all of them who have gone before us. Let us honor their lives and their martyrdom with a structure worthy of their memory."

"I shall need funds and men to accomplish the task."

"Whatever you need, you shall have."

"Bless me, Father, as I begin this work. I am not worthy."

The Holy Father stood and put both hands on my head. "The Lord bless you as you enter into this most holy work. May God give you and all who labor here strength for the days ahead. In the name of the Father, the Son, and the Holy Ghost. Amen."

"Thank you, Father. We dedicate our labor to the glory of God and to the memory of those who shed their sacred blood for the cause of Christ."

Kalend of May

The crew is hired and the work has begun. In shoring up the walls of the old house, we have found it necessary to dig into the original foundation. My workmen have been instructed to salvage whatever objects the digging uncovers. So far, they have found pottery and cooking pots from the original kitchen area, and combs and a bronze enameled mirror which must have been used by the women of the house. I must tell them to tread carefully and to be alert to small, valuable objects. This was the house of a wealthy family. We cannot know what might come to light. My men are honest. I intend to keep them that way. I keep my eyes open.

Kalend of Sextillis

Today we found a part of an ivory screen. It must have been a magnificent piece of art when it was new. The masons have come to begin the heavy foundation work. We begin each day's work with prayer. We are aware of the sanctity of this place.

Kalend of November

Our cache of objects grows daily. The Holy Father says they will be displayed in the new church, along with relics of the saints. Today we found a small bronze box with jewelry inside: an enameled ring, a buckle of silver, a gold talisman of some sort. The walls of the church are rising.

THEIRS IS THE KINGDOM

"Saint Praxed's ever was the church for peace."
Robert Browning, "The Bishop Orders His Tomb at
Saint Praxed's Church" (351-354)

"The four children of Pudens and Claudia, Timotheus,
Novatus, Praxedes and Pudentiana, with their father
Pudens, sealed at different times their faith with their blood
in Rome, and were, with Linus, the first Britons who were
added to the glorious army of martyrs. And, Pudens ex-
cepted, they were not only martyrs, but royal martyrs; and
martyrs of the most patriotic and heroic blood in Britain."
Andrew Gray, *The Origin and Early History of Christianity in Britain* (35)

THE BASILICA   2003 *AD*

MARIANNE BOOKER SPEAKS:

 My friend, Evelyn, and I approached the *Chiesa de Stanta Prassede* through the side door. "It's 'The Church of Saint Praxedes' in English," I said. "I really want to see this basilica. It's not on the regular tourist list of 'things to see,' but it was the inspiration for Robert Browning's poem 'The Bishop Orders His Tomb at Saint Praxedes Church.' It's the price you pay for doing Rome with an Old English and Victorian literature professor." We stepped over the threshold of the basilica and stopped a moment while our eyes adjusted from the glare of the sun to the dimness within.

"I don't mind at all. I might learn something. Doesn't that poem say something about *lapis lazuli?*" Evelyn looked toward the great curve of the apse.

"Go to the head of the class. It does, indeed."

"Well, look at the mosaic in the apse. That's about the bluest blue I've ever seen." Evelyn gazed upward. We sat in the second pew staring at the ornate mosaic, two mature women, grateful for a place to sit down and for the cool silence against the heat and noise of the streets. "Who was Praxedes, anyway?" Evelyn asked.

"I don't know. I'm going over to see if I can buy some post cards. Maybe they have a pamphlet about her." I walked to the alcove near the side entrance, chose a half dozen postcards from the rack, smiled at the volunteer behind the counter, and pointed to the booklet in English entitled *The Basilica of Saint Praxedes.*   I paid my Euros and returned to find Evelyn trying to translate the Latin inscription beneath the apse mosaic. "Okay. This ought to tell us something," I looked at my friend squinting into the Latin. "Oh, look. The guidebook says she was the daughter of Senator Rufus Pudens, and she had a sister, Pudentiana. 'The sisters are often depicted soaking up the blood of martyred saints.' Good heavens. Let's take a walk around and see what we can see."

"What does the book say about the large painting in the apse under the mosaic?" continued Evelyn, still taken by the apse.

"Let's see. Here it is–page nine. It is one of five by Domenico Maria Muratori (1662-1749); it represents St. Praxedes intent on collecting and preserving the blood of the martyrs in a well." I felt squeamish at the thought.

"I wonder if one of the other women in the painting is supposed to be her sister. What a gory task they set for themselves. And, I imagine it was dangerous. You know those Roman emperors were hell-bent on wiping out every vestige of Christianity." Evelyn stared at the painting.

"Um. Hell-bent–a good way to describe it. They took a dim view of those who wouldn't recognize the emperors as gods." I rubbed my tired legs as we walked around the church looking at the chapels, the paintings, the frescoes. "Look. There is a fresco of Pudens, the senator, dressed in military garb. He must have served in the Roman army at some time during his life."

Evelyn took the guide book and turned the pages. "Here on page fifty, it says that this chapel was dedicated to St. Praxedes in 1721. 'The altar piece is by an unknown painter of the eighteenth century and represents St. Peter's visit to Senator Puden's house in the presence of his daughters, Praxedes and Pudentiana.' St. Peter's visit? My goodness. That would be twenty or thirty years after the crucifixion. Senator Pudens may very well have had one of the early churches in his house. I wonder what happened to him."

"He is called 'Saint Pudens.' That means he was martyred. Both Praxedes and her sister are called 'Saint,' so I assume they also died for the faith."

Evelyn said, "Let's go ask the man in the book shop what happened to St. Pudentiana." We walked back to the shop near the side door where we had entered. "How is your Italian?"

"Not great. My Latin is not bad and my Spanish is fluent." We approached the gentleman behind the counter. "Pardon me. Do you speak English? Habla Espanol?"

"Italiano."

"Saint Pudentiana. . ."

"Ah, *Santa Pudenziana–La Chiesa de Santa Pudenziana. . .*not far. *Via Urbana 601*." He wrote it on a slip of paper and handed it to me.

"Thank you. *Grazie*." I turned to Evelyn. "Well, it looks like there's another church. Get out your map. Where is *Via Urbana*? He says it's not far."

"'Not far' in Rome can mean anything from a block to ten miles. Everything here is uphill or upstairs. Here it is on the map. I'm game. Let's go." We walked uphill the twelve or so city bocks to the address we had. From the street it was not possible to see the church. We entered the gate and went down two flights of stairs to a courtyard leading to the main entrance. The place looked somewhat bedraggled. The sanctuary was smaller and much less imposing than Saint Praxedes. To the left of the entrance was a man conversing in French with a young woman who had just purchased post cards. We waited. She left.

"Do you speak English?"

"Yes, a little."

"Do you have a guidebook we might see?"

"Yes. One Euro."

I dug out my European coins and paid him. We took the booklet into the sanctuary and sat on the back row.

I read aloud: "The church of *Santa Pudenziana* was rebuilt by Pope Siricius who reigned from 384 to 399. He changed the church from a hall into a three-aisled basilica.

The date of its original founding is not known. Tradition ascribes it to Pius I who was Pope between around 142 to 154. He ordered the first church built on this present site– oh, gosh–*over the ruins of the house church of Senator Rufus Pudens."* I looked up. "We might be on to something really exciting here." Evelyn took the guidebook from my hands. She picked up the reading:

"Pudentiana and Praxedes were the daughters of Rufus Pudens and his wife, Claudia Rufina. The plaque on the floor at the main entrance was placed there in the fifteenth century. It is a copy of the original which dates from the second century. It is, of course, inscribed in Latin. The translation is this:

'In this sacred and most ancient of churches, known as that of Pastor, dedicated by Sanctus Pius Papa, formerly the house of Sanctus Pudens, the senator, and the home of the holy apostles, repose the remains of three thousand blessed martyrs, which Pudentiana and Praxedes, virgins of Christ, with their own hands interred.'"

We stood up and turned around to see the plaque in the entryway. We walked to it, stunned.

"Can you imagine what they must have experienced. We owe such a debt to all of them–three thousand Christian martyrs. Just think of it."

"And think of going out to collect their bodies and bringing them home to bury. That's where the idea of the sponge to soak up the blood of the martyrs comes from. What else does the book say?"

Evelyn read, "Eleven of the members of Senator Pudens' family were martyred, he, in 96 AD under Nerva. His wife, Claudia, died of natural causes a year later, the only one of the family not martyred. All of his children died for the faith, Pudentiana in 107 under Trajan in the third persecution. The two brothers, Timotheus and Novatus, and their remaining sister, Praxedes, in 139. This church has been known by many names through the centuries: *Domus*

Pudens, the *Paladium Britanicum, Apostolorum,* Titulus, Pastor, and most recently The Church of Saint Pudentiana."

We sat again, needing time to absorb all this information. The only other person in the church with us was a young nun who was kneeling in prayer in front of the apse. She raised her head, crossed herself, and walked toward the rear of the sanctuary. Evelyn quickly stood and walked back to intercept her.

"Pardon me, Sister. Do you speak English?"

"Yes."

"Can you tell us about this church?" She smiled and nodded.

"Forgive me. I'm Evelyn St. Claire, and this is my friend, Marianne Booker. And you are?"

"Sister Pearl. I have been here a year and a half. I have been assigned for three years. This is the official church in Rome for all Filipino Catholics. We do not offer mass in Italian, but only in our language of the Philippines. We serve one hundred thousand Filipinos who live in Rome."

"What do you know of the history of this church?"

Pointing to the front of the church, she said, "We are most famous for the mosaic in the apse. It dates to the time of Pope Siricius. Pope Hadrian I between 772 and 795 had the mosaic restored. In 1588 it was trimmed around the curved margin when the apse was narrowed. A portion of the lower part was removed later by the erection of the *baldacchino* and in 1831–I believe that was the date– the right side was done over. It is the earliest and most beautiful apse mosaic in existence. As you can see, in the center, Christ is dressed in a tunic of gold and is seated on a throne. The open book he holds is inscribed: 'The Lord, Guardian of the Church of Pudentiana.' Originally, the twelve apostles were on either side of the Christ, but the outermost figure on each side was lost when the apse was narrowed. Peter stands at the right and Paul at the left. Behind each of the two apostles stands a woman clothed in gold, holding over his head a crown of laurel. These women are believed to represent the Jewish Church, *Ecclesia ex Circumsisione*, and the Gentile Church, *Ecclesia ex Gentibus*. The Church of the Circumcision was, of course, the church of Jewish converts to Christianity. You probably know the names of Aquilla and Priscilla, who were the leaders of that church. The Church of the Gentiles, which the Apostle Paul mentions in the last chapter of his letter to the Romans, was the house church here on this property. The basilica is built over the ruins of a first century house believed to be the house of Senator Rufus Pudens. The original walls of the house were used as foundation, so we know that the first century house was as big as the church is."

"Can you show us the first century house–Senator Pudens' house?"

"It is underneath this floor, not open to the public, and only partially excavated. The Italian government owns the rights to it. We are not permitted to take visitors there because there might be some danger–snakes, perhaps. I can take you up to Mary's chapel, though. It is not generally shown to visitors, but I'll take you there, if you like."

"Oh, yes. We'd be delighted. Thank you."

"Wait here. I'll come back for you." She stepped out of the sanctuary and soon returned with a ring of keys. "Follow me. Watch your step." She led us up a curved stairway into a small alcove. On the wall behind a simple altar, we saw a fresco of Mary and the infant Jesus. Flanking them are two women–Praxedes and Pudentiana. "The fresco is eleventh century," Sister Pearl explained. We were overwhelmed by the simplicity and the beauty of this small chapel. "Would you like a closer look at the mosaic in the apse? I can take you to the choir loft."

"Oh, yes. Thank you. You are so kind." She led us to a small loft to the right from the apse. We were almost within reach of the beautiful mosaic. She said, "It is the most

THEIRS IS THE KINGDOM

ancient mosaic in existence."

"Why is this church not on the list of places tourists should visit?" Evelyn turned to our guide.

"A good question. Pudens and his family are mentioned by Paul in his second letter to Timothy. He wrote that letter from what we know as the Mamertine prison. It was not called the Mamertine until much later. His greeting to Timothy from Pudens and his family is the last thing the Apostle Paul wrote. I do not know all the details, but in the seventeenth century, Pudens and his children were taken off of the list of saints. I understand there was some discrepancy in the dates of Pudentiana's death. They say there is not enough proof of their existence, but this is his house and the first, or among the first, of the gentile churches. It seems to me that every Bible scholar would want to visit here."

"Absolutely. This is just incredible."

"Look." She pointed to the mosaic. "Behind the depiction of Christ is the rock of Calvary. The cross is jeweled. Above in the clouds are the symbols of the four evangelists. This is the first time they appear in art: the man, lion, ox, and eagle representing the four gospel writers: Matthew, Mark, Luke and John. The man is the symbol for Matthew who wrote of the incarnation. Mark is the lion because his gospel begins with John the Baptist in the desert. Luke is the ox. His gospel begins with the story of Zacharias and the priestly sacrifice. John is the eagle. He writes of Christ, the light of the world. The eagle is the only bird that can fly straight into the light of the sun."

We followed her back down the stone stairs to the basilica.

"If you are really interested in seeing the first century house church, come back to Rome. Call me for a reservation. Bring a big emergency light with you–not just a flashlight. I'll take you down–just one or two at a time. Come look at our little museum. We have some artifacts taken from the lower level." She ushered us through a door and

279

dismissed herself. "Take your time. If you will excuse me, I have some work waiting."

We entered the small museum with its glass cases filled with ancient artifacts–oil lamps, a cooking pot, a fragment of a marble frieze, writing implements, a comb, a metal mirror, a few pieces of jewelry.

"Look at this, Evelyn. It's some kind of amulet." Absorbed by the early Christian atmosphere, I added, "It must be Christian. Look at the fish shapes."

"No, it couldn't be. The card says it's pre-Christian, Druid in origin."

"Of course! It's a Celtic knot. How could I have missed that? Those designs of unending lines that curve in and around have been in regions of Celtic culture for centuries."

"Where?"

"Celts were in Europe, but they flourished and endured in the north and west of England. By the Old English era, the influence of their art was prominent. English cathedrals reflect it, especially these lines in their stonework. I look at this and it reminds me of the masonry, the lacework, it is called, in the ruins of Tinturn Abbey. You know, the subject for Wordsworth's poem."

"I wonder how it got to Rome? I wonder who wore it–maybe a warrior."

"It is too small for a warrior's insignia. The card suggests it was a necklace. I suppose it was worn by some lady–too much to hope that it belonged to Praxedes or Pudentiana." We lingered, held by some mystic sense of the importance of the objects spread before us in the display case. As we collected our things to leave, I said with determination, "I intend to research this period when I am back on campus. In particular, I am going to work on the Celtic knot model of the one in the case."

Evelyn nodded. "If these objects could speak, think what a story they could tell."

AFTERWORD

"About this time, there lived Jesus, a wise man, if indeed one ought to call him a man. For he was one who wrought surprising feats and was a teacher of such people as accept the truth gladly. He won over many Jews and many of the Greeks. He was the Messiah. When Pilate, upon hearing him accused by men of the highest standing among us, had condemned him to be crucified, those who had first come to love him did not give up their affection for him. On the third day he appeared to them restored to life, for the prophets of God had prophesied these and countless other marvelous things about him. And the tribe of the Christians, so called after him, has still to this day not disappeared."

Josephas, *Jewish Antiquities xviii* (63-64)

"Wherefore, seeing we also are compassed about with so great a cloud of witnesses, let us lay aside every weight, and the sin which doth so easily beset us, and let us run with patience the race that is set before us, looking unto Jesus the author and finisher of our faith; who for the joy that was set before him endured the cross, despising the shame, and is set down at the right hand of the throne of God."

Hebrews 12:1-2 KJV

ROBERTA M. DAMON

GLOSSARY OF WORDS

Amphiteatrum Caesarium – The structure known to moderns as the colloseum, begun by Vespasian and finished by Titus in AD 80

AUC: ab urb condita – from the founding of the city (Rome)

Apostolorum – sanctuary in the home of Rufus Pudens for the apostles and other believers travelling to Rome

Arcus Claudii – the Arch of Claudius

Auditori – Listeners at the door of the Senate chamber in Rome

Caer – Old English for 'castle'

Caldarium – the steam room in the Roman baths

Castra – Roman military base of operations

Carcer – prison

Concubitus – sexual relations

Consensus – consent

Curia –the building wherein the Roman Senate conducted business of state

Damnatio memoriae – "damned in memory," an official act expunging a person and his acts from the historical record

Decurio – an official serving in a specific capacity in a Roman province

Divus – divine

Domus – house

Domus Aurea – "golden house," Nero's opulent palace

Epithalamion – Greek and Roman wedding poem extolling the virtues of the marrying couple

Fasces – a bundle of rods with an ax blade projecting; a badge of authority in ancient Rome

Flammeum – "flame," the word for the sheer red veil of a Roman bride

Ichthus – Greek for "fish," the symbol of secret followers of Christ in the early days of Christianity; the letters of the Greek word form an acrostic: Jesus Christ Son of God, Savior

Ides – fifteenth (sometimes the thirteenth) day on the Roman calendar

Insulae – apartment houses in first century Rome

Kalend – the first day of the ten Roman months: March (named for Mars); April (L. *Aperire*–"to open); May (named for Maia, goddess of growth); June (named for Juno); July (named for Julius Caesar) was originally Quintillis (fifth); August was orginally Sextillis (6th); September (septem, 7th); October (octo, 8th); November (novem, 9th); and December decem, 10th)

Libra custodia – free custody; a prisoner was free to go about the city or other specific territory, but not beyond those boundaries

Modum, pl. modii – Roman measure corresponding to tons

Nubo – form of "cloud"

Nuptius – marriage ceremony, nuptuals

Palladium – palace

Passum – sauce made from wine or grape juice used in Roman foods

Paterfamilias – The man of the house who held life and death power over his wife and children

Pax – peace

Pronuba – the faithful wife of a living husband who prepared the bride for the marriage bed

Siluria – ancient name for Wales

Sine manu – If a wife married 'sine manu, she would retain inheritance rights from her parents

Spectatori – spectators

Triquetra – Latin for. 'three cornered;' a symbol which is at least 5000 years old, used in many cultures and religions

Tutulus – cone to hold a Roman bride's braided hair and her veil

Urbs Romana orbs humana – Rome is the world

GLOSSARY OF ICONS

ALPHA AND OMEGA: The first and last letters of the Greek alphabet–used to represent Christ, the beginning and the end.

BUTTERFLY: Symbolic of transformation from death to eternal life–the larvae is hidden in the chrysalis awaiting life in a new form, as the body is hidden in the tomb awaiting resurrection.

CHI-RHO: The first two Greek letters in "Christ."

CIRCLE: Universal symbol of eternity.

CROSS: Symbolic of Christ's atonement for the sins of the world–an "emblem of suffering and shame." While Rome was not the first to employ crucifixion as a means of execution, Christ's death is associated with the Roman cross.

CROSS AND CROWN: The crown is the emblem of victory, honor and sovereignty. When the cross is displayed with it, it symbolizes the reward of the faithful in the life after death. This symbol is often associated with martyrdom.

CROZIER: A pastoral staff conferred on bishops at their installation. In Western Christianity, the top of the staff is curved as is the shepherds' crook reminding the bishop of his pastoral care of the people entrusted to him. He is to keep watch over his flock, sustaining the weak and faltering, confirming the wavering in faith, and leading back the erring.

DOVE: The symbol of the Holy Spirit and of peace.

FASCES: A cylindrical bundle of elm or birch rods bound together by red bands, from which an ax head projected. The fasces was borne by attendants (lictors) before a consul or high magistrate as a symbol of authority. The Emperor Claudius had twelve lictores bear the fasces before him when entering a caputred town in Britannia.

FISH: A secret sign used by the early persecuted Christians to identify each other as followers of The Way. The initial letters of the Greek words "Jesus Christ, Son of God, Savior" spell the Greek word for fish–Ichthus.

FLAME: A symbol for Pentecost and a universal symbol for light.

GRAPES AND WHEAT: Shown together, the grapes and wheat signify holy communion. The grapes represent the blood of Christ and the wheat represents the Bread of Life–the body of the Savior.

LAMB: Symbol of the Lamb of God who takes away the sins of the world. This symbol has its roots in the Jewish Passover when the blood of the lamb was sprinkled on the doorposts to assure that the death angel would pass over that house. It is also a symbol of innocense and purity.

LAMP: A symbol for the Word of God which illumines the understanding.

LAUREL WREATH: Ancient symbol of victory. In Rome, the laurel leaf is from a tree which produces what is generally known as the bay leaf used in cooking.

MENORAH: A holy candelabrum of seven candlesticks associated with the Jewish Temple in Jerusalem. It is the earliest symbol of Judaism.

SCROLL: Made of parchment or vellum containing ancient writing. It is the symbol of learning.

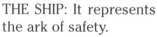

THE SHIP: It represents the ark of safety.

SUN OF RIGHTEOUSNESS: This symbol consists of a circle with rays. It depicts Christ, the light of the world.

TRIQUETRA: Literally, "three cornered:" The symbol dates back five thousand years. It signifies balance, the ebb and flow of life, the phases of a woman's life–maiden, mother, and crone.

TRIANGLE: Symbol of the triune God.

TRISKELL: A common widespread symbol in Britain having many meanings: the cycle of life, the three elements (water, air, earth), the path of the sun. The triskell, if turned to the right, represents day, or the positive. If turned to the left, it represents night or war.

ROMAN EMPORORS · 27 BC - 117 AD

27 BC - 14 AD	AGUSTUS CAESAR
14 AD - 37 AD	TIBERIUS
38 AD - 40 AD	CALIGULA
41 AD - 53 AD	CLADIUS
54 AD - 68 AD	NERO
68 AD	IULIUS VINEX
68 AD	CLODIUS MACER
68 AD - 69 AD	GALBA
69 AD	NYMPHIDIUS
69 AD	OTHO
69 AD	VITELLIUS
69 AD - 79 AD	VESPASIAN
79 AD - 81 AD	TITUS
81 AD - 96 AD	DOMITIAN
97 AD - 98 AD	NERVA
98 AD - 117 AD	TRAJAN

LIFE OF PAUL · FROM CONVERSION IN 34 AD TO 64 AD

34 - 35 AD	Paul is converted - *Acts 9:1-19*
37 - 38 AD	Visits Jerusalem - *Acts 9:26-29*
48 AD	Second visit to Jerusalem - *Acts 11:27-30*
48 - 50 AD	First missionary journey (Cyprus, Galatia) He writes Galatians - *Acts 13-14*
50 AD	The Council at Jerusalem - *Acts 15*
51 - 53 AD	Second missionary journey (Galatia, Macedonia, Greece). He writes I and II Thessalonians - *Acts 16:1-15:22*
54 - 57 AD	Third missionary journey (Greece, Macedonia). He writes I and II Corinthians, Romans - *Acts 18-23-21:14*
58 - 60 AD	Arrest in Jerusalem; Tried and imprisoned in Caesarea - *Acts 21:15-26:32*
60 - 63 AD	Paul in Rome writes Philemon, Colossians, Ephesians, Philipians
64 AD	Final imprisonment and death. He writes I Timothy, Titus, II Timothy

FAMILY CONNECTIONS · RELATIONS EXPLAINED

EMPEROR CLAUDIUS
CLAUDIUS was married four times.
He married URGULANILLA
 They had no children.
He married AELIA, a marriage in name only.
He married MESSALINA when she was 14 and he was 57
 The had two children: BRITANNICUS and OCTAVIA.
He married AGRIPPINA, who brought NERO, her son
from a previous marriage.

EMPEROR NERO
NERO married OCTAVIA.
 They had no children.
He married POPPEA, but had her put to death when she
was with child.

CARADOC (CARACTACUS)
CARADOC (CARACTACUS) married ERGAIN.
 They had four children: CYNON, LINUS, ERGAIN and
GLADYS (CLAUDIA).

AARON
AARON married PRISCILLA.
 They had two children, SAUL (PAUL) and REBECCA.
PRISCILLA was widowed and then married QUINTUS
CORNELIUS PUDENS.
 They had one son, RUFUS PUDENS.

RUFUS PUDENS
RUFUS PUDENS married GLADYS (CLAUDIA).
 They had four children: TIMOTHEUS, NOVATUS,
PRAXEDES, and PUDENTIANA.

WORKS CONSULTED

Allen, Clifton, ed. *The Broadman Bible Commentary, Acts-1 Corinthians.* Vol 10. Nashville: Broadman Press, 1971.

Allen, Clifton J. ed. *The Broadman Bible Commentary, 2 Corinthians-Philemon.* Vol 11. Nashville: Broadman Press, 1971.

Balsdon, J.P.V.D., *Romen Women: Their History and Habits.* Westport CT: . Greenwood Press, 1962.

Baedae. *Opera Historica–Bede Historical Works.* Ed. T. E. Page. Trans. J. E. King. *Ecclesiastical History of the English Nation Based on the Version of Thomas Stapelton, 1565.* The Loeb Classical Library. Vol 1. New York: G. P. Putnam, 1930. 26-27.

Beard, Mary and Michael Crawford. *Rome in the Late Republic.* Ithaca, NY: Cornell UP, 1985.

Bellingham, David. *An Introduction to Celtic Mythology.* Manchester Center, VT: Apple Press, 1990.

Browning, Robert. "The Bishop Orders His Tomb at Saint Praxed's Church." *The Brownings: Letters and Poetry.* Ed. Christopher Ricks. NY: Doubleday, 1970. 351-354.

Caesar, Julius. *Commentary on the Gallic War.* Tr. H. J. Edwards. Cambridge: Harvard Press, 1966.

Cahill, Thomas. *Desire of the Everlasting Hills.* New York: Doubleday, 1999.

Capt, Raymond. *Stonehenge and Druidism.* Muskogee, OK: Artisan, 1979.

—. *The Traditions of Glastonbury.* Muskogee, OK: Artisan, 1983.

Carmichael, Alexander. *Carmina Gadelica*. Hudson, NY: Lindisfarne Press, 1992.

Chadwick. *The Celts*. New York: Pelican, 1979.

Crossan, John. *The Birth of Christianity*. San Francisco: Harper, 1998.

Cummings, John, ed. *A New Dictionary of Saints*. Collegeville, MN: Liturgical Press, 1994.

DeVane, William Clyde. *A Browning Handbook*. New York: Appleton-Century-Crofts, Inc., 1963.

Elder, Isabel. *Celt, Druid and Culdee*. London: Covenant Publishing, 1973.

Ellis, Peter. *The Celtic Empire*. London: Constable, 1990.

—. *The Druids*. Constable: London, 1994.

Finegan, Jack. *Light from the Ancient Past: the Archeological Background of the Hebrew-Christian Religion*. Princeton: Princeton UP, 1946.

Foxe, John. *The New Foxe's Book of Martyrs*. Rewritten by Harold Chadwick. Gainesville, FL: Bridge-Logos Publishers, 2001.

Gallio, Paola. *The Basilica of Saint Praxedes*. Genova: Trib. Genova, 1998.

Graves, Robert. *I Claudius*. New York: Random House, 1934.

—. *Claudius, the God*. New York: Random House: 1935.

Gray, Andrew. *The Origin and Early History of Christianity in Britain*. 1897. Thousand Oaks, CA: Artisan Sales, 1991.

Griffith-Jones, Robin. *The Four Witnesses*. San Francisco: Harper, 2000.

Haywood, Richard Masfield *Ancient Rome.* New York: David McKay Company Inc., 1967.

Howell, James. *Servants, Misfits, and Martyrs: Saints and Their Stories.* Nashville: Upper Room Books, 1999.

Jones, Prudence and Nigel Pennick. *A History of Pagan Europe.* New York: Barnes & Noble, 1995.

Josephus. *Jewish Antiquities.* Trans. Louis Feldman. Cambridge: Harvard UP, 1956.

—. *The Jewish War.* Gaalya Cornfeld, ed. Grand Rapids: Zondervan, 1982.

Kelly, Sean and Rosemary Rogers. *Saints Preserve Us!* New York: Random House, 1993.

Kiek, Jonathan. *Everybody's Historic England: A History and Guide.* London: Quiller Press, 1988.

Lanciani, Rodolfo. *Pagan and Christian Rome.* New York: Benjamin Blom, 1892.

Laing, Lloyd. *Later Celtic Art in Britain and Ireland.* UK: Shire Publications, 1987.

Martial. *The Epigrams of Martial on the Spectacles.* Tr. Walter C. A. Ker. Ed. T. E. Page. The Loeb Classical Library. Cambridge: Harvard UP, 1961. (MCMLXI)

Martial. *Epigrams.* Trans. Walter C. H. Ker. Cambridge: Harvard UP, 1943.

Morgan, R. W. *Saint Paul in Britain, or The Origin of British Christianity.* 1860. Muskogee, OK: Artisan Sales, 1984.

Muggeridge, Malcolm and Alec Vidler. *Paul: Envoy Extraordinary.* New York: Harper & Row, 1972.

Payne, Robert. *Ancient Rome.* New York: Simon and Schuster, 1966.

Piggott, Stuart. *The Druids.* New York: Thames and Hudson, 1968.

Ricotti, Eugenia. *Dining as a Roman Emperor.* Rome: L'ERMA di Betschneider, 1999.

Ritchie, W. F. *Celtick Warriors.* UK: Shire Publishers, 1985.

Roberts, Alexander, and James Donaldson, eds. *Ante Nicene Fathers: Translations of the Fathers to AD 325.* Grand Rapids, MI: W.B. Erdsmans Publishing Co., 1956.

Rutherford, Ward. *The Druids: Magicians of the West.* Northhamptonshire: The Aquarian Press, 1978.

Saint Pudenziana's Basilica. Rome: Tipolitografia Trullo, 1988.

Saint of the Day. Leonard Foley, ed. USA: St. Anthony Messenger Press, 1974.

Stough, Henry. *Dedicated Disciples.* Muskogee, OK: Artisan, 1987.

Suetonius. *The Lives of the Caesars.* Loeb Classical Library. Ed. T. E. Page. Trans. J. C. Rolfe. New York: G.P. Putman, 1930.

—. *Lives of the Twelve Caesars.* Tr. Pilemon Holland. New York: Heritage Press, 1965.

—. *Vita Claudius* The Loeb Classical Library, Tr. J. C. Rolfe. NY: G.P. Putnam's Sons, 1930.

Tacitus. *Annals and Histories.* Ed. Robert McHenry. Trans. Alfred John Church and William Jackson Brodribb. Chicago: Encyclopedia Britannica, 1952.

—. *The Annals.* Ed. E. G. Warmington. Trans. John Jack son. Vol. 1-5. The Loeb Classical Library. Cambridge: Harvard UP, 1970.

Taylor, John. *The Coming of the Saints: Imaginations and Studies in Early Church History and Tradition.* 1906. 1969. Thousand Oaks, CA: Artisan Sales, 1985.

Tertullian. *Apology.* Tr. T. R. Glover. NY: G.P. Putnam's Sons, 1931.

The Basicilia of Saint Praxedes. Rome: Tipolitografia Trullo, 1988.

The New Encyclopedia of Christian Martyrs. Ed. Mark Water. Grand Rapids, MI: Baker Books, 2001.

Toulson, Shirley. *The Celtic Year.* Rockport, MA: Element Publishers, 1996.

Walker, Barbara G. *The Women's Dictionary of Sacred Symbols.* San Francisco: Harper, 1989.

Wallace, Susan Helen. *Saints for Young Readers.* Boston: Saint Paul Books and Media, 1995.

PERTINENT WORKS OF THE SIXTEENTH-NINETEENTH CENTURIES

Armin, Robert. *The Valiant Welshman, or, The True Chronicle History of the Life and Valiant Deedes of Caradoc the Great, King of Cambria, Now Called Wales.* London: Imprinted by George Purslowe for Robert Lownes and are to be solde at his shoppe, 1615.

Bruty Tywysogion: The Gwentian Chronicle of Caradoc of Llancarvan. Transl. by Aneurin Owen. London: Printed for the Cambrian Archaeological Association, J.R. Smith, 1863.

Lysons, Samuel. *Claudia and Pudens, or, The Early Christians of Gloucester: A Tale of the First Century.* London: Hamilton, Adams, 1861

Williams, John. *Claudia and Pudens: An Attempt to Show that Claudia, Mentioned in St. Paul's Second Epistle to Timothy, Was a British Princess.* London: Llandovery, W. Rees, 1848.

Powell, David. *The Historie of Cambria, Now Called Wales, A Part of the Most Famous Yland of Brytaine, Written in the Brytish Language above Two Hundreth Yeares Past.* London: Imprinted by Rafe Newberie and Henrie Denham, 1584.

INTERNET SOURCES

"A Few Thoughts on Garabandal, Plus. . ." www.ourlady.
ca/events/BishopsAccount.html 8/26/2002

Alpha and Omega (in Scripture)" http://www.newadvent.
org/cathen/01332a.htm 1/17/2004

"Ancient Gynecology: Ancient Roman Theories on Conception," http://bama.ua.edu/-bindo001 8/14/2002

"Ancient Rome," www.roman-empire.not/maps/map-
rome.html 8/11/2003

"Ancient Roman Clothing," www.dl.ket.org/latin 1/things/
romanlife/ancientp 15.htm 9/21/2002

"Ancient Roman Marriage," www.pogodesigns.com/JP/
weddings/romanwed.html 9/21/2002

"Antique Roman Dishes–Collection," www.2.cs.cmu.edu/-
mjw/recipes/ethnic/historical/ant-rom-coll.html
9/21/2002

"Arch of Claudius," http://itsa.ucsf.edu/smlrcsnlrc
encyclopaedia_romana/britannia/boudica
claudiusarch.html 2/3/2003

"Bible Study: Emperor Claudius," www.execulink.com/-
wblank/20010829.htm 1/26/03

"Calamistrum,"www.jukans.edu/history/index/europe/
ancient_rome/E/Roman/Textssecondary/SMI...
4/11/2003

"Catholic Encyclopedia: Early Roman Christian Cemeteries," http:// www.new advent.org/cathen/03510a.htm 8/26/2002

"Catholic Encyclopedis: Saint John Lateran," www.new advent.org/cathen/09014b.htm 8/26/2002

"Chiesa de Santa Prassede,"www.romaonline.it/Rol/ Turismo? Cultura/RMSchede. cfm?CMD=ViewDET&ID =415 9/6/2002

"Chiesa de S. Prassede," www.romeartlover.it/Vasi 127a. htm 11/11/2002

"Churches of Rome: Santa Prassede," http://home.on line.no/cynborg/prassede.html 5/14/2003

"Churches of Rome," www.romeartlover.it Churches.html 11/11/2002

"Churches of Rome: Santa Pudenziana," http://home.on line.no/-cnyborg/pudenziana.html 9/6/2002

"Claudius as Emperor," www.geocities.com/AthensParth enon/7094/claud2html 2/3/2003

"Claudius Invades Britain," www.stephen.j.murraky.bt interet.co.uk/invade.htm 2/3/2003

"Convento dei Padri de S. Bernardo e Chiesa di S. Pudenziana," http://www.romeartlover.it?Vasil27.htm 11/11/2002

"Daily Life in Ancient Rome," http//members.aol.com/ Donnclass/Romelife.html 9/21/2002

"Early British Christianity," www.write-on.co.uk/history/ early_british_christianity.htm 12/2/2002

"Ecclesia Anglicana-A history by Rev. Guy Hawtin, St. Stephen's Timonium" www.ststephens-md.org history.htm 12/2/2002

"Emperor Claudius Timeline," http://ancienhistory. about.com/ibrary/blbl_time_claudius.htm 1/26/2003

"Essay–Dear Sister Wendy," www.benito-mussolini.com/domine.html 7/27/2002

"Fasces (laurum de fascubus)" http://home.uchicago.edu/~janie/fasces.htm 1/17/2004

"Folk Stories," http://members.aol.com?EverettPet/st/spring2000/4.htm 12/2/2002

"From Christ to Constantine," http://asis.com/-stagx2 consta.htm 2/12/2003

"Gloucester, Is there a Biblical Link?" http://uk.geocities.com/oldglos/page1.html 6/9/2003

"Greek Approach to Women's Illness, Pregnancy and Childbirth,"www.womenintheancientworld.com/health%20in%greece.htm 8/24/2002

"Gregory Flood's Roman Gods and Goddesses," http://ancienthisoty, about.com/library/bl/blgregorygods2.htm 9/23/2002

"History of the Christian Altar," www.ewtn.com/library/LITURGY/01362A.TXT 8/26/2002

"Italy, Rome, Santa Prassede," www.mcah.columbia.edu/cgi-bin/dbco...publicportfolio?portfolioid'852&x%0D=18&y=1 9/6/2002

LacusCurtius and Rodolfo Lanciani, "Pagan and Christian Rome,"www.ukans.edu/history/index/eurose/ ancient_rome/E/Gazetteer/Places/Europe?Italy/ 5/14/2003 and 6/16/2003

"Mamertine Prison and Chapels," www.fcsn.kl2.nd.us/ Shanley/broanth/mamertine.htm 8/26/2002

"Marbles from Antiquity," www.rnw.n/culture/html/ marbles020121.html 8/24/2002

"Nero," www.roman-empire.not/emperors/emperors. html 6/24/2003

"Nero's Character: Good Looking and Short Sighted," ww.bible-history.com/nero/NERONeros_Character. htm 6/25/2003

"Nero's Downfall," www.ecnet.net/users/gemedia3/nero/ nero.html 6/24/2003

"Newsletter of the District of Asia: Roman Pilgrimage, August 5-19,2000," www.sspxasia.com/Newsletters/ 2000/Sep-Oct/Rome-Pilgrimage-Day-1-3.htm 8/26/02

"Paul and Pudens," www.childrenofyahweh.com/ Teaching%20Letters/letter_15.htm 8/26/2002

"Paul and Tentmaking," www.salvationbygrace.org/ QandAPaulAndTentmaking.htm 12/2/2002

"Paul, the Roman Citizen," and "Triads of Paul the Apostle," http://chrisitanparty.net/ stpaul.htm 8/26/2002

"Peter (Simon)," http://www.biblepath.com/peter2.html 8/26/2002

"Roman Architecture," http://library.thinkquest.org/
11402/uitgelicht.html 8/26/2002

"Roman Calendar," www.wikipedia.org/wiki/Roman_
calendar 1/1/2003

"Roman Emperors: Claudius," www.roman-emperors.org/
claudius.htm 7/3/2002

"Roman Gods," www.gwydir.demon.co.uk/jo/roman/
9/23/2002

"Roman House," www.vroma.org/-bmcmanus/house.html

"Rome, Italy: The Arch of Titus and Reliefs, Via Sacra,"
www.bluffton.edu/-sullivanm/titu/titus.html 8/16/2003

"Romans in Britain: The Celts and Celtic Life," www.
romans-in-britain.org.uk/clb_celts_ and_celtic-life.htm
5/26/2003

"Royal Soap," http://asis.com/-stag/royalsoap.html
12/9/2002

"Sanctuary Windows 1987" http://www.sunrise
presbyterian.org/AStainedGlass.htm 1/17/2004

"Santa Prassede," www.holidayinrome.com/history/
santa_prassede.html 9/6/2002

"Santa Prassede," http://home.online.no/-cnyborg/
prasssede.html 9/6/2002

"Sex and Childbirth in Ancient Rome," www.afn.org/-
afn32612/Childbirth.htm 8/24/2002

"Smith's Bible Dictionary: Rome," www.studylight.org/
dic/sbd/view.cgi?number=T3675 8/26/2002

"Suetonius on Nero's Suicide," www.bible-history.com/ nero/NEROSeutonius_on_Neros_Suicide.htm 6/25/2003

"Symbols of Christmas" http://www.beaufortgazette. com/features/lifetimes/story3140191p-2840346c.html 1/17/2004

"The Jewish Tradition"http://faculty.evansville.edu/r/29/ art105/f02/art105-3.html 1/17/2004

"The Fasces" http://www.legion.org/fasces%20page/ 1/17/2004

"The First Church of Rome," www.thepilgrimcompany. com/pages_20items/pt3_first_church_ rome.htm 2/19/2003

"The Forum," http://library.thinkquest.org/11402/ uitgelicht.html 8/26/2002

"The Gallic War (De Bello Gallico) Book V," www.romans online.com/souces/dbg/Ch05_20.asp 2/9/2002

"The Names of the Months," www.infoplease.com/ipa/ A0002067.html 9/21/2002

"The Port of Claudius," http://index.waterland.et/navis/ Musea/Ostia/Fiumicino_English.htm 9/21/2002

"The Roman Makeover," www.geocities.com/sallypointer /makeover/ 2/11/2003

"The Slaves' Role in the Family," http://bama.ua.edu/- dunla003/family.html 9/21/2002

"The Star of David" http://www.menorah.org/starofdavid .html 1/17/2004

"The Triskell" http://www.bretagne-celtic.com/an/
symbole_an.htm 1/17/2004

"The Synthesis of Ancient Languages: Latin," www.unil.
ch/imm/docs/LAIP/LAIPTTS_old_lang.htm 9/23/2002

"The Triquetra," www.museumoftalkingboards.comtri.
html 4/26/2003

"The Welsh Triads or Trioedd Ynys Prydein," http://
camelot.celtic-twilight.com/triads/index.htm
1/17/2003

"Triquetra Pendant," www.wildwisdom.net/triqpend.htm
4/26/2003

"Victorian Cemetery Symbolism" http://www.vintage
views.org/vv-tl/MtHope/Sym0142.html 1/17/2004

ANCIENT ROME (100B.C. - 300 A.D.)
areas of interest

Camp of the
Pretorians

Tiber River

Quirinal
Hill

Pantheon

Viminal
Hill

Capitoline
Hill

Equiline
Hill

Domus Pudens
(also known as the
Paladium Britanicum)

Arch of Titus

Palatine   Colosseum
Hill

Site of Golden
House of Nero

Caelian
Hill

Tiber River

Aventine
Hill

PORTA
OSTIENSE

PORTA
APPIA

SAINT PUDENZIANA'S BASILICA
above Domus Pudens, villa of Senator Pudens

original le
of the
thermal ro
with rema
of baths

ground level
of basilica

remains of the
mosaic floor of the
ancient church,
Titulus Pudentis

galleries of the
thermal room

side courtyard
and remains of
mosaic floors of
the ancient house

Schematic adapted from R. Lanciani artwork in *Saint Pudenziana's Basilica*, 1988, owned by St. Pudentiana's Rectorate.